Raven shuddered and completed the final steps to stand at the man's table. She slipped the menu in front of him and smoothed down her thick cotton apron. The entire time, his focus remained trained on the now-silent, mini-frat party.

Raven cleared her throat.

Nothing.

"Welcome to Dan's Diner. Our special tonight is—"

The man turned his attention to her, and the music and lighting returned. His Otherness rolled over her in a sweet, dangerous wave. His skin shone like smooth porcelain, contrasting sharply with his dark features and ink-black hair. His gaze enthralled her—piercing eyes, pools of black, as if the pupil bled into the iris, leaving only a sliver of silver along the edges. She could easily fall into the murky depths and not care if she ever resurfaced.

Eyes of the Underworld. Like hers.

Praise for novels of J. C. McKenzie

Shift Happens

"SHIFT HAPPENS has excitement, intrigue and lots of danger. I love the whole cast of characters and how they played a part in the story"

—Fresh Fiction

Beast Coast

"I loved this book as much as the first. There are secrets, surprises, and all manner of supernaturals." *—Paranormal Romance Guild*

Carpe Demon

"The story keeps the adrenaline pumping and spine tingling tension building throughout the story with well written scenes full of vivid details that capture the imagination and make it easy for the reader to become engrossed..." *—Literary Addicts Book Community*

Shift Work

"It's a terrific series and if you like supernatural reads, with a side of romance, the sort with solid and intense plots, gripping and very real dangers, hard choices, supernatural people some of whom can be selfish, cruel and bloodthirsty...You'll be hooked." *—Jeannie Zelos Book Reviews*

Beast of All

"This time out, J. C. McKenzie has outdone herself with high-velocity action, soul deep emotions and one of those finishes that you want to replay over and over!" *—Tome Tender*

Dangerous Dreams

"This new world promises to be an adventurous one full of snark, passion, thrills, romance, danger and wonderful characters and I can't wait to read the next one." —*Stormy Vixen Reviews*

Dangerous Liaisons

"Loved this story and loved Raf and strong, stubborn Lara and I can't overlook Lara's dragon who brought humor to this story." – *Paranormal Romance Guild*

The Good Griffin

"THE GOOD GRIFFIN is as addictive as a double shot of espresso, only without any of the withdrawal symptoms." –*N. N. Light*

The Shucker's Booktique

"Is there anything sexier than a man who wants to do more than just twine his aura together with another woman? Because if there is I simply don't know if I can handle that kind of blatant sexuality." —*Romance Novels For The Beach*

Be My Love

"When this book ended I think I actually sighed. Not because I was happy it was over! No, it was just so darn sweet I couldn't help it." —*Romance Novels for the Beach*

Books by J. C. McKenzie

Conspiracy of Ravens
Nevermore
Queen of Corvids

Shift Happens
Beast Coast
Carpe Demon
Shift Work
Beast of All

Dangerous Dreams
Dangerous Liaisons
Dangerous Decisions

The Good Griffin

The Shucker's Booktique

Be My Love

CONSPIRACY OF RAVENS

A RAVEN CRAWFORD NOVEL, BOOK ONE

J. C. McKENZIE

This is a work of fiction. Names, characters, places, and incidents are either the product of the author's imagination or are used fictitiously, and any resemblance to actual persons living or dead, business establishments, events, or locales, is entirely coincidental.

Conspiracy of Ravens

Contact Information: jcmckenzie@jcmckenzie.ca

Cover Art: Eerilyfair Design
Raven vector artwork: Yauheniya Piatrouskaya
Raven in nest artwork: Chad Keith
Reading Ravens: Dmitriy Sladkov

Publishing History:
First JCM Publications Edition, 2019

ISBN: 978-1-9992394-0-4 (print)
ISBN: 978-1-9992394-1-1 (ebook)

To my friend Megan,

She's nothing like the Megan in this story
(my Megan is way more awesome),
but she let me use her name anyway.

Author's Note

As I'm Canadian, and this story is set in Canada, I will subject all my fabulous readers to the wonderful, and sometimes confusing, world of Canadian spelling. We use a combination of British and American spelling in the True North. It's "colour" not "color" and "organization" instead of "organisation." We love the letters U and Z. Please keep this in mind when you're reading. It's not that I can't spell or didn't have a fabulous editor, it's that I'm demonstrating complex Canadian spelling.

Also of note: Although we are technically a metric nation, our proximity to our American neighbours (see how I spelled that?) means we are well versed in the imperial system. Many of us still use feet and inches to describe our height and pounds for our weight. I'm not being inconsistent in my world building, I'm being realistic and reflective of the community I was born and raised in.

Canadians...we're complex and full of layers.

Like onions.

"I fly upon the blackest of wings,
I soar through the dark night sky,
I answer to no call but my own,
I alone forge my reality,
for I am the Raven,
Child of Odin."

~ Viking Proverb

Chapter One

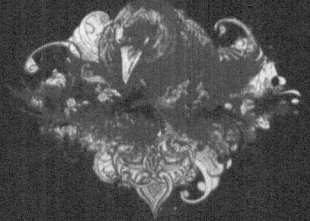

"The trouble with the rat-race is that even if you win, you're still a rat."

~Lily Tomlin

The bell above the entrance door chimed and Raven's impending doom walked into Dan's Diner. She froze with a coffee carafe in one hand and an empty mug in the other.

The cool night air washed into the twenty-four-hour restaurant in North Burnaby. Anywhere else the breeze would be welcomed, bringing in subtle hints of late summer, like the honeyed perfume of fragrant night-blooming flowers. Not here. Instead, gasoline and gloom from the neglected division of the city accompanied the oily scent of Dan's Diner with the arrival of their newest customer. Victim was more accurate. But neither customer nor victim described the latest patron.

Tall, dark and dangerous. TDD.

A shiver ran along Raven's spine as she took in the late-night patron. Well over six feet, with broad shoulders, his presence commanded attention. The sweater's hood covered most of his face, but dark jeans and a hoodie failed to hide his powerful build or how he moved with the confidence of a well-trained fighter.

The lights flickered and the music playing over the speaker faltered briefly before the static cleared and the low voice continued serenading the customers.

"My coffee?" The surly customer at the table in front of Raven scowled. He wore a stained wool sweater and smelled of sawdust and old coffee grounds. This particular regular never tipped and always looked at her as if everything he hated about his life was somehow her fault.

She plunked his mug on the table and straightened to greet the newcomer. "Grab a seat anywhere and I'll be right with you."

TDD nodded and stalked past the counter, his black boots meeting the cheap tile without a sound. His silent progress mesmerized her. She got the impression he'd take care of everything and anything. If mountain trolls attacked the diner at this very moment, he'd eliminate the threat with cold, quick efficiency.

"Waitress." The surly regular lifted his empty

coffee mug and waved it in the air.

Oops. Raven flipped her long ponytail out of her way, the dull black hair trailed greasy strands along her neck. Her mane's lustre disappeared a while ago, along with hope. She turned back to the customer and his potent glower and forced a smile on her face.

Snatching the customer's ring-lined mug, she filled it. If only she could wave a magic wand and look her best. Her power didn't work like that, though, so instead, her forearm shone under the artificial light with a thin layer of grease from working close to the kitchen. She smelled like vat fat even when she wasn't working.

She needed to drop off the carafe and pick up a menu for the new customer. And perhaps deliver a better greeting than staring at him with wide eyes and an open mouth.

"Miss?" A woman snapped her fingers a few booths over.

Raven clamped her mouth shut and turned to the middle-aged woman and her miserable husband. She'd drawn the short straw for customers tonight—and every night—but she needed this job and the potential tips that came with it. She repeated her "be nice" mantra in her head and smiled at the customers.

The woman raised both hands and mimed writing on paper. There should be a degree in waitressing sign language—probably the only qualification Raven could now afford. She'd given up her dreams of getting an actual degree years ago. Now, she busted her ass to pay off someone else's debt.

"I'll bring the cheque right over," Raven told the woman. She returned the coffee carafe, printed the cheque and slipped a menu under her arm. Her skin prickled with unease as the tiny hairs on her arms stood. Was TDD watching her every move?

Get a grip. He wanted a menu.

TDD took the small booth on the far end of the restaurant. Table Fifteen, used mostly by late-night lovers for tonsil hockey or loners for brooding. She gulped and resisted the urge to look at him. *Act normal.*

Normal? What in the Underworld was that? Stale coffee coated her tongue. She popped another mint in her mouth and walked like a drunk lumberjack toward the table with the demanding wife. The loose change in her apron jingled with each step.

The longer Raven served the general public, the more she hated people in general. The drunken frat boys at table six yelled at each other over the static speaker crooning oldies. Their excessive banter appeared to impress the young women hanging off them but did little to endear them to Raven.

"Here you go." She placed the cheque down on the table along with two mints in front of the middle-aged couple, and left before the woman could demand anything else. Taking a deep breath did little to quell Raven's nerves. She pulled the menu from under her arm and turned in slow motion to the booth across the diner. With a pace closer to a shuffle than a hustle, she made her way over to the new customer's booth. Her black pants grew tight and her white work blouse suddenly felt frumpy.

Instead of staring her down, as she expected, the man's gaze focused on the window to take in the nightlife of North Burnaby. The corner of his full lips tugged up in a slight smirk as if he found something amusing. Raven found nothing about working at this crappy restaurant amusing.

Unfortunately, any decent job these days required a bachelor's degree at minimum. Dan's Diner required the ability to speak passable English and had flexible hours that allowed her to work for the family business on the side.

Raven clutched the plastic menu tightly and closed the distance. One of the drunken frat boys spoke as she walked by. Something about her ass. Her step faltered. It wasn't the first time, nor the last, a customer commented on her body. Positive or negative, it was always unwanted, but she needed the tip, so she let it slide. The size of her ass had never prevented her from taking orders or delivering food. Fitting into certain clothes, maybe. Avoiding table corners that seemingly jutted out of nowhere, certainly. But never waitressing.

The others at the table snickered.

Screw them.

TDD stiffened and his gaze flicked first to her and then to the rambunctious, entitled group of wealthy students behind her. His face darkened and an eerie sense of foreboding filled the diner—as if rage itself flowed from his pores and radiated through the grease-laden air. The lights flickered and the room dimmed. The music stopped.

The table behind her went quiet.

Raven shuddered and completed the final steps to stand at the man's table. She slipped the menu in front of him and smoothed down her thick cotton apron. The entire time, his focus remained trained on the now-silent, mini-frat party.

Raven cleared her throat.

Nothing.

"Welcome to Dan's Diner. Our special tonight is—"

The man turned his attention to her, and the music and lighting returned. His Otherness rolled over her in a sweet, dangerous wave. His skin shone like smooth porcelain, contrasting sharply with his dark features and ink-black hair. His gaze enthralled her—piercing eyes, pools of black, as if the pupil bled into the iris, leaving only a sliver of silver along the edges. She could easily fall into the murky depths and not care if she ever resurfaced.

Eyes of the Underworld. Like hers.

Raven's scalp prickled as if all the hair on her head decided to stand up and say, "Take me!" Mom had kept her and her brother away from anything remotely connected to the Underworld, and all the realms within its domain, going as far as making them wear contacts to hide their nature. Raven and her brother grew up pretending to be fox shifters like the rest of the family.

The man's black brows rose. "You were saying?"

His deep gravelly voice danced along her skin.

Oh, sweet baby Odin. No. The low rumbling timbre made her want to do all sorts of things. Dirty things. Naughty things. She squeezed her thighs together.

Within five minutes, not even, this man turned her into a mewling kitten with three words. Raven mentally cursed. Instead of what? A bitter, late-twenty-something waitress with a mountain of debt? Ugh.

Grandma Lu always said Crawford women had strong backbones, not wishbones. She'd throw punches in her casket if she saw her granddaughter now.

Raven smoothed her apron. "The special is—"

"I'll have a coffee, black."

"Like your soul?" The thought slipped through her lips before she could stop it.

He blinked.

"Any food?" Good save.

He narrowed his eyes and shook his head.

"One black coffee, coming right up." Cheap ass. She snatched back the menu and walked away to get his order. The weight of his gaze pressed against her skin like a strong wind.

Server Pet Peeve Number One, Campers. Raven hated customers who ordered one of the cheapest items on the menu and nursed it through her whole shift—essentially taking away a perfectly good table where other, potentially higher tipping customers could've sat. Campers pitched a tent, laid claim to their campsite and stayed for a relaxing, extended vacation.

Raven slapped the useless menu back on the pile. Making numbered lists helped soothe her and the restless dark energy she harboured inside. It was an old habit. She wrote down all sorts of lists in her notebook at home, and if she took a deep breath and closed her eyes, she could see the lined page containing all her Server Pet Peeves as if it lay in front of her. Raven lacked many skills, but memory wasn't one of them.

Raven's gaze scanned the near-empty diner and sighed. One good-looking, if not ominous, camper wouldn't destroy her already-dismal tip prospects tonight.

Or any night.

Raven grimaced. At this rate, she'd never pay her way out of the hot mess money hole her useless sack of an ex dumped her in.

Hot coffee spilled over the mug's edge and burned her hand.

"Odin's balls!" She sucked in a breath and pulled her arm back. Flapping her hand in the air didn't help. The skin stopped screaming and settled to a dull ache while the surface bloomed a lovely shade of red. Raven slammed the coffee pot back on the burner.

After sopping up the mess with a rag and delivering the cheque to the now mute party table, she made her way back to TDD.

Behind her, the frat guys and their groupies slapped money on the table and cleared out of the diner in under a minute flat. No jeers, leers or otherwise typical behaviour of the early-twenty-somethings trying to use alcohol to find themselves.

"Here you go." She placed the mug on the table.

This time, she managed not to flinch when he looked up.

"Can I get you anything else?" she asked.

He continued to study her unblinking.

She turned to walk away.

"Yes."

She froze.

"As a matter of fact, you can." His voice rolled over her like a slow-moving thunderstorm, offering all kinds of dark secrets and salacious promises.

She pivoted toward him.

"A moment of your time?" He waved his hand, palm up, at the bench across from him.

Raven hesitated. She didn't need to look over her shoulder to know they were alone. Even Mr. Grumpy Pants from table ten had left. At least Mike was in the kitchen.

Right. Like her pimple-faced brother, who weighed maybe a buck fifty soaking wet, would stop the barely contained hurricane in front of her.

"Uh..."

He raised a brow and his gaze briefly swept the empty diner behind her. His kissable lips twisted into another grin. "Unless you're busy?"

Ass.

She pursed her lips and crossed her arms. Her cheap blouse pulled at her shoulders. She took a deep breath and instantly regretted it. This close, his scent cut through the grimy stench unique to Dan's Diner and wound around her. He smelled like a mysterious forest, laden with magic, before the sun slipped away and the shadows took over, when light started to play tricks on the mind and made up monsters from errant branches.

Raven shivered.

"Will you sit with me?" Something in his chiselled face dared her to object.

She slipped into the booth. Her polyester pants slid smoothly along the synthetic leather seat. "If you're looking to hook up, you're looking in the wrong place."

His eyebrows shot up.

Why did she say that? Heat flooded her cheeks. Grandma Lu would be proud, but from his amused expression, not quite the right thing to say.

"You mistake me." His gaze sparkled with silent laughter. "I'm not looking to *hook up*. I'm looking for your brother."

Raven leaned back. "My brother?"

"Yes."

"You want to see Mike? Why didn't you say so earlier? He's in the kitchen." Raven scooted to the end of the booth. "Go bother him."

The sparkle and interest drained from his face. "I'm not looking for Mike."

And then she knew without any uncertainty. Even if she had more than two brothers, she'd know exactly who this man sought. She slumped in the booth. Just as she knew this wasn't a social call. Dread swamped her, coating her skin. The twisted emotion sank into her flesh. Her heart slowed and beat heavy. Her skin prickled.

This dark fae wanted her brother, which meant one thing.

He was in trouble.

As if the stranger sensed her inner dread, he nodded. "I'm looking for Bear."

Chapter Two

"Most women are attracted to the simple things in life. Like men."

~Henny Youngman

The last words Raven spoke to TDD echoed through her head. *The coffee's on me. You can leave now.* She squeezed her eyes shut. Nope, it didn't work. Opened or closed, she saw his dark Other eyes blaze, the black pools crashing like an angry ocean, before he got up and left the diner without a word.

The rest of her shift had been uneventful, boring even. After the mysterious man left, she caught herself more than once staring out the diner's greasy windows into the dark abyss of the night to fantasize what it would be like to run her hands down TDD's hard chest. She'd spoken with him for a few minutes, but apparently, that was all the time her libido needed to obsess over him. Where was he now? Where did someone foreboding like TDD lurk in his spare time?

Mike shoved the door to the restaurant closed until it clicked and turned to her. "Are you going to stand in the alley with that garbage all night?"

Raven scowled at her brother and turned to fling the last bag in the dumpster. She released the heavy lid of the bin as fast as possible, letting it slam closed. Too slow, the smell smacked her in the face. Overheated, spoiled refuse had a gross smell category all its own. Raven sucked on her mint and tried to will the peppermint flavour to drive away the assault on her nose. No luck.

After double checking the door had locked, Mike stepped from the security light and into the inky darkness with her. He'd pulled on a light jacket, but even in the dark, the white of his kitchen uniform stood out.

Mike shoved his work key in his back pocket. "You want me to walk you home?"

She bit back a laugh. *Oh, Mike. You sweet, sweet boy.* "You're my little brother. Shouldn't it be the other way around?"

His chest puffed out. "I'm nineteen."

She folded her arms. She didn't bother with a sweater or jacket. Her shirt and pants stuck to her sweaty limbs and the idea of pulling more clothing made additional sweat break out across her skin. The "fresh" breeze added notes of sea scum and stale fish, instead of clean ocean and pine, but the wind would help cool her down.

The bustle of the nearby street trickled down the empty and otherwise silent alley. Normally, neither of them lingered in the alley after work. Already, the stench of rotting garbage left too long in the summer heat and old, pungent urine smothered her senses.

"I'm a badass fox," Mike continued.

"You are, but you also have class in about five hours. You're not going to become a software engineer if you flunk out. You need to get home." Part of her wished she could follow. Her parents had offered her old room but moving back to her parents' place was one step her pride wouldn't let her take.

"Like you should talk. You work two jobs. When's the last time you slept for more than five hours? The bags under your eyes are bigger than your bank loan."

She blinked. "Low blow."

"Relax. The semester just started. Half the class is still mentally on vacation, including the prof, and the other half is made up of gamers. Everyone's tired. I'll fit right in." He flashed the wide grin she loved, but it quickly dissolved. He hesitated. "You sure you don't want me to walk with you. That last customer seemed to..."

Seemed to melt off my discount-bin panties and scare me at the same time? Raven shivered. She pulled the elastic band from her long black hair and shook out the ponytail. She ran her hands through the strands and whipped her head around enough to look like a head-banging lunatic at a free music festival. If she didn't, the grease would keep her hair in place as if the elastic still held it together. "Seemed to what?"

Mike glanced down the dark alley before unchaining his bike. "Unsettle you."

And nothing unsettles you. He didn't say the words. He didn't need to.

"And he creeped me out." Mike gave a fake shiver.

You and me, both. TDD wasn't too happy getting stone-walled and kicked out of Dan's Diner. The sensation of impending doom only intensified when her twin brother, Bear, didn't respond to her texts or calls. Not unusual, but not a good sign, either. Especially not with TDD somewhere out in the night looking for him.

"Well, he's gone. Besides..." She winked. "I'm pretty badass, too."

Mike laughed and crammed the last of the chains and locks for his bike into his bag. Thieves in the Lower Mainland were ruthless. They'd steal an unlocked wheel out of spite. Somewhere in Vancouver, a master thief slept on a pile of useless bike parts.

Mike wouldn't have to keep his bike in a dark alley full of criminals if Dan let him stash it inside. Health violation. Go figure.

"Okay, Rayray. See you Sunday?"

She snorted. "Like I'd miss roast night."

Mike's smile returned, and he pushed off on his bike and rode along the uneven concrete. She watched him head toward the warm glow of the main street's lights before turning to go the opposite way. She ran into a concrete wall.

No, not a wall, the hard chest of a man. The soft fabric of a sweatshirt smushed into her face and provided no buffer to the solid muscle beneath. An iron grip clamped around her arms.

"TDD," she breathed. His alluring scent of promises whispered at twilight slammed into her senses.

His dark gaze widened. "Tee-Double-Dee?"

She snapped her mouth shut.

He let go of one of her arms and caught a strand of her loose hair. "So, Rayray. What kind of badass are you?"

Ice seared her veins. He heard them? How? The alley was empty. They would've heard or smelled him. Well, maybe not Raven—her sense of smell was mediocre at best—but Mike? Nothing got past that sly fox.

The shadows clinging to the alley seemed to gather and surround them like a cold cloak, shrouding their figures from prying eyes. Raven shook her head. The gloomy lighting in the alley returned to normal. Her mind must've played tricks on her. Shadows didn't move like that.

TDD tilted his head. "Some sort of shifter? Fox, like your brother, maybe?" He let the long dark strand slip through his fingers. "I really wish you'd gone with Option A."

Raven clenched her hand and drew her free arm back.

"I don't want to do this," he continued.

Raven's fist connected with his jaw. His head snapped to the side, and his shoulders jerked. Pain lanced down her arm from her knuckles.

TDD's head whipped back to her. "Is that the best you've got?"

Her fist throbbed. "Well, yeah, kind of."

He grabbed her free arm and the shadows enveloped them.

Chapter Three

Normal moms preach "Always wear clean underwear in case you get in an accident." My mom says, "Always wear clean underwear in case you get lucky."

~Raven, wallowing in the hardships of her life

Raven blinked and three things became apparent. One, TDD had mesmerizing eyes and flawless skin. Even with the hint of stubble, his face held an undeniable rugged appeal— too rough to be pretty, too chiselled to be soft, but cutting, smouldering and devastating in a deadly way. His cheekbones appeared carved from granite with a precision scalpel. His ink-black hair contrasted with his porcelain skin, almost severely. The only soft features on his face were lush, kissable lips, the colour of delicate rose petals. If she leaned forward and kissed him, would he taste like sin?

TDD hovered about a foot away and peered at her as if assessing her mental state.

Good luck. She'd given up trying to figure out her brain long ago.

Two, even though the grime still clung to her skin like greasy moisturizer, without the stink of the diner masking his scent, TDD smelled unbelievably delicious. The fragrance of a mysterious forest at night pooled around them, threatening to drown her and she couldn't muster any concern. Instead, she fought the urge to fling out her arms and fall back into the waiting depths.

She licked her lips.

His gaze flicked to her mouth and tracked her movements. He leaned forward, gaze darkening.

And three, they weren't in Kansas anymore. Okay, not Burnaby, not Canada, and certainly not the Mortal Realm.

Along with TDD's scent, dark magic wound around them with its seductive power and allure. It tugged at her own essence, deep within her core. Like the neighbourhood boy no one wanted their kids to hang out with because they suspected he'd end up a serial killer, the potent energy cajoled and beckoned her to come out and play. And she wanted to. Oh, did she want to, despite knowing she shouldn't. Just within reach, her fingers itched to wrap around the power, to wield it, despite having no clue how to do so. And just like that devious child, if she did surrender to the unrelenting call and play with the destructive magic, her actions would lead to trouble and heartache.

Darkness blanketed the room, but the air tasted of scandalous promises and lust.

The Underworld.

"Before we get started..." TDD's voice rumbled and trailed off. He still held her arms, but his grip loosened. The inexpensive material of her blouse stuck to her oily skin. "Explain what or who Tee-Double-Dee is."

Heat rushed to her face again. Just great. Like she wanted to explain her pet nickname for her good-looking captor.

TDD watched her, his body still, arms tense, gaze flicking back and forth to take in details. Slowly, his stern face softened, and the corners of his lips tugged up. "Fine. We'll revisit that topic later."

She relaxed.

"Nice hair, by the way," he said.

What in the Banshee did he mean by that? Her hands drifted up with a mind of their own and patted her hair. Normally straight and sleek, her hair had poofed out in...waves? Did the potent energy of the Underworld act like some sort of magical diffuser? Is that why her scalp tingled?

"Where's your brother?" TDD asked.

She dropped her arms to her sides. "If I didn't tell you before, what makes you think I'll tell you now?"

He stepped back, and the shadows in the room

rolled away. The expanding light revealed their surroundings. They stood in a small, sterile room. The shadows continued to recede and uncovered metal bars. They were in a jail cell. The fluorescent light above them flickered. A low hum settled over the room from somewhere outside, suggesting a generator. An off-the-grid jail cell in some dark realm within the Underworld.

Fabulous.

"Do you know where we are?" he asked.

"The Underworld." If Mom knew, she'd have a fit. Half of Raven's childhood memories contained lectures about the evils of this place and the importance of avoiding it, compliments of Mom. Oh heck, Mom would rage if she knew an unknown man held her eldest daughter captive in a jail cell in any of the realms, including the mortal one.

He nodded and turned to walk away. His feet hit the concrete and created an echo.

Before Raven moved, shadows burst forth and wrapped around her wrists and ankles. Like stiff rope, the dark bands materialized into something physical and held her in place.

Her own energy coiled within her, ready to spring.

Raven froze. She'd never heard of anyone manipulating shadows like some sort of rhythmic gymnast gone bad. At least not as a common skill. But she also knew very little of the Underworld, and not all Others ventured into the Mortal Realm.

"Who are you?" After his shadow trick, possibilities

ran through her head and none of them were good.

He ignored her, stepped from the jail cell and shut the door. The hinges creaked. "Take them out."

"Excuse me?"

"Take out whatever haywire human contraption you have shielding your eyes."

She blinked.

"Your contacts. Remove them."

He knew. He must've sensed her Otherness somehow. The boring brown contacts she always wore muted her natural eye colour, the one thing holding her apart from any other rundown waitress.

"I'm not taking my contacts out," she said. "One, you'd have to release me from these shadow cuff things, which I'm guessing you won't. And two, my hands last touched garbage bags and a dumpster. Eyes are, like, the number one site for infection."

He pulled off his hoodie. The black shirt underneath tugged up to reveal smooth abs before he pulled it back down. He tossed the sweater on a nearby bench and crossed his arms over his wide chest.

Don't stare at his muscles, don't stare at his...

Oh crap!

The thin fabric of his simple T-shirt pulled tight across his chest and biceps when he folded his arms. If dehydration-induced delirium from excessive drooling counted as an interrogation style, she was doomed.

A slow smile spread across TDD's face as the bands grew tighter and the shadows melted off the walls and flowed over the floor toward her.

What in the Underworld was wrong with her? Drooling over her captor like some Stockholm victim. Ugh. Sorry, Grandma Lu.

"Let's try this again. Where is your brother? I don't wish to hurt you," he said.

"Then don't. I have no idea where he is."

"He's your twin." He spoke his statement as if it provided some grand explanation. It didn't. The shadow bands around her arms tightened again.

"Yes, my twin. My twin who alienated himself from the entire family, myself included." The truth turned sour on her tongue.

He clenched his jaw. "I find that hard to believe."

She released a deep breath and some of the tension in her chest and shoulders eased away. "Look. Part of me wants to be difficult just to spite you for kidnapping me, but I have a low pain tolerance and no delusions of grandeur. I honestly don't know where he is. He hasn't returned my last three texts and I haven't seen or heard from him in a week." No need to mention she normally heard from him every other day, unlike anyone else in the family. TDD was right. Bear was her twin, and no matter how wayward he went, she loved him.

"A week?" TDD's lips twisted into a frown, and he stepped away from the cell to grab something.

"That's my bag!"

The cold look he gave her over his shoulder dismissed her outrage. Pulling out her phone, he tapped on the screen. Really, what did she expect? A kidnapper with morals?

"What's your passcode?"

"What's your name?"

His eyebrows rose.

Really? His name? Out of all the things she should be concerned about in this situation, she decided to find out what to call him first? Face palm.

"Cole."

"Cole?"

He grunted.

"The big, bad manipulator of shadows is named Cole?" Not exactly original, or fear-inducing. Then again, her name was as unoriginal as it got.

"Would you prefer *Beul na h-Oidhche gu Camhanaich...*"

He pronounced his name: blah blah blah kaym-hay-nitch.

"Lord of Shadows, Master of Darkness, Keeper of Secrets, Patron Fae of Assassins, Bastard of Erebus, Born of Chaos?" His gaze flashed with silver shards of lightning and his mouth clamped in a firm line.

"Err." Obviously, he had some daddy issues. He certainly wore an annoyed expression as he waited for a more intelligent response. Then his words sunk in. Holy fuck. A dark fae lord had kidnapped her. Dread cleaved up her spine. "It's 2-3-2-3."

Cole grunted and punched in the numbers.

"A really scary dude came looking for you tonight?" Cole read her last text to her brother, his black eyebrows creeping up.

She shrugged.

After scanning the screen and scrolling through her messages, he tossed the phone back in her bag. He flicked his fingers and the shadows dispersed, retreating to the corners and crevices of the room.

Raven stumbled forward, now a mere foot from the bars. Cole swung open the prison door and motioned for her to come closer. Her heart chose now to beat hard, hammering away like some spastic punk rocker on a new drum set.

"You expect me to come closer?"

"Do you want to go home?"

No. Yes. Ugh. Her lady parts needed a slap in the face.

A cheeky voice in her head piped up—*it's not a slap they need.* Heat crept along her neck to her cheeks.

"Unless you can get home on your own?"

She took a deep breath before stepping forward.

Cole smirked and closed his muscular arms around her. Immediately surrounded by his intoxicating scent and intimidating warmth, Raven swallowed and held her breath. His shirt brushed against her face, reminding her of the hard chest and abs underneath. A chuckle rumbled from Cole sending tingles to all the right places. Shadows swirled around them and closed in.

Her head grew light and her vision swam as the world around her seemed to tilt and bend. When the shadows withdrew, Raven found herself alone in the damp, dark alley behind Dan's Diner, with her bag unceremoniously dumped at her feet. "Goodbye,

Cole."

The darkness answered her with silence. The summer breeze brushed past her. The nightlife of North Burnaby bustled along the nearby street.

She should be glad. His departure meant she'd never see him again. Right? Yet, longing clouded the thought of never seeing his handsome features and lethal grace. Her fist still ached from hitting his titanium-plated jaw. She bent to retrieve her bag and turned down the alley to make her way home. Her limbs grew heavy. Not in all her twenty-seven years had she felt so suddenly and unmistakably alone.

Chapter Four

"I need to go where there's no responsibilities or shoes required."

> *~Raven Crawford, every day on the way to work*

Raven balanced a cardboard tray with two coffees in one hand and yanked open the door to Crawford Investigations with the other. The familiar smell of paper, copier ink and gun oil washed over her along with the cool office air.

"Hey, Rayray." Terry Crawford, her stepfather, glanced up and shot her a warm smile. His kind brown eyes crinkled at the corners and his bald head exposed from his receding hairline shone under the fluorescent lights.

"Hey, Dad. Glad you got the air conditioner fixed. It's going to be hot today." She glanced at the door to his office. He'd pulled it shut, which meant the client had already arrived. On the drive over, in between worrying about the new whining sound coming from her car's engine and what hot mess her brother had dumped her in, she debated what to tell Dad about last night, and when.

Now was not the time. There might never be a right time. How did she tell the man who loved and raised her and Bear as his own that in his continued act of defiance, Bear had done something so spectacularly stupid a dark fae lord kidnapped her for information on his whereabouts? At least she didn't have to worry about Cole attacking any of her other siblings. Though she had a younger brother and sister, Cole's assessment of her relationship with Bear was correct. She was the closest to him. If she didn't know where he was, no one in her family did.

Bear would probably resurface when the danger passed. She'd rip into him then. Right now, she needed to focus on the task at hand. She leaned down and whispered, "I hope this job pays well."

Dad nodded and gave his office door a weary look. "I know it's before ten o'clock, but I could use your help on this one."

She straightened and the weight of sleep deprivation slid off her. "Person or thing?"

What Raven lacked in fighting skills, she made up for with her unique abilities. She specialized in finding things and tailing people. Dad usually called her in for searches or when he needed to follow a questionable spouse more covertly than a car in Vancouver traffic allowed.

Dad scratched his jaw. Evidently, he hadn't shaved in days, and now salt-and-pepper stubble speckled his face. "Thing, I think."

Her brows shot up. "Interesting."

"I don't know much. I'll fill you in after the interview." He grabbed the folder in front of him. "Hey, did you hear about the kidnapping at school?"

Her head snapped up from smelling her coffee. What? At Juni's school? Why hadn't her sister texted her? Was she okay? "What? No."

"It's okay." Her dad cracked a large smile. "She woke up."

Raven groaned and plunked the tray down on the table. Always the comedian. Dad had a knack for telling terrible jokes regardless of whether the timing was appropriate or not. He usually waited until she was fully awake, though. And caffeinated.

She held one coffee out for him and took the other for herself. It was never too hot for coffee. Anyone who said otherwise couldn't be trusted.

"Thanks." He took the offered coffee, and they walked toward his office. The thin carpet muffled their footsteps. Dad rarely had her walk in blind to a client meeting. Something about this one had already set him on edge. He told a dad-joke before noon.

"I don't want to keep this guy waiting." Her dad

reached forward to hold the door to his office open. "Shall we?"

A tall man in a designer suit, tailored to fit his large body perfectly, stood and turned at their entrance. Automatically, his attire and demeanor set him apart from their normal clientele, and contrasted with her own business pants and blouse, both in cut and cost. This guy should be downtown at a fancy restaurant, or in a boardroom, not in a rundown PI business in North Burnaby. They generally worked cases involving insurance fraud and cheating spouses.

No wonder Dad was on edge.

Raven stepped forward and offered her hand. "Hello. I'm Raven Crawford, one of the associates here."

Up close, she realized he was a lot bigger than she originally pegged him for—his large frame and wide shoulders masked by the expensive cut of his suit. "Luke Bane."

He gripped her hand in a firm handshake and his amber gaze locked on hers. The rough skin and strong grip of his hands indicated he worked hard at something manual. The character trait didn't match his smooth exterior or polished scent. Hard angles gave his attractive face enough edge to prevent him from appearing pretty.

The man leaned forward with amusement pulling at his lips. His subtle cologne wound around her. Oh yeah, this guy knew he was handsome. Was she supposed to swoon? Not happening. He was totally

Megan's type. Until she got married and started popping out babies, her friend always went for the smooth operators.

As good looking as Luke Bane was, something seemed off. His expensive suit and handsome features acted as a smock to cover something else. Something dark, twisted and hostile lurked below the smooth veneer of his flawless skin.

Cold ice slithered along her spine and her scalp prickled. An Other. From the menace radiating from his bulking frame, she'd bet a night's worth of tips he hailed from the Underworld. She had no proof, but she possessed a pretty decent "faedar."

The air conditioner whirred in the background with a steady hum.

"A pleasure." She pulled her hand back a little too quickly.

His gaze paused on her for a moment longer before switching to her dad.

Dad waved his hand at the two seats on the guest side of his desk.

Luke adjusted his tie and sat back down. Every hair on her body stood at attention. Along with his size, the smooth way Luke Bane moved and conveyed confidence screamed predator. His gaze gleamed in the streaks of light through the dusty blinds.

Dad took his seat on the opposite side of the desk. As a fox shifter, Dad quelled the innate instinct to flee from large predators all the time. Otherwise, he'd be an absolute mess walking around current society with streets full of supernatural beings. It certainly wouldn't bode well for business, either, if he scurried away and hid under the desk every time a powerful client came in with a potential job.

Raven could've pulled up another chair to sit beside her dad, but the last thing she wanted was to place herself in a more vulnerable position. Besides, she looked to the skies for escape, not lurking low and pressed to the ground like Dad. Instead of sitting, she moved to stand behind her dad's left shoulder, and took a long sip of coffee. The heavenly aroma encased her face and the smooth creamy goodness coated her tongue.

"Thank you for coming in Mr. Bane. You said very little over the phone." Dad folded his hands on the desk in front of him. "I haven't had a chance to brief Raven on this case, yet, so let's go through the details again and see if we can be of assistance to you."

Huh.

Guess Dad couldn't suppress all his instincts. He only folded his hands like that when his nerves ate at him.

A slow smile spread across Luke's face, as if he tasted their unease.

Strike one, asshole.

"I would like you to locate the *Claíomh Solais*," he said.

Raven frowned at the fae word. "An object of light...or something?"

His unsettling gaze flicked to her. "Or something."

"Mr. Bane." Dad took a deep breath. "We can't help you if we have limited information. We'll need to know more than the name of the object. If you're holding back—"

"A week ago, the Claíomh Solais was stolen. I want it found and brought to me."

A week ago. Dread flittered along her skin and sunk into her muscles with barbed spikes. Raven didn't believe in coincidences. Two menacing Others within twenty-four hours—one looking for her brother, the other searching for a stolen object, and both missing for a week.

Coincidence?

Nothing involving Others and the Underworld ever resulted in coincidences.

Oh, Brother Bear, Brother Bear. What have you done?

"I assume you're not the only one looking for this object?" She squinted at Luke.

He relaxed into his chair. "You are correct, Miss Crawford. Once news of the theft became known, many parties have taken an interest."

Cole being one of them. Great. She took another sip of coffee, but the java failed to drive away her unease.

"Why come to us?" Dad asked.

"It is known your agency is excellent at finding stolen goods."

"It is known?" Raven held back a snort and shuffled her feet instead. They ached a little after her long shift last night.

He nodded. "As is your discretion."

Huh. Raven couldn't deny they had a great track record when it came to retrievals, but Crawford Investigations paled in comparison to the big agencies downtown, both in noteworthy cases and in resources.

Again, no coincidences with beings from the Dark Realms. Mr. Luke Bane came to them because he knew of the connection between the object and her brother.

"We need to know more about the object," Dad insisted. "What does it do? Where was it taken from? How did the thief steal it? Is there a police report?"

Luke laced his fingers together and rested his forearms on the chair's armrests. Unlike Dad's nervous habit, Luke's actions held the practiced air of a smooth-talking politician.

Strike two.

"The Claíomh Solais can dispel darkness."

The fae couldn't technically lie, but this guy could probably talk circles around the truth without a misstep. His statement answered none of the questions

"Is there any special handling instructions? Will it harm us?" Dad flapped his hand in fast circles, motioning for more information. This would be a long interview if he had to prompt Mr. Bane for every snippet of information.

"You have to deliberately set off the Claíomh Solais. And even if you managed that, absolute light shouldn't hurt you." His gaze flicked to Raven. "Unless you're from the dark."

Raven frowned. If the Claíomh Solais was an object

of light, why did a dark fae want it?

"One more thing." Luke's smooth voice interrupted her thoughts. "I require both the Claíomh Solais and the thief brought to me. Unharmed, of course."

Anger sliced through Raven's veins. She knew without hesitation her brother was involved in this hot mess. Luke most likely didn't realize she knew of the connection. With his last condition, if they accepted this job, she'd have to haul in and hand over her own twin brother to this dark fae and whatever evil punishment he planned. Sadistic fuck.

Strike three.

"I'm afraid we can't help you," she said.

Luke's eyes widened, and he turned to Dad. "I have more information to provide."

Tempting, but no. She stepped back. "There's no need for more information. We're not taking the job."

Maybe she spoke too soon. Maybe she should've let Dad try to pry more information from this douche canoe first. But she couldn't. He'd essentially ordered the capture of her brother and the smug bastard treated them like clueless minions. Every additional second she spent standing in his presence without hurling office supplies at his head made her stomach acid bubble up.

She lifted her takeaway cup to her face and inhaled the coffee without taking a sip. In and out. In and out. The warm scented steam caressed her face. *Do not attack the dangerous fae. Do not engage.*

"As I said on the phone, I pay well." He looked slowly around the room, lip curling up. "Something I think your business would benefit from."

Asshole.

The air conditioner groaned in agreement.

Dad's body stiffened. He pushed away from the desk and stood. His khaki pants and blue polo did little to hide his lean, non-aggressive runner's frame. "My daughter is correct. I'm afraid we're unable to assist you at this time. Thank you for coming in. I can recommend some of the bigger agencies downtown. They have excellent reputations and more resources. They will be better equipped for this task."

A tight smile replaced Luke's relaxed expression. He stood and fastened the top button on the jacket of his expensive suit. "No need. I have some contacts."

After shaking her dad's hand, he grasped Raven's, his grip still strong and warm. What had she expected? A lightning bolt? A flash of images containing mutilated bodies?

Mr. Bane's gaze locked her in pace. "Take care, Miss Crawford. Till we meet again."

He gave her hand an extra squeeze before releasing it and walked out of the office. She didn't breathe until the building door closed. His parting words sent numbing cold to every limb. *Till we meet again.* His unsettling gaze held promise—not the warm fuzzy kind, the cold psychotic kind.

Raven's life held a lot of uncertainties. Most people's lives did. But she knew one thing for sure. She had no wish for her future to have Luke Bane in it.

"I hope you have a good reason for turning down

such a high paying job," Dad said. "The guy might've been a prick, but he was right about one thing. We could use the money." Dad's voice held no anger, only questions.

She nodded and turned to her Dad. "Bear."

"Bear?" He choked on his coffee. "What does he have to do with this?"

"He's the thief."

Chapter Five

"Naked acrobatics are on my résumé."

~*Miles Teller*

Raven eyed the murky waters of Burrard inlet. The full moon overhead cast eerie, glitter-like strands of pale light reflecting off the rippling surface of the ocean. The shore on the south side remained clear, but the eye of the storm was always calm before chaos reigned.

Chaos.

Born of Chaos.

Beul na h-Oidhche gu Camhanaich, Bastard of Erebus, Born of Chaos. Master of heated looks and panty-melting voice.

Her heart skipped a beat.

Ugh. She needed to get out more and rid her mind of Cole and all the things she'd thought of doing with him. It had been two days since he'd kidnapped her and not even twenty-four hours since Luke Bane visited the family business, but the quiet didn't fool her.

Bear still hadn't returned her calls or texts, and she needed to find him before Cole or Luke did.

After the interrogation from her parents about the kidnapping, Bear's potential involvement, and another eventless shift at the diner, Raven made her way to the banks of Vancouver Harbour with the sole purpose of seeking out her brother and getting answers. Once beautiful and prosperous, filth and debris lined the shore. The remains of previous oil spills had long since congealed into black sludge. The tip of a tanker jutted out of the rippling water as a visual reminder of a long-ago Titanic-esque tragedy. The casualties of this event were "inconsequential" sea life though, not affluent travellers who'd have beautiful Hollywood actors portray them years later. Dead fish and other sea life floated in the black abyss like a jelly fruit cake gone wrong. Luckily, she didn't plan to swim across the channel.

Without a doubt, the most used route to the North Shore involved the Lion's Gate Bridge. It was the only way to cross on foot or with a vehicle after a horde of banshees took out the other bridge, but Lion's Gate wasn't necessarily the safest option. Now run by trolls, she either had to pay a fee she didn't have, owe a favour she would be stupid to grant or risk the eighteen hundred meter dash. At least two of the three options resulted in death. Luckily, Raven had another plan.

She pulled off her jeans and black T-shirt, folded them, and made a neat pile on top of her shoes. Her underwear quickly followed, and she tucked them into the fold of her pants. She could've flown directly from her house or work, but she chose not to.

One, she never flew from her house or her parents' place, if given a choice. The shifter community would ostracize her family even more than they already did if anyone discovered Raven and Bear were part fae, not fox shifters like everyone believed. Shifters could be really snooty and condescending to beings from the Other Realms, believing their Mortal Realm origins made them superior somehow.

Two, although suspiciously absent, she didn't trust Cole or Luke. Both probably watched the house. Flying directly from there showed her hand, and she wasn't ready for that.

Three, bigger, badder things lurked in the shadows, both on land and in the air. Once shifted, she was more vulnerable to predation. Better to scope out the water first and then cut across quickly.

And four...though she used her shifting to carry out work for her dad, she tried to limit shifting on her time off.

A heavy weight settled on her shoulders and pulled her limbs toward the ground. No. She couldn't let these thoughts consume her.

She shook her head, letting the long strands of her midnight-black hair caress her naked skin. Although she disliked parts of her body, predominantly the jiggly parts, she found standing naked on the shore freeing. She faced the ocean and let the Salish Sea's breeze flow past her. Despite the cesspool of garbage and oil, the wind carried fresh air from beyond the inlet where magic kept the ocean clean. The heat from the hot summer's day had lingered well into the night and even the wind off the water held some warmth. The water lapped the smooth stones at her feet.

With a deep breath, Raven focused inward. She found the animal essence waiting beady eyes focused and alert.

Pushing deep, she ripped the essence from her center until it morphed, melting into her bones and limbs, consuming her human shape like a ravenous beast. Her mind shattered, fracturing into multiple pieces as her body erupted into a conspiracy of ravens. Sleek and black, the harbingers of death held her mind together as a collective consciousness.

She nudged them forward, and the swarm of black birds headed to the opposite bank.

Nine birds.

Last time she'd shifted, there'd been ten. She'd lost another one. She'd started out with over twenty. After Bear had "accidentally" offed one of her ravens with a sling shot when they were twelve, they learned the loss of a bird didn't cause any long-term damage. Her consciousness housed in the once-living bird redistributed to the remaining ones instead of disappearing into the ether. Losing the bird hurt like a full-body super-powered bra-snap and left a lasting sting, but when she shifted back to human form, she retained all her body parts, and arguably, her sanity.

One needs to have a mind in order to lose it. A memory of her brother's teasing flittered through her head.

Bear hadn't harmed any more birds since that day, and she had no explanation for the recent decrease in her congress. The birds were a manifestation of her Other nature, so obviously over the last year her power had dwindled, but why? And although losing ravens might not have any lasting physical or mental impacts on her human form, if she kept losing birds until none remained, would she retain the ability to shift at all? Did her power have a critical mass requirement or threshold? Would she start to lose body parts and her mind if her conspiracy dropped below a certain number? If she only had one bird left and someone or something killed it, would she die without another bird to transfer her mind to?

An offshore breeze gusted down the inlet. The air pushed against the strong wing spans of her birds. A group of ravens formed a conspiracy, congress or unkindness, not a flock, technically, but people rarely used the correct term these days, and she'd given up correcting her family long ago.

Oooooh. Shiny.

One of her birds swooped down and plucked something from the water's surface. The bird crushed and palpitated the food in its bill. The cold texture of dead fish meat crashed through the hive mind. The salty taste coated her senses. Metal. Toxins. Bad. The bird spat out the food. What remained of the fish hit the surface of the murky water below with a plop.

A dark cloud moved in front of the large moon and cast the murky waters of Burrard Inlet in darkness. A perfect response to her thoughts. Wolves howled in the forests north of the city. Real wolves rarely travelled this far South. With the full moon, though, werewolves roamed the wooded areas. Witches worked dark spells with their covens, and supernatural creatures in general let the lunar energy soak into their essence.

Tonight was a night for the powerful and wicked. A night the Others would dance, celebrate, and revel in the waves of energy as the bands flowed along, perfect for tethering and manipulating.

Raven should be in bed.

She had none of those skills. She could split her essence into an unkindness of ravens. A neat parlour trick and handy for searches, her power still paled in comparison to the rest of the supernatural community.

Last time she checked, though, she hadn't angered or crossed anyone important, so she should be left alone. No, if anyone pissed off the powerful, it would be Bear. And she was flying straight to his den to find him.

Chapter Six

"If you wallow with the pigs, expect to get dirty."
    ~Pretty much every father everywhere

The inside of the sweatshirt chaffed Raven's bare skin. Too much time on the drying rack had left this old high school sweatshirt somehow starchy instead of soft and worn.

Bear always made sure to leave a spare set of clothes on his apartment building's roof for her. The naked state might be natural but standing around in her birthday suit in front of her brother was awkward. For both of them.

She yanked on the sweatpants and folded the waistband over a few times. They still fell to the ground. Raven hoisted the pant legs up and padded across the roof to the fire escape. Despite the warmth of the summer's day lingering well into the night, the metal bars remained cool to the touch. Mist crept down the North Vancouver mountains, cascading toward the twinkling city lights. Rain drizzled down and left Raven's skin dewy. Typical Vancouver. It always rained. Dark and damp should be stamped on the city's website. It constantly surprised her that she hadn't started to mold yet.

After scaling down the fire escape ladder, Raven stepped onto the second-floor balcony of her brother's place. She rapped her knuckles on the sliding glass door and waited.

The rain fell heavier, pattering against the balcony's smooth surface, soaking through the crappy sweat suit and running down her clammy skin.

She knocked again.

Nothing.

Her heartbeat picked up. While Bear tended to ignore his phone and the front door buzzer, he *never* ignored her on the balcony. They had a silent pact. Raven never showed up like this unless she really needed him. Last time she'd arrived à la balcony, she interrupted her brother and his latest conquest. Bear hadn't hesitated, kicking the dagger-glaring redhead to the curb to let his bedraggled and distraught sister clamber into his home like some desperate rat on a sinking ship.

Twins before wins, he always said. His equivalent

of "bros before hoes." He probably still wished sometimes she'd been born a boy. He spent a lot of their childhood lamenting her girliness.

"Answer, Bear," she hissed.

Still nothing.

She leaned back and peered over the balcony. She'd already circled the building to ensure nobody lurked around, but a second look never hurt.

No one.

Well, almost no one.

Two large ravens perched one level down on the railing of the balcony of the apartment across the street. Their beady eyes tracked her movement.

"Don't judge me," she hissed.

They croaked and launched from the railing. A flutter of wings broke the silence of the night. The birds flapped their wings with strong powerful strokes to carry them into the inky darkness of the night.

The watchful presence of corvids might creep out the average person, but Raven wasn't average. She'd grown up with birds her entire life. Her dark energy somehow drew ravens and crows to her, more so if her brother was around.

Raven crouched by the flower pots and dug into the damp soil of the nearest one. The petals of this particular plant had turned brown and hard, drooping to the ground. How did Bear keep this thing from disintegrating? It had appeared dead for years.

Her fingers struck metal and she pulled out the key for the sliding door. Taking a deep breath, Raven unlocked her brother's place and stepped inside.

Her brother arrived into this world seven minutes and thirteen seconds before her with a chip already etched into his shoulder. With an absentee biological father and a mother working through her own issues, he grew up hating the world, and everything and everyone in it...except Raven.

When they came into their power at puberty— Raven transforming into a conspiracy of ravens, and Bear calling the death birds to him—he suffered another blow to his ego, and another loss, another rejection. He'd always hoped to gain something valuable from having an Other as a father. And instead, he essentially became the bird equivalent of a dog whistle. His words, not hers. She'd love him even if all he could do was drool.

Raven never doubted her twin's love for her. Ever. But without words, she knew he felt the divide in their powers sharply.

The cool night breeze followed her into Bear's living room, displacing the stale taste in the air. Her heart skipped with each step. Normally, when Raven was in close proximity to her twin, their magic pinged off each other. She hadn't sensed his presence outside on the patio and gaining entry to his apartment didn't change the growing sense of doom. The silence of Bear's place, along with the stale air, confirmed what her heart already knew. Bear hadn't been here for a while.

A tasteful two-bedroom apartment on the North Shore greeted her searching gaze. Sure, the area was run down, but what part of the former Metro Vancouver area wasn't, aside from some areas in West Vancouver and Downtown? Bear's tasteful furnishings and clean aesthetics confirmed he made more money taking the less than savoury jobs. He'd offered to help pay her debt once. She refused. Her own stupidity got her into her money problems, her grit and determination would dig her out.

Raven wandered around the living room. Her wet feet left tracks in the soft carpet. Bear might not be here, but hopefully a clue was. She glanced around his sparse decorations and show-home-esque décor and sighed. Bear never left anything out of place in his apartment. He had few truly personal belongings. On his bedside table, he had a picture of the two of them together, laughing their butts off at some lame joke Dad had told.

The summer after high school ended and before university began for Raven, her parents took the whole family—all four siblings—to Vancouver Island and they'd spent the day at Rathtrevor Beach without squabbling once. Raven and her twin had their whole adult lives ahead of them and hadn't realized the harsh reality that awaited them. Mom had snapped the candid photo, and somehow captured the love between the twins. Raven kept a copy of the same picture in her apartment.

A sound came from Bear's spare room. Raven froze. She strained to listen, letting the sounds from outside the apartment building fall away until only the living room buzzed around her.

There!

Like something sliding across a table.

She turned toward the room and tucked a loose strand of wet hair behind her ear. Tension clamped along her spine and her brain whirred with possibilities.

At least she'd left the sliding door open for a quick escape.

Thump, thump, thump.

Her heart beat so hard, it drowned out any other possible sounds. She pushed open the door. The hinges moved with a low, grinding creak.

Raven winced.

Nothing stirred in the room. No more sliding sounds. Not even her heart dared to thump. She shoved open the door the rest of the way.

A loud screech pierced the air. At the same time, a fluffy black object sprang from the top shelf of the nearby closet.

Raven squealed and leapt in the air. Her feet caught in the soggy ends of the sweatpants. She stumbled, and her back slapped the wall. Her heart hammered again and sweat broke out across her skin.

Kissa, her brother's deranged cat, hissed at her. Back arched, fur puffed out. With one last threatening yowl, the cat streaked past and ran off into her brother's living room.

Raven slumped against the wall. She took deep breaths until her heartrate slowed down. His cat. His stupid, moody cat, not some evil villain lurking in the shadows.

That *thing* had never liked her.

Well, good riddance.

Raven headed for the garbage next. The idea of scouring her brother's trash turned her stomach, but the study of garbage, or "Garbology," as Dad called it, was one of the best sources for information for a detective. Any half-decent private investigator slapped on latex gloves and went digging.

Bear's garbage was empty. Either he was an excellent housekeeper, or he purposely emptied his trash and cleaned up before he left for a job. Bear kept things neat and tidy but not this tidy. He didn't want any evidence left in his home.

Argh. What are you up to, Bear?

She puttered around her brother's apartment looking for clues. No more signs of Kissa. The demented hell-beast probably slipped out the sliding door. She'd worry, except that nasty creature probably took down fully-grown, rabid coyotes for sport.

She popped her head outside but couldn't spot Satan's spawn. She re-hid the key and stepped back into her brother's apartment. If she couldn't find any clues in his home, then she'd have to expand her search. She closed and locked the sliding door from the inside.

The shadows in the room shifted position as the traffic passed the building on the street below. Her sweat suit had started to dry, but the damp material still stuck to her limbs. Raven sighed and plucked a few paper clips off Bear's desk. She turned toward his front door and hesitated.

"Odin's balls!" Just in case her brother's beloved pet hid in the apartment, Raven scooped some food in an empty bowl. Not for the cat, but for Bear's sake.

She wiped the cat crunchies from her hands on her sweatpants. The crumbs remained glued to the cloth like large gritty sand at the beach. She kept wiping, but the action only smeared the crumbs deeper into the material and stirred up the slightly fishy smell of the cat food. With a groan, she left her brother's place through the front door. Thankfully, he'd installed one of those keypad locks. One push of a button and Raven secured her brother's home without a key.

The damp cuffs on her pants slapped the floor. The hallway walls of the building reeked of stale popcorn, sweat and that disturbing old man odor she could always identify, yet, never accurately describe beyond "old man." No matter how much fresh air she got afterward, the smells of this place gripped the inside of her nostrils for hours after visiting Bear.

Raven pulled up her sweatpants to prevent them from dragging as she walked. The carpet did little to dampen the sound of her bare feet padding toward the entrance. Fairly lean from shifting with a side of curves, Raven wasn't heavy, but the echo of her footsteps made her sound like a cyclops thundering down a runway. The material had long been stomped down to a threadbare sheet of fabric with a worn, dirty trail leading down the middle. All this place needed was a flickering light at the end of the hallway.

Not trusting the elevator, and knowing Bear didn't either, Raven hopped down the stairs. She stepped into the main entrance and peered into the night through the glass front door and windows.

Nothing. The glow of streetlights and the occasional car chugging down the street. Bear didn't live in a rich neighbourhood. Hardly anyone in the Mortal Realm did anymore. The Others made sure of that. Desperate people did desperate things.

Raven turned her back to the front entrance and walked around the corner to the small nook housing the tenants' mailboxes. Technically, even with permission from the owner, breaking into someone's mailbox counted as an indictable offence in Canada, but Bear wouldn't report her, and the police had bigger crimes to solve than a mailbox break-in. She pulled back the long sleeves of her sweatshirt and bent the paper clips into the shapes needed.

She paused, holding one of the warped clips a few inches from the lock.

At least she hoped Bear wouldn't report her. Sometimes, she felt like she didn't know her own twin anymore, and she was the closest person to him.

With a shrug of her shoulders, she turned her attention to picking the lock. Generally, Bear specialized in the unsavoury, less-than-legal PI jobs, not Raven. His ambivalence toward the law was one of the main reasons he no longer worked for the family business. Not only did he butt heads with Dad, but their dad didn't approve of her twin's methods or the jobs he picked up.

Raven's heart ached. She didn't like Bear distancing himself from the family. From her.

Click.

Raven's lips twitched as she swung open the tiny mailbox door and pulled out the contents. Junk. Junk. Bill. Junk. Bill.

A black card fell from the stack of white envelopes and fluttered to the floor. She bent and picked the business card from the cold tile.

Huh. This looked interesting. A solid black card, front and back. The only writing was a large, stylized "O" in silvery font on one side. She flipped it back and forth, willing some invisible ink to activate. Nothing. She sniffed it. Regular card-stock paper. No trace scents from the handler. At least none that she could detect. She'd have to let Mike sniff it.

Raven stuffed the card in her pocket and shut Bear's mailbox.

Heavy footsteps thumped up the front steps outside. Someone fiddled with the lock. The tinkering didn't sound like a drunk person fumbling to get their key in the door. It sounded like...

She stepped forward in time to see the front door swing open and reveal a dark figure crouched on the other side. Before she could hide or scream, or do something, anything, the shadows behind her flowed out, like a rising tide. Dark strands materialized and wrapped around her.

Raven gasped and lurched forward.

A large hand clamped around her mouth. The shadows pulled her back. Her body slammed into something hard. Someone. The shadows materialized into strong arms, holding her in place.

"Shhhh, *Einin*," a deep rumbling voice tickled her ear.

The manly scent of a magical forest at dusk caressed her senses. Cole. She lurched forward again. Or at least tried. His arms tightened around her stomach and held her in place. Her scalp tingled. Again. Banshee's tits. Her hair must respond to potent dark energy somehow.

The crouched figure from the main entrance stood, tall and looming, before walking into her brother's building. With the hood of his dark blue sweater pulled up and his head down, Raven couldn't make out his face. If Cole was behind her, who was the intruder?

The man lifted his chin and pulled back his hood. From across the entranceway, his familiar features rang all sorts of warning bells.

Luke Bane.

Chapter Seven

"The biggest problem with red flags is I'm drawn to them."

~*Bulls and Raven Crawford*

The imposing man loomed in the entrance of her brother's building. He stood with confidence instead of cowering like the lock-picking menace he really was. What type of ever-loving Underworld trouble had Bear joined now?

Luke's dark gaze, edgy with Otherness, scanned the foyer. She watched from the shadows, cocooned in Cole's heat, heady scent and strong arms. The Lord of Shadows behind her remained relaxed. A thin veil of darkness shielded her vision, almost as though Cole had thrown some sort of invisibility cloak over them. Tension knotted Raven's shoulders.

The smooth veneer of Luke's polished business image slipped away, and his piercing gaze roamed the entrance. She flinched when it reached her. Instead of tensing or letting out some sort of dark fae war cry, Luke's menacing gaze passed over her and Cole without hesitation.

Luke glided across the floor. No other word described his progress. Technically, he moved one foot after the other and his boots hit the old tiles of the foyer, but he walked with a fluidity only an Other could pull off. He flowed across the room without effort, like one of those dancers on TV, just without the fancy footwork.

He paused at the elevator. He tilted his head and stared at the closed metallic doors for a minute. Raven held her breath. Instead of pushing the button for the elevator, Luke pivoted and took the stairs.

The fluorescent lights in the lobby buzzed. One flickered. When the second-floor door creaked to announce he'd arrived on her brother's floor, Raven let out a long breath. The tension eased from her body, and she slumped against Cole.

Against the Patron Fae of Assassins.

Instantly, the tension returned. She bolted forward.

The strong arms anchoring her in place released her. She stumbled a few steps and flung out her arms. Her hand slapped the wall, and she stopped her forward-propelling body before completely face-planting.

She spun around.

The shadows withdrew, revealing Cole in all his drool-worthy glory. Amusement danced in his dark, intense gaze, only a foot away.

"You smell of the rain," he whispered.

Her breath caught, and her heart convulsed. Memories of her dreams from the last two nights, dreams featuring the man within touching distance in front of her, came rushing back. Her face heated. A buzzing sensation settled around them as if someone pushed the world's pause button and grabbed some popcorn to watch the show.

She shook her head. Focus. What was he doing here? What was Luke doing here? What was Bear doing if he wasn't here? She opened her mouth to demand answers.

He raised his fingers to his lips.

She glared at him.

He pointed at the ceiling, indicating the second floor, with his index finger.

Her jaw snapped shut. No fair. He got to speak. Then again, he whispered. The words bubbling up her throat required more expression. She yanked up her soggy sweatpants and tip-toed out of the building. She wanted to stomp, but her two remaining brain cells told her that wasn't a good idea. The cool night air along with the scents of late summer hit her face. Cole followed, close at her heels, like a dark looming shadow, until she ducked into the nearest alley. Her bare feet slapped the cold, damp pavement. She squeezed her eyes shut for a second. Her life had sunk to a new low. She willingly walked into a nasty alley barefoot. And it was all Cole's fault.

"Start explaining." She spun to face him.

Cole arched a dark brow. His ink-black hair framed his porcelain face, and once again, he wore jeans and a black hoodie. She wanted to rip off his clothes and see the powerful body beneath.

"I like your eyes like this," he said. "Natural."

She stifled a moan. Why couldn't the Lord of Shadows be a willowy old man with a cane? And why'd he have to comment on her eyes? She'd left her contacts in their case in the car because they wouldn't shift with her. "Why are you here?"

"Looking for your brother, obviously."

Oh no. His voice. She'd forgotten the potency of that deep rumbling baritone. The sound vibrated through her bones and turned her insides to goo. He could reach forward and mold her, play with her like putty in his hands.

"Why is Luke here?"

"Luke?" His lips twitched. "Is that what he's going by now?"

Her legs shook. She resisted the urge to kick him in the shin. Barely. "Maybe I should go ask him for some answers."

She waited, but Cole continued to watch her, gaze darkening.

Fine. Let him stand there looking every bit like the

God of Darkness. Maybe Luke would actually give her answers. Even if he scared the beejeezus out of her.

With a huff, she stomped past the Lord of Shadows.

"If you think the Lord of War will gift you with anything other than pain and suffering, you deserve the punishments awaiting you in that building."

She froze, her back still facing Cole. "Lord of War?"

"Bane, to be precise."

Luke Bane. Bane. The ruthless fae lord from the Realm of War she'd read about in her school books. She shivered. "Crap."

Shadows ebbed and flowed along the alleyway. With each tide-like surge, the darkness crept forward, edging closer to where she stood. She spun around. Cole's unsettling ink-black gaze met hers.

"And what awaits me here?" she asked. Her heart hammered against her breastbone.

Cole strode forward, stopping a foot away. The darkness folded in, dousing her in shadow. "What would you like?"

Dear Odin, he better not read minds. *Please, please, please, don't read minds.* Images of their entwined naked bodies writhing against each other flooded her mind. Her mouth went dry.

He waited, shoulders tense, as if ready to pounce. Part of her—the long repressed sexual part—wanted to call his bluff and see what happened. Would those lips hinting of carnal knowledge live up to their promise and make her nerves sing? Would his hands light her skin on fire?

Gah!

His self-satisfied smile grew, as if he followed her entire mental dialogue.

Oh no. Please, please, please, don't read minds. "Answers," she sputtered. "I want answers."

He continued to wait, as if silence alone would break her will. It probably would if he continued to look at her like that. She ground her teeth and willed her hands to keep to themselves.

As if reaching a silent conclusion, Cole straightened, and his gaze grew distant. "A shame."

She dug her hands into the pockets of her damp sweatpants.

A car drove down a neighbouring street, the slick tires rolling down the uneven asphalt. Instead of a low hum, or steady drone, the vehicle thumped down the road. The wind travelled down the alley and brushed past them.

Cole cleared his throat.

Two could play this game. She continued to wait.

"That's a shame," he repeated. "I'm also seeking answers."

In other words, TDD refused to help. She crossed her arms. He might search for answers, but he knew a lot more than she did. "No, you're not. You're looking for my brother."

Cole sneered. "He stole something."

"He has a habit of doing that. Get in line."

"Something of mine." His voice dropped.

"The Claíomh Solais?"

Cole lunged. Without warning the shadows closed in from all sides and slammed her against the dirty wall of the nearby building. Giving her no chance to escape, or breathe, Cole followed the wave of shadow, clamped his strong hands on her arms, and pressed his hard body into hers. His earthy scent coiled around her, deep and lush.

She swallowed a moan. Her whole body ached to touch his.

Dear Odin, the man had already kidnapped her, and now he practically assaulted her in an alley and all she wanted was to rub against him. What was wrong with her?

The black of his irises bled out to stain the white of his eyes. His ominous gaze pinned her down. Her lungs ached. Then she remembered to breathe. What had she done wrong?

Nothing.

The answer hit her brain cells. Besides wanting to touch him in a highly inappropriate way, she'd done nothing wrong.

"You have to stop doing that," she said.

He blinked.

"You're not in your shadow world or whatever questionable Underworld realm you hail from. You can't go around grabbing women. It's assault. And not nice."

"Okay, Einin." His grip softened, but he kept her against the grimy brick wall with his body.

He'd called her Einin twice now. If she survived

this encounter, she'd look the term up on the internet.

She glanced down the alley. Her hair stuck to the wall. She winced. No one on the street to help her. Though, the way Cole controlled shadows, even if someone did walk by, she doubted they'd spot her.

"What do you know of the Claíomh Solais?" His voice held sin and promise, rumbling deep and low, sending tingling sensations along her skin.

"Why should I tell you anything?" Her mind scrambled. Someone had lied to her, and fae didn't lie. They couldn't. Cole said Bear stole something of his, but Bane made a similar statement. They couldn't both be telling the truth.

His gaze narrowed.

"If you're willing to kidnap and assault me for merely sharing DNA with Bear, you have worse planned for my brother."

He opened his mouth.

"Don't insult my intelligence and claim otherwise."

He closed his mouth.

"What does Einin mean?"

"What does Tee-Double-Dee stand for?"

Her cheeks burned.

He leaned in. "I'll tell you mine, if you tell me yours."

Oh, sweet baby Odin. She squeezed her eyes shut. His innuendo sent all sorts of dirty thoughts racing scandalously through her mind.

"No deal," she said. No way could she tell him the nickname she gave him. He'd use it against her somehow. His sinful voice and powerful body already made her weak in the knees and in the mind. If he knew how badly she yearned to feel his body sliding against hers...Game over. She'd end up his puppet to seduce, manipulate, and ultimately, control.

Isn't that what she wanted?

He chuckled softly and shook his head. "You would risk your life to save your brother?"

She nodded.

"From what I understand, he's the scourge of your family. A blemish on an otherwise clean slate."

Fire raced through her veins and heated her face. She clenched her hands into fists. The sleeves of her sweatshirt slipped down her arms and covered them. Her brother's distance wasn't entirely his own fault. He had his reasons. Although she didn't approve, she understood. Raven lifted her chin. "He's my brother."

The dark gaze flicked back and forth, taking in her expression. Cole released her arms, placing his palms against the wall on either side of her head. He grimaced and took a step back. He looked down at his open hands, now covered with tar-like grime, and scowled.

Raven smirked.

He rubbed his palms down his dark pant legs before taking another step back. "I have a proposition."

Her mind squealed with delight. *Um, hello? Don't forget the early not-so-subtle threat.* If she could bitch-slap her libido, she'd do it. *Focus.*

"I'm listening." She straightened and pushed off the wall. Her sweater and her long black hair peeled off the sticky surface with a wet Velcro-like sound.

Cole flinched.

She continued to glare at him as she pulled the last stubborn strands of hair from the brick.

"You work for your dad's PI business, which according to the website specializes in finding things. Let me hire you. You want to find your brother anyway."

He'd obviously researched her and her family. Her skin prickled. What information had he found? "And you want the Claíomh Solais."

His jaw clenched. "Yes."

"No."

"No?" He recoiled. "I'm offering you a job."

"No."

"Why not?"

"Do I need to mention the kidnapping, assault and future plans to torture and possibly kill my brother?" Hopefully, she sounded angrier than she actually was. Part of her still wanted him to kidnap her just to see what he'd do with her. How twisted was that?

He grunted. "You were returned intact."

"Intact?" she sputtered.

"What if I promise to spare your brother?" He leaned in, his deep voice ran over her skin like a caress. "That's not a small compromise. He stole from me."

Tempting, but no. One thing her mother instilled in her at a young age was a healthy mistrust of Others. Pun intended.

She shook her head.

Cole leaned forward. "I will find him, one way or another. And then you'll wish you had made a deal."

She lifted her chin. Maybe, maybe not. If she found Bear and the Claíomh Solais before anyone else, she could make a deal to save her twin's life. Cole would use her for information to get Bear first. If that happened, she'd have nothing to barter with. The black card burned in her pocket. Nope. *I'm not telling this guy a thing.*

Cole straightened and pulled out a card. Like a shady street performer, one moment his hand was empty, and the next he pinched a black business card between two fingers.

Another black card? Like the one from Bear's mailbox?

She plucked the sleek card from his fingers and flipped it over. Charcoal gray, not black. A stylized "C" instead of an "O." And a number. She ran her finger over the smooth card stock and along the embossed letter.

She raised her brow and ignored the quailing of her lady bits. "Your number?"

"Call me."

Before she could think of a snide remark, Cole disappeared. A second before, he'd loomed in front of her, vibrating with a potent sexual energy while his sardonic smile mocked her. With the next blink, he dissolved into the shadows.

Did he watch her from the dark? If she waved her hands around the space where he'd stood, would they smack into his hard body? Her arms itched to test the theory. She clenched her hands and held her arms stiffly by her side. No way. If he watched from somewhere else and saw her batting the air like a deranged tourist at a mosquito infested park, she'd, well, she'd...

Raven sighed. She should push Cole from her mind and focus on helping her brother.

Her gaze wandered up the grimy wall of her brother's building. Despair settled on her shoulders like a lead shawl. She'd have to scale the wall to return her clothes. She didn't have a key for the building's front door, only Bear's apartment.

She glanced around the alley.

Or she could strip down here, exposing not only her body to potential watchers, but the card she found and her abilities as well.

Raven groaned and flung one arm across her chest to stretch it.

Climbing it was.

Chapter Eight

"You're going to be fine. You come from a strong line of lunatics."

~Unknown, probably a fellow lunatic

Despite washing her hands in the ocean and donning the clean clothes waiting for her back on shore, Raven couldn't shake the dirty feeling clinging to her skin. She twisted her still-damp hair into a top-knot out of desperate hope the updo prevented the miscellaneous, sticky substance in her hair from getting on the car seat. She drove a 2002 Grand Am, which, according to an article published on her favourite "news" website last week, was number ten on the list of "The Top Ten Shittiest Cars on the

Road Today." Awesome. But not wrong. Affectionately dubbed, Jean Claude, the vehicle already bordered the line between useful and train wreck. She didn't need to add "mysterious goop smell" to the list of Jean Claude's features.

Her contact case sat on the passenger seat. She examined her hands. Crap. Pulling some baby wipes from the glove box, she scrubbed her fingers more thoroughly before popping the contacts back in. Her dry eyes itched in complaint. They needed a break. Raven squirted in some drops before turning the key to the ignition.

After a long, tiring, stinky drive, she pulled up to the back entrance of Crawford Investigations. Her father's small office sat at the end of a rundown strip mall. She needed access to her father's database and visiting tonight meant no interruptions or questions. She'd tell Dad about Bear's disappearance soon enough, but she wanted to delay the worry that would settle on her parents' shoulders. They raised her to hope for the best and plan for the worst.

Before she set out to Bear's place, she'd hoped her twin wasn't responsible for stealing the mysterious Claíomh Solais. She hoped to find him binge-watching the latest show on television. She hoped he had nothing to do with the dark fae lords now running amuck in her life. After Bane's appearance at his apartment, though, she had to accept her fears were correct and plan accordingly. Bear's involvement moved from probably to positively. Maybe this was a simple misunderstanding, and she'd solve the problem quickly and retrieve Bear unharmed, but she needed to plan for the worst.

If she couldn't figure out something tonight, she'd go to Dad. No way would she risk Bear to save her pride or his.

And that's how she differed from her twin brother.

Raven turned the car off and popped open the door.

A scream pierced the night.

Raven froze.

Another short, explosive scream. A cold sheet of ice ran along her spine. Her blood chilled. She'd know that sound anywhere. Mike.

Raven broke into a run for the forest behind the strip mall. Her jeans pulled as she stretched her legs out to run faster. Most people mistook the cry of a red fox as the screams of someone in distress. A few years ago, Mike had been a little too impressionable with friends a little too eager to exploit his desire for acceptance. He'd created panic and hysteria in their community by running around in fox form screeching while his friends laughed and continued to encourage and prod him along. He sounded like a woman under attack and nearby citizens either ran out to empty streets to help or cowered behind closed curtains thankful it wasn't them.

What does a fox say?

Grounded!

At least that's what Dad said when he discovered Mike was behind the sudden increase in police calls regarding unconfirmed attacks.

This, though. This cry was different. The pain in Mike's screeching bled through. Raven stumbled on an exposed root and hit the ground hard. Her hands broke her fall, slamming against the packed dirt with roots and upturned rocks. Her worn jeans ripped at the knee. Her head snapped forward and smacked the dry ground. A headache bloomed.

Raven grunted and leapt back to her feet. Her palms stung, and her knees ached. She ignored the pain and pressed on. The sweet cedar smell of the forest in late summer burned her nose. Moonlight streaked through the trees and illuminated the deer path like some mystical fairy tale...or a horror movie before things got messy.

She wanted to yell, to cry out and reassure Mike as she ran as fast as she could, but what if someone held him? She bit back her words and pushed harder. The closer she got, the stronger her scent would be.

He couldn't be far. As a fox, he had a phenomenal sense of smell and he'd know her approximate location. With a strong survival instinct, much like a normal fox, Mike wouldn't risk drawing the attention of predators unless he knew help was nearby. And since Raven's senses were muted and subpar in human form, he had to screech for her to hear him.

A branch lashed against her cheek. Her skin sliced open. Her eyes stung.

Keep going.

She reached a small clearing. A furry body of orange

and red huddled near the base of a large bush. The fox turned at her arrival and whimpered. A leg-hold trap clamped his foreleg, his limb bent at an awkward angle. Matted with sweat, and missing small patches, his fur had lost its usual fluffy look. He sat in the center of a small circle of trampled dirt, about two feet in diameter.

How long had he been here? Dad sent him to do some filing at the office hours ago. Had he gone for a night run? Or had something lured him into the forest?

"Mike." She rushed forward, knelt down beside her brother.

He whimpered. His little fox body trembled. "Shhh. It's going to be okay. I've got you." She brushed his patchy, matted fur back. Despite wanting to gather him in her arms and hold him close, moving him right now would only add to his pain. She smoothed down his fur, instead. "I'm here. I'll get you out.'

When his quivering subsided, she pulled away and straightened. Her shirt plastered to her sweaty body. She placed a foot on each side of the trap and pushed the springs down. The rusted metal groaned. When the trap released its hold on Mike's damaged leg, she pulled his shaking body into her arms. As soon as he was clear, she removed her feet and the trap snapped shut.

Her blood boiled, and her body vibrated. Traps were normal dangers for shifters. Much like large predators, they learned at a young age to be wary and careful. But this...

This was illegal. No respectable trapper would set traps within city limits. Someone had deliberately set this leg-hold close to a known shifter's place of business.

Red stained her vision. She clutched Mike hard to her chest, glad he hadn't tried to shift back to human form while caught. He hadn't panicked. That was good.

Mike whimpered. She eased off crushing his body to hers. He was safe. Everything would be okay.

Shadows encased them. Her scalp prickled as if someone reached out and gripped her head with giant fingers. Raven twisted around to find a large figure blocking out the moonlight.

"You!" she hissed.

"Move." Cole's deep voice punctured the quiet forest and silenced Mike's whimpering.

Before she could demand answers, Cole flowed forward, gathered them both in his arms and pushed them into the darkness of the trees. A shadowy film settled over them, much like the dark cloak when Cole had pulled her into the shadows at Bear's apartment.

A branch snapped down the deer trail to the right.

Cold settled over her skin.

Moments later another large, looming figure entered the clearing. Luke. Again. She couldn't lose these two dark fae. They kept hopping back into her life like rabid fleas.

Wearing the same clothes as before, Luke crouched by the trap that had held her brother moments ago. He used his forefinger and thumb to pick up the leg-hold by one of the springs and lifted it in front of him.

Her body tensed. Fury wiped away the momentary fear. One of these men had set a trap and Lord of War or not, she was going to find out what was going on. She pushed forward.

Cole's arms tightened around her.

She stilled and clamped her mouth shut. She held Mike closer. Dammit, without even speaking, Cole was right. This wasn't the time to confront Luke. There might never be a right time to confront the Lord of War. She stood silent and useless while her blood simmered.

With a sneer, Luke tossed the trap to the side and stood. His gaze swept the clearing and the surrounding trees, not pausing over where they hid.

"Did you keep the shifter for your own sport, Camhanaich?"

Raven tensed. Mike went rigid. Did Luke mean Mike or Bear? Surely, he saw the patches of fur in the trampled circle and knew which shifter he caught. Bear couldn't shift, anyway.

"I sense you, *Lord of Delinquents*. I feel your shadows lurking in the darkness like some contagion. No matter. I will find the Claíomh Solais, and then you will answer to me."

Luke pulled out a red object shaped like a flattened rugby ball, only smaller, the odd stone-like surface glittering under the moon. He threw the disc on the forest floor and a portal formed, sucking the air from their surroundings like a giant vacuum. Without hesitation, Luke stepped into the portal and it snapped shut behind him. The trampled dirt where Bane had stood appeared just as it had before. No disc. It must've been sucked into the vortex with the Lord of War.

Cole shifted his weight behind her and tightened his hold around her waist. Was he enjoying this?

Raven threw her elbow back, connecting with hard abs. Cole grunted and his hold slackened. Still clutching the small, shaking form of her brother, she stepped away and whirled around to face the Lord of Shadows.

"You!" she hissed again. "You better start talking."

Still clad in black, Cole folded his arms across his considerable chest. "You better start being thankful. Or at least reasonable."

"Reasonable?" She hefted Mike a little. He was heavier than she remembered.

Cole's gaze flicked briefly to the fox before returning to study her face. "I had nothing to do with the traps."

Traps. Plural. She quickly scanned the area. Trappers used old dirt and leaves to cover the springs and teeth of a trap, leaving only the trigger pad exposed. She couldn't see or smell anything, but that didn't mean much. Traps rarely worked when shiny and new. The one clamped on Mike's leg was rusty and slathered with grime.

Cole sighed and picked up a stick. He threw it near another opening in the bush.

Snap!

Raven jumped. Another trap triggered. The powerful teeth sank into the old bark with a crunch.

Raven and Mike flinched.

Cole turned to face them. If only she could punch that smug look off his face. She wasn't much of a fighter. At least not the type that could take down a man like Cole. A couple of self-defence classes, and a childhood playing fisticuffs with brothers. Neither qualified her as a ruthless warrior. She was armed with snark...and that was about it.

"What exactly is the Claíomh Solais?" she asked.

"Does it matter?"

"Yes." Very much so. Both Bane and Cole wanted her help to find it, yet, neither wanted to give her any information.

"Well, among other things, stolen," he said.

"Mr. Bane seemed to believe he'd control you if he gained possession of this object. Is the Claíomh Solais some sort of crazy dark fae remote control?"

"Not even close."

"Then why won't you or Bane tell me what it is? Or what it does?" she asked.

"Knowledge is power. Neither of us will freely grant said power to an Other with no ties or loyalty to us."

"That's not helpful. I need to know why Bane would set a trap for my family. Is this revenge because we wouldn't take his job, or is there something else going on?"

Cole sighed and gestured to Mike with a wave of his hand. "Your brother would've provided Bane with an excellent bargaining chip. I'm sure you'd do anything for this brother as you would Bear. I'm not the only one looking for the Claíomh Solais. I'm just the only one who's decided to play nice. Have you reconsidered my deal?"

Raven took a deep breath and held it. So, Bane wanted leverage. That wasn't good. How would her family stay safe? She glanced at Cole. Bands of moonlight broke through the shadows cloaking him to illuminate his pale skin. He could keep them safe.

Had she reconsidered his deal?

Raven tensed. No. He purposely evaded her questions. He definitely held back something important and couldn't be trusted. "I'd like you to leave."

Shadows streaked out from the dark forest and wound around the Patron Fae of Assassins, coating him like liquid chocolate covering a juicy strawberry in one of those fondue towers. The dark bands rushed away, and Cole no longer stood beside her.

Chapter Nine

"Raisin cookies that look like chocolate chip cookies are the main reason I have trust issues."

~Unknown, but obviously someone awesome

Raven's scalp prickled when the shadows consumed Cole and completed his "disappearing into the night" magic trick. She squeezed her brother to her chest and stomped through the forest toward their dad's PI business. Twigs snapped under her feet.

"Hey, Mike." She shifted his thankfully-not-dead weight in her arms and dug out the mystery card she found at Bear's apartment from her pocket. "Smell this."

Mike whined, but dutifully craned his neck and sniffed—short successive inhales followed by a long exhale. He repeated the scenting action a few times and turned to her with his wide soulful eyes.

"Recognize it?"

Mike shook his head and snuggled into the heat of her body. His bent forearm resting over hers.

Raven sighed and went back to plodding along the deer path. How far had she run? She had the physical stamina of a sea slug in cold water, but adrenaline played funny games on the mind. Already tired and sweaty, her muscles ached, her joints complained, and her arms screamed for mercy. Much like his human form, Mike hadn't finished filling out. He was on the small side for a male fox, and last time they dropped him on a scale, it read thirteen pounds. Mike had definitely put on some weight since then.

Weight.

Technically, weight was a measurement of the force of gravity acting on an object.

Her grade twelve physics teacher's nasally voice resonated in her memories, explaining how to draw a vector diagram for the forces involved in holding up a glass of water. Her teacher had cast his big eyes behind bigger glasses to explain how it didn't matter if the glass was half empty or half full, it required a force equal but opposite to the force of gravity acting on it to hold it up. The more weight, the more force required. Basically, the fatter Mike got, the more tiring it was to hold him, and she didn't need to take a physics class to figure that tidbit out.

Raven had barely passed that course. But she still remembered the glass analogy, though it did little to provide fuel or give her strength to carry her brother much farther. It just made her thirsty. She licked her lips and pressed on.

The next physics unit had been on the discovery of magic. The unearthing of an additional force a hundred years ago had allowed scientists to move past the barriers between the Mortal Realm and the Other Realms. They called the newly discovered force "magic," because apparently, they lacked any imagination.

Much like the discovery of electrons behaving both like particles and waves in the early 1900s, this revelation created mass excitement within the scientific community along with loud voices of detractors. Eager to prove their theory with more than equations and proofs, the physicists gave little thought to the ramifications of their actions as they dismantled the barriers with some crazy scientific voodoo crap way too complex for Raven to understand. Once the scientists created access to the Other Realms, though, they couldn't reinstall the barrier. Their actions, all in the name of science, caused an imbalance. A real-life disturbance in the force. Pun intended.

And if Raven learned anything in her high school science courses, it was nature always tried to maintain balance.

Hordes of vicious entities whose existence had

inspired myths, legends and religion in the Mortal Realm waited on the other side of the barrier. The Others had learned how to manipulate the Force of Magic, or Fm, long ago but hadn't figured out a way to take down the barrier. They visited the magic-less realm for short vacations filled with debauchery and hijinks, but never stayed long. The relative stability on the mortal side of the barrier, and limited access to the source of their powers prevented them from permanently moving to the Mortal Realm.

When the barrier fell, however, crazy moved down its gradient from an area of high concentration to an area of low concentration, and chaos ensued.

Since the initial hysteria, an uneasy equilibrium had been reached. Things had settled...somewhat.

Raven stepped over a log.

Mike's leg bounced against her arm. He whined.

"Just a few more steps, buddy."

The lights from the street illuminated the dark path ahead. Before breaking free from the cover of the woods, Raven paused in the safety of the shadows. Her T-shirt, now doused with sweat, clung to her body. Jean Claude Grand Am sat under the warm glow of the building's security lights—the engine off and squeaky door open, as she'd left it. The gentle summer breeze blew through the branches. Some dogs barked a few blocks over. In all appearances, the short distance to the relative safety of Crawford Investigations looked clear and safe.

Raven stilled. Her skin itched. Her power pressed

from within, demanding release. Something was wrong. Something dark lingered nearby. Was it Cole? Or was it Luke? Or something else just as sinister? If she stepped out of the forest, she'd leave herself and Mike exposed, without backup. Besides stern words and Raven's questionable abilities to fight, nothing prevented someone from snatching them away at any time.

They were defenseless.

Raven sniffed the air. Nothing. Should she risk it?

She glanced down at Mike. His amber eyes met hers—soulful and deep, creased with pain. Her baby brother. He'd waited in a dark forest injured, vulnerable and alone, hoping someone he trusted would arrive before the person who set the trap. She'd arrived in time, only minutes before Bane. What if she'd taken longer? What if she hadn't made the light at Boundary? What if she stayed in the alley longer with Cole? Her eyes stung. She squeezed Mike again.

Raven swore. Her skin itched, as if the magnitude of her decision threatened to explode from within. Despite appearing clear, she couldn't risk her brother more than she already had. She pulled out Cole's card and hesitated. She might regret this, but she'd rather endanger herself than her family. Any day. Any way. There was no other choice. She shifted Mike in her arms and reached for the phone in her pocket.

He picked up after two rings. His rich voice flooded her senses. "Yes?"

"Can you protect my family?"

Cole paused. "To an extent. If the entire Underworld came for them, there's nothing I can do."

She nodded. "If you protect my family to the best of your abilities and promise not to harm Bear when we find him, I'll work *with* you, not for you."

Silence met her proposal.

"Take it or leave it. You don't have any leads. I do." He wouldn't have offered a deal otherwise.

"Deal. But in return, you promise to disclose everything you know. You promise not to hide anything from me. No too-stupid-to-live moments where you run off after a lead without me. No stashing your brother away. And no keeping the Claíomh Solais for yourself or getting some altruistic feelings and donating the Claíomh Solais to some scam of a charity or museum."

"Deal."

"One moment." He hung up on her. The dial tone cut off any response she could make.

What the hell was she thinking? Making a deal with a fae lord? They'd been one of the most ruthless groups of Others when the barrier fell.

Cole materialized out of the shadows. His forest scent brushed past her.

Too late to go back now. She made a deal. She shut her mouth and stuffed her phone into her pocket. "Do we shake on it?"

Cole frowned. "That is not how we seal a promise."

"Pinky swear?" She rotated her hand and stuck her pinky finger out.

He shook his head and stepped in. His large hands slipped to each side of her face, and he leaned over Mike to bring his mouth down on hers. Dark shadows wove around them and sunk into her skin as the promise of more than their deal raced through her veins. The forest faded away. Her brother dissolved. All that existed was where his body met hers. She wanted to run her hands up the smooth fabric of his shirt and splay them against the hard muscles of his chest. He tasted like a chocolate bar after a month-long sugar-free diet. She wanted to ingest, absorb and inhale him all at once. His lips, soft yet firm, pressed and played, while his hands threaded through her hair and gripped the back of her head. Her nerves hummed at the tease of his tongue. Heat pulsed in her limbs. All her worries fell away.

Cole pulled back with a self-satisfied smile.

Mike let out a string of guttural yelps, unimpressed with being the meat in a fae sandwich, apparently.

She licked her lips. "Surely, you don't go around making out with men and women every time you make a deal." Or did he? Not sure how she felt about that, but she did know his kiss had melted her bones. His dark Other energy pulsed so close to her, strong and more crystalized now. If she reached out, she could trace it with her fingers. Her body swayed and the thought of moving right now didn't appeal to her at all. If she tried to walk, she'd probably face-plant.

"Of course not." He leaned in. "But this is more fun."

She snarled at him.

Mike continued to chatter. "Gekkering" was commonly used among adult fox in aggressive encounters. He was definitely not happy, but as broken and small as he was in fox form, it just came across as cute. Raven knew better than to tell him so. She hugged Mike's fuzzy body closer instead and used the time to regain enough composure to look Cole in the eye. She could still taste him.

He chuckled. "So, Miss Private Investigator. What's *our* next step?"

"I'm taking my brother to the hospital." She'd have to get him clothes first without their parents knowing, but that reply lacked the snippiness she wanted.

He grunted. "After that."

She clutched Mike to her chest with one arm and dug out the card she'd retrieved from Bear's mailbox. "We find out who this card belongs to."

Cole stiffened. "There's no need."

"Why?" She swallowed the lump in her throat. His ominous tone meant she wouldn't like the answer.

"It's the calling card of Odin."

Chapter Ten

"When you're young, you think your dad is Superman. Then you grow up and realize he's just a regular guy who wears a cape."

~*Dave Attell*

Mom and Dad's house was sandwiched between two bordellos of crazy. An Other-hating crone lived on one side in the house with the deceptively nice looking garden, and a—

Raven flung out her hand and slapped her palm against Cole's chest.

Odin's balls, he was solid muscle.

Cole stopped and frowned.

She pushed him to the side of the house and into the

shadows a second before a man walked out onto his patio on the house neighbouring her parents' place.

"Who's that?" Cole whispered.

"We call him Tarzan," she whispered back. "He has an aversion to clothes."

Cole grunted.

Tarzan stretched, raising his arms into the air and pushing his bare chest out. His golden skin glowed in the moonlight.

When the Crawfords first learned of his nightly naked jaunts to the balcony, they figured he went shirtless because of the summer heat. Nope. This was an all year performance.

Tarzan sighed and shuffled back into his house, pulling the sliding door closed behind him. Raven didn't hate Tarzan like she despised Mrs. Humphreys, but he'd still call the cops if he spotted them lurking around the side of her parents' house, and the authorities detaining her and asking questions right now was a complication she didn't need.

"Come on." She motioned Cole forward and they rounded the side of the house to the backyard.

Raven hoisted Mike on her hip and eyed the second-floor window. Suddenly, her plan to break into her parents' home at night undetected didn't seem so great.

"Why don't you just go in the normal way? Your parents are going to find out about your brother's accident either way." Cole's dark brows furrowed. "He lives with them."

Mike snarled in her arms.

"Are you kidding me?" she hissed. "Have you met our mother?"

"Obviously not."

"Obviously not." She shoved Mike into his chest and gave the Lord of Shadows the option of either holding Mike or allowing the injured fox to fall to the ground.

Cole wrapped his arms protectively around her brother and glared at her. "This is ridiculous." He stage whispered over Mike's matted fur, "You're both adults."

"Well, neither of us are particularly good at adulting." Raven retied her long sticky hair into a topknot and flexed her fingers. "The formidable Elizabeth Crawford is easier to face when we show her a productive solution instead of the problem in the middle of its hot mess stage. Ever heard of the expression, 'it's better to ask for forgiveness than permission'? That's pretty much the Crawford kids' motto."

"Productive solution?"

"Taking care of Mike's injury without asking for parental assistance."

Cole eyed the second-floor window. "I could go for you."

"Absolutely not." It was one thing to break into her own parents' house, but an entirely different thing to stand by and send a stranger to do it. Besides, Cole might not survive the state of Mike's room if unprepared, and they didn't have time to give him a crash course.

Despite explaining her rationale on the way over, Cole offered to go in her place. Repeatedly. If she didn't know any better, she'd think the Great Lord of All was worried about her proposed B&E. He didn't know how often she used to sneak in and out of this house with Bear. In any other circumstance, she'd tease him about his concern, but her mind still reeled from his kiss. She wanted to avoid any interaction with the fae lord until she could forget the taste and feel of him.

"Besides," she said. "Shouldn't you be setting up a meeting with Odin for us? You can't do that if you're breaking into my parents' house."

They blinked at one another. A loud bleat fractured the silence of the backyard. Raven jumped. Cole spun around. A black and white goat stood a few feet away, stared at them and chewed something in its mouth.

"Mike?" Raven whispered into her brother's fur. "Do I want to know why there's a goat in our parents' yard?"

Mike whined.

So, the answer was probably not. She turned back toward the tree.

"I can't exactly text the Allfather and arrange a coffee date." Cole continued the conversation as if a random goat hadn't interrupted them, moments ago. Points to him. "There's a process for requesting an audience. It takes time and finesse."

Raven gripped the bark and thumped around with

her feet for the familiar footholds. "Shouldn't you be *finessing*, then?"

"I'd rather be accompanying you right now." He paused.

She glanced over her shoulder to find him frowning at the tree.

"Couldn't you just lend him some of your clothes?" he asked.

Mike growled again.

"Just shut up and hold my brother." Without waiting for a response, Raven hauled her tired body up the tree and scaled the large branch reaching out to Mike's second-story window. Her hands clutched the rough bark and her arm muscles screamed in protest. Despite wearing jeans, the knots dug into the tender flesh of her inner thighs when she used her legs to clamp around the tree to anchor herself. Her tight jeans made it a little more difficult than she remembered. The summer night grew cooler and the cold air scorched her lungs. Her throat burned by the time she scooched down the thick tree limb extending to Mike's bedroom window. With a well-practiced finesse, she shimmied the window open.

Sure, she could've lent Mike some clothes. As someone with many siblings capable of shifting, she had plenty of extras lying around her own place, but Mike would want his own. The break was bad, and his body was going into shock. Having something of his own would help with the painful and upsetting transition back to his human form.

Cole grunted.

Something thudded.

Mike yipped.

Halfway into Mike's dark room, Raven spun to look down. The leaves and branches rustled, allowing only a small glimpse of the shadowed figures below under the moonlight.

"What's going on?" she hissed.

"Nothing," Cole said.

She waited, but no further explanation came. Whatever. She'd find out when she returned with Mike's clothes. She slipped into the darkness of her youngest brother's room. Various objects loomed before her, illuminated by the night sky and the lone streetlight outside. The air skimmed by her, fleeing the pungent mix of body odour, stale pizza and empty pop cans.

Most people were surprised to learn natural foxes gave skunks a run for their funk. Not only did they secrete a pungent oil from their sweat glands, but they used the smell as vile cologne to distinguish themselves from others, convey their status and mark their territory.

Fox shifters weren't quite as bad in the odour department because they had their human nature to override the baser instincts of the fox, but some shifters, adolescent males, especially, struggled to keep the stink contained.

Mom and Dad gave up trying to get Mike to keep his room clean long ago. For much of the same reason their parents left Raven to flounder and find her financial feet, the Crawford's believed in "hands off" parenting and let Mike wallow in his own filth. They hoped he'd grow from his mistakes given time.

Honestly, they were probably happy as long as he showered, and the stink didn't leave the room with him. And at least he didn't urinate in the house to mark his territory.

Now, where in this jumbled mess would she find his clothes? The low hum of his computers answered her. He never turned them off. A dresser sat on the opposite end of the room, with its drawers open and random clothes hanging out.

For someone with such a sharp mind, Mike sure was a slob.

She tiptoed over to the dresser. Her foot caught on something and she flailed forward.

"Oomph." She caught herself on the edge of the desk, forehead inches away from one of his many beloved computer screens. She pushed away from the desk and straightened. She didn't have time to rummage through a garbage heap or flirt with dark fae lords. Maybe she should've faced the wrath of her mother and gone through the front door instead.

An image of her mom's rage-filled gaze pierced her memory.

Maybe not.

She plucked the first T-shirt and pair of sweatpants she found. She learned long ago never to rifle through a brother's room. Disgusting beasts.

She turned toward the open window. The bedroom door flew open behind her, and the light flicked on.

Raven froze, arms out to each side clutching Mike's clothes.

"Rayray?" Juni's voice sang. "What are you doing?"

Raven spun to face her fifteen-year-old sister. Clad in unicorn pajamas, the teenager's tightly coiled red curls sat wildly around her head, held back with a purple headband.

"Shhhh!" Raven waved her hands. "Keep it down."

"Mom and Dad are still out for their date night." Juni folded her arms. "What do you need? Practice was intense and I want to sleep."

Raven straightened. "You made the volleyball team?"

"Yup." Juni cracked a smile. "And a herd of elephants trampling through the house couldn't have woken me. Which is what you sound like, by the way. Only louder. Don't try to make a living from B&Es."

Raven rolled her eyes. Fox shifters. So prickly.

"You must be really busy. I posted like a zillion photos," Juni added.

Her youngest sister, the baby of the family, had just turned fifteen and started Grade 10 a couple of weeks ago. She'd agonized all summer about volleyball tryouts and worrying about what she'd do if she didn't make the junior volleyball team.

"Are you still doing that puckered lip thing? Duckface? Trout pout? Whatever it is you kids call it today," Raven asked.

"Maybe." Juni lifted her chin.

"That's why I don't check your profile. All your photos are part of your face, on an angle, with duck lips. Once I've seen one, I've seen them all."

"You're a terrible sister."

"Am not."

"So why are you breaking into our brother's room, hmmm?"

Raven held up the clothes. "Can you keep a secret?"

Raven stepped away from the front door and made her way around the side of the house where she'd left Mike and Cole. The goat bleated a greeting and went back to munching grass.

As soon as she rounded the corner, Cole stepped from the shadows with Mike in his arms. "Everything okay?" he whispered. "We saw lights and heard voices."

"Huh?" Raven turned from the mystery goat and turned to Cole and Mike. "Yeah. You can drop the whispers, I forgot tonight was date night. Juni busted me but promised to let us break the news to our mom and dad after we fix up Mike."

"What did that cost you?"

"An outfit." One of her only nice ones. "She'll technically borrow it, but I'll probably never see it again unless I want to scrap for it."

"Interesting." Cole hefted Mike in his arms. He'd

pushed up the sleeves of his hoodie to reveal toned forearms as pale as his face. They stood out in the dark under the moonlight. A few angry red puncture marks marred the smooth skin.

"Is that a bite mark?"

Cole sighed. "Maybe."

"From Mike?"

"Maybe."

That explained the grunting and yipping from earlier. "Why did my brother bite you?"

"Apparently, I admired the view a little too much."

"What view?" The tree? The house? "We're in the middle of suburbia." Did Tarzan come out to beat his bare chest at the moon again?

He gave her a pointed look.

Mike snarled.

Oh. That view. He must've checked out her ass when she climbed the tree. Her cheeks warmed. She shouldn't like that. Nope. Most definitely shouldn't feel all warm and fuzzy from the idea of the Lord of Shadows being attracted to her. She should slap him or something.

Her overactive imagination decided now would be a good idea to provide her with images and ideas of what *something* could entail.

Her face grew warmer.

Cole's gaze darkened, and he leaned forward. "Red suits you."

She spun away and stomped to the car with Mike's clothes in her hand. "Shut up and hold my brother."

Chapter Eleven

"Only time can heal your broken heart, just as time can heal his broken arms and legs."

~*Miss Piggy, Raven's spirit animal*

The emergency doors to the hospital opened, blasting Raven with cool air, slightly musty from the overworked and underserviced air conditioners, and heavy with disinfectant. The bright fluorescent lights beamed down and burned her eyes. Raven stepped from the summer night into the cool, bright hospital.

Mike shuddered in her arms. He'd pick up a lot more than cleaner and mould, especially in his fox form.

She'd traded Cole for her brother. The Lord of Shadows now held Mike's clothes and eyed the building with unease.

"It's so bright." Cole clutched the outfit in one hand. Blood trickled from his bite mark and soaked into the soft material.

"Well, they need to see what they're doing."

They quickly checked in with reception and provided Mike's health card to the registration clerk before heading to the triage nurse. A middle-aged woman in teal scrubs looked up from the desk as they approached. A halo of loose brown hair had escaped her tight ponytail and framed her face. Her name tag read, "Martin." The nurse scanned Raven and Mike when they approached her desk. "Shifter?"

Raven sighed. Not because the nurse was wrong in her assessment, but because of her bone-weary voice and haunted eyes. Too many injured shifter cases had hit the ERs in the Lower Mainland lately. So many, the news actually felt compelled to run a piece on it, all of a minute and twenty seconds, but the existence of the report, not the length, said more than any of the words the reporter actually said. Someone or something was targeting the shifter community.

The nurse's gaze cut to Cole and raked his body. Her tired, over-worked expression disappeared, and her eyebrows rose. She straightened her plump figure in her office chair. "And you, love? Are you in need of medical assistance?" Her voice somehow deepened to a more sultry tone.

"I'm fine," he said.

"You're bleeding."

"A scratch."

"A bite from a ferocious beast, no doubt." She pushed away from her desk and scurried around the counter. The security door flung open and she rushed to Cole's side.

He frowned.

Raven eyed her torn up palms from her fall in the woods. She had more blood on her hands, literally not figuratively, than Cole. Would the nurse care about her wounds, too?

Nurse Martin tsked and held his arm gingerly in one hand while the other stroked the smooth skin around the wound. "We should get this treated immediately."

Did the provincial health care system cover dark fae lords? They weren't considered residents. Raven hefted the fox in her arms. "Um, my brother?"

Mike whined loudly. Whether he did so theatrically or for real, Raven appreciated the dramatic effect.

"Yes, Yes." Martin waved Raven off. "Have a seat. Someone will be with you shortly to assess and triage accordingly."

Cole pulled his arm back, but the nurse had latched on.

Nurse Martin turned her wide doe-like eyes up to him. "You, my dear, you come with me."

"There's no need." He shifted his weight. His gaze cut to the exit.

One of the nurses called out. "Mary, are you—"

"I'm taking care of this!" Mary screeched. "Cover me."

Cole's gaze darkened. His jaw clenched. The shadows pooled in the room, spreading outward from the corners.

"Cole," Raven warned.

He sneered.

"Don't."

Cole glanced at Raven. His gaze softened. His expression relaxed. "Fine."

The nurse pushed a scowling Cole toward the admittance doors without inquiring about his medical card or following proper registration procedure. Raven lifted a hand and finger waved. She found something oddly satisfying with watching a swooning, five-foot-nothing, middle-aged nurse manhandle the mighty Lord of Darkness into submission.

Raven and Mike sat like two lumps of useless clay. With each loud tick of the second hand on the generic, antiquated clock on the stark waiting room wall, Raven became more and more livid. Her hands shook. At this rate, they'd be here until the morning and well past the critical healing point for shifters. The gunk coating her hair from her brother's building had ripened, and every few minutes she got a waft of the funk. She smelled like the dumpster outside Dan's Diner. The busy waiting room held at least ten other patients and their friends and family. Accidents rarely waited for a convenient moment and school nights were no exception. A gentle din of conversation settled over the drafty room, punctuated with sirens and gusts of night air rushing in from the automated emergency doors.

The other nurse had finished assessing Mike and took his vital signs with bored disinterest, robotic even. Mike still hadn't been called when Cole re-entered the emergency waiting room wearing a crisp white bandage on his forearm, a bright red lipstick smear on his cheek, and an intense glower threatening severe violence to anyone who dared comment on either.

Heads snapped in his direction. The sneezing, whining and coughing stopped. The shadows flowed behind him and eased into the room, darkening the corners and entrance. All conversations ceased. Raven's hands stopped shaking.

Men stiffened and straightened. Others cowered. Most of the women preened, while others grabbed their children and scurried from the room. For an assassin who counted on stealth and subterfuge, Camhanaich's presence demanded attention when he wasn't hiding. Luckily, the late-night patrons of the hospital emergency room seemed too intimidated to approach him.

Well, except Nurse Martin. In the background, the nurse returned to her desk, settling into her cushioned office chair with a satisfied sigh and a happy wiggle.

Cole spotted Raven and headed in her direction.

His focus trained on her as he moved with deadly grace around the frozen patients. Raven clamped her jaw shut and swallowed. *No drooling here.* Yet, her body didn't care one bit what she tried to tell it. Her heart rate still picked up and her cheeks warmed.

Oh, who was she kidding? Though she barely knew him, she wanted Cole to look at her the way she looked at a travel brochure. The second she laid her contact-covered eyes on him she wanted a piece. But he wasn't for her. He probably had a complicated relationship with a powerful voodoo priestess who controlled the souls of the dead. She knew the type. Power always attracted more power, and those with lots of it wanted more. Like a drug, the power they possessed was never enough.

Raven held no illusions regarding her own abilities. Her skills might be a neat trick, but in the supernatural community, she was small potatoes. If Cole even looked her way, it would be fleeting, and for a casual night or two, a blip in a long string of women.

Sweet Odin, it would almost be worth it.

Mike whined in her arms and she gave him a squeeze, hugging his furry little body to her own. "Shouldn't be much longer."

He shivered.

If someone didn't get them soon, she might lose what little self-control she had left. Ogling Cole was a nice reprieve, but barely contained rage simmered under her skin. Not only had her baby brother been hurt, he now faced further injury if he wasn't treated soon. How could they make him wait? What were they doing? "Maybe Casanova here can pull some strings for us."

Cole closed the distance between the doors and where they sat. The room let out a collective sigh when he sat down beside them and the shadows in the room settled.

"Have fun?" Raven asked.

"Don't." He rubbed at the lipstick smudge on his cheek.

"Will you survive the vicious attack from the ferocious beast you vanquished for mankind's collective safety?"

"Please, stop."

"Did the night nurse give you some healing? Sexual healing?" She waggled her eyebrows. Hmm. Making fun of Cole made her feel better and eased some of the fury vibrating her bones.

He turned his glower on Raven

She mock-flinched. "We were worried."

He grunted. "How do you stand these human centers of disease?"

"They save lives here, and their services are covered under our provincial health care. Not everyone can wave a magical wand and heal all their wounds."

The scowl eased from his face, replaced with a slow spreading smile. He leaned in. "It's been called magical before, but I don't know if I can claim healing capabilities."

Heat infused her face. She refused to look away

from the deep depths of his intense gaze. "Just..."

"Shut up and hold your brother's clothes?"

She pressed her lips together.

Cole's face scrunched up. "What's that smell?"

"Me, unfortunately."

His gaze travelled up her body and lingered. "I prefer when you smell of the rain."

"I'll try to keep a bottle of that handy in the future." She shifted in her seat. "It's the tar-like gunk from the building you threw me against. It's still in my hair."

A couple of patients in the waiting room turned to her with wide eyes.

A smile crept along Cole's face, like the memory warmed the cold recesses of the big bad fae lord's heart.

"And sweat," she added. Lots and lots of sweat. Her skin itched from the dried perspiration, and her legs ached. She'd worked out more in the last twenty-four hours than she had all last month. She'd suffer a two, if not three, day burn from this exertion. She ran her hand through Mike's patchy fur, smoothing the orange fuzz down.

Cole continued to watch her, and she fought the urge to squirm in her seat.

"So..." she started.

His eyebrows rose.

"Tell me about yourself." She cringed. Really? Did she honestly ask the Lord of Darkness to talk about himself? Next, she'd ask him what he was thinking.

Mike whined and shoved his snout under his paws.

Cole cringed. "Aren't you a PI? Why not search me

on the internet or one of your databases?"

She pursed her lips. "That would undoubtedly lead me to hordes of fanfiction and smut based articles." Not that she was opposed to either. Hmm. Come to think of it. That wasn't such a bad plan. She'd have to wait for her next night shift off and she had excellent source material sitting next to her to help fuel her imagination. "Access to information doesn't necessarily lead to true facts."

"There's textbooks."

"Look at you. So sure of yourself. You're probably not even worth a bold font or index listing."

Shadows pooled around them. "I'm sure you can find a chapter or two on the Shadow Realm, as I'm sure I warrant at least a brief mention in its history."

"So, you're not going to tell me about yourself?" Geez. Tough crowd.

"No."

"No?" She ran her hands through Mike's fur again. "Would it ruin your man of mystery image?"

Cole shrugged but didn't look away. Instead, the smile continued to slowly grow, and he leaned closer. Voluntarily. "I'd rather discuss you. Tell me, Rayray, why do your cheeks turn rosy every time I'm near?"

A male nurse walked through the receiving doors. "Crawford? Mike Crawford?"

"Here!" Raven sprang to her feet, holding her brother close to her chest.

Cole chuckled and shook his head.

The tall nurse had broad shoulders and wore his

scrubs a little on the snug side. Dark bags under his eyes and a day's worth of stubble suggested he'd been on shift for a while. His nametag read, "Jordan." His gaze travelled over their group before pivoting back toward the way he came. "Follow me."

Mary batted her eyelashes and waved at Cole as they passed. The mighty Lord of Darkness grumbled. He'd effectively distracted Raven from an unseemly and unproductive outburst in the waiting room, though, so bonus points for him.

Nurse Jordan led them to an examination room and retook Mike's vitals. His dark brows furrowed. "Have you been through this before?"

"A broken limb?"

He nodded.

"Not my brother, no." Her mother, father and Juni on the other hand, many times. Not something she wished to repeat any time soon, especially not with Mike, yet she had a feeling she'd be back with Juni in the future.

"But you know what to expect?" Nurse Jordan asked. His dark skin shone under the bright fluorescent lights.

Raven nodded. All shifters did, even though she was technically different than the rest of the family.

"As a nurse, I'm unable to legally obtain consent from the patient so the ERP—"

"ERP?"

"Emergency Room Physician." He took a breath and continued. "Anyway, the ERP will obtain consent once he arrives, but I'll go through the gist of it now while we're waiting and start the IV. We'll sedate Mike, set the break in the animal form, and then your brother will attempt to shift after we pull the IV from him." His glanced at the clothes Cole clutched. "You brought something familiar with his human scent. Good. With any luck, the transformation will accelerate the healing process and maintain bone alignment."

She waited. No one in her family claimed to have good luck.

The nurse took another deep breath. "If the bones move too much during the shift, we'll have to reset the break, again, once Mike is in human form."

She nodded. She'd heard this before.

"There is a small chance, the bones might shift too much and the injury will result in permanent disfigurement and possibly future transformational hindrance."

In other words, difficulty or inability to shift again.

"And there's also a chance Mike may get trapped in the transformation, especially now that we're drawing close to critical injury time. It's good that he has family and his own clothes here. It will help. He should be fine. Have you signed the waiver?"

She had and knew from experience once the doctor arrived they'd video Mike giving his consent as much as a man in a fox's body could. She ran a hand down his patchy fur again.

"Okay, well, your doctor tonight will be Dr.

Fleming."

Her head snapped up. Fleming? Her heart hammered in her chest. No. It couldn't be. Her mouth grew dry. There had to be other Flemings in the Lower Mainland working as doctors. It couldn't be...

Two knocks preceded the door swinging open to the examination room. A classically handsome man in his mid-thirties, with thick brown hair and light brown eyes walked in. Despite having a straight nose, it appeared perpetually turned up at the end as if he constantly looked down on others. A white lab coat partially covered his mint green scrubs, and his white sneakers shone under the harsh fluorescent lights. He either buffed them after every shift or they came straight from the box.

Doctor Robert Fleming. If she required urgent care and the only options for a medical professional was this guy, Dr. Lecter or Dr. Jekyll, she'd choose one of the others. Sure, she might end up with no skin or someone else's body parts, but she'd rather those possible outcomes to spending any time with Robert. The idea of placing herself in a vulnerable position with him near sent shivers along her skin. He'd already proven himself unworthy of her trust.

"Robert?" She stiffened in her seat. She'd planned on looking like an absolute smoke show the first time she saw her ex post break-up, not like a sweaty, dumpster-diving drowned rat. Her jeans stuck her to legs with some unflattering bunching going on near her crotch and thighs and her ripped shirt was drenched with sweat and covered in fox fur. Her scraped hands ached to reach out and throttle the doctor.

Mike growled.

Robert halted. His hands gripped the clipboard and he scanned the forms instead of meeting her glare. His eyebrows furrowed and his jaw clenched.

The douche-canoe had actually done it. He'd finished med school after declaring bankruptcy and left Raven to scramble and clean up after him. Anger flashed through her veins. He'd achieved his dreams, and she...and she...

Well, she hadn't.

Cole perked up from his resting place leaning against the wall. His hoodie did little to hide his large, imposing frame and his dark jeans emphasized the strength of his thighs and made Raven drool. Despite his "civilian" wardrobe and casual stance, he continued to radiate lethal purpose. The shadows pulled in around him.

"Well, this is..." Robert's voice trailed off.

Unexpected? Awkward? Unpleasant?

"A routine procedure. Hardly something requiring my specialist expertise." He finally looked up from the clipboard and his gaze swept the room, somehow still managing to avoid direct eye contact.

Why was he an expert in shifter medicine? He had no supernatural abilities that she knew of, besides being an epic loser, maybe. Was there even such a thing as a specialist in Emergency? Didn't they all have the same training?

The nurse frowned.

"Nurse Jordan here will get you one of the many, fine, generalist doctors at Burnaby General to assist you."

"There's no such thing as a—" the nurse started.

The dark look Robert cast him stopped the words from tumbling out.

Raven didn't need Nurse Jordan to finish his sentence. Understanding hit her like a two-ton brick. She was right—all emergency doctors had the same training. Robert was no more or less qualified to reduce a bone than any other emergency room physician. He was attempting to run away while still coming across as superior. She knew reassigning a doctor would take time, too much time. They still had to videotape Mike's consent, sedate him and call a respiratory therapist to manage his airway while he was under sedation.

The longer they waited, the more difficult the transition would be for her baby brother. He already approached the critical point for seeking "standard" medical attention. After twelve hours, magical assistance was required, and as an elective procedure, basic medical insurance wouldn't cover the expense. No one in Raven's family could afford the extravagant procedure, and Mike might never shift again, or regain full use of his arm.

There woa a chance Robert knew nothing of this time factor despite his bullshit "specialist expertise" claim, or maybe he missed the time of injury or the red stamp on the form reading, "TIME SENSITIVE," when he scanned Mike's medical forms. There was a chance he just wanted to save both of them an awkward encounter. Or he was just a coward and couldn't, or wouldn't, face her.

There was a chance he wasn't a complete dickwad, but Raven doubted it. Robert wanted her to beg.

Every cell in her body vibrated with anger, demanding to be rid of his presence, or lash out. Under any other circumstances, she'd applaud Robert's cowardice and revel in the glow of his quick retreat.

Not tonight.

Not when her brother's health counted on Robert's assistance. She'd grovel for him to stay if she had to.

Odin's saggy ball sack! She had to. They couldn't wait for a new doctor, and setting the bones herself had other medical implications, mainly a giant messed up debacle.

Raven swallowed her rising stomach contents and straightened in her seat. She bit down so hard, she tasted blood. It was going to be okay. It had to be okay. *Do this for Mike.* With a deep breath, she flashed a tight smile to Cole and gathered Mike in her arms to stand up. "Robert."

Cole's gaze flicked between her and Dr. Douche. He moved so smooth and fast she didn't see him take a step. One moment he stood by the wall, and the next, he loomed over her ex.

Robert blinked.

"You will heal this shifter, and you will do it now." The shadows gathered around Cole

Robert's hands tightened on the clipboard again as he held it to his chest like some sort of body armour. His jaw clenched.

She knew the look. Robert was pissed.

"I don't know who you think you are," Robert started. "But you have no power over me."

Cole took a step to stand in front of Raven. She couldn't see Cole's face, but she could see Robert's when she leaned to the side to peer around Cole's hulking body. The normally healthy colour in her ex's cheeks drained. He lost his pissy face. Whatever Robert saw in Cole's expression scared him. The room dimmed.

"You're mistaken," Cole said.

The shadows lurking in the corners of the room shot forward and slammed the door to the examination room shut. The lights flickered.

Robert jumped.

The strands of shadow lengthened and snapped around the doctor's wrists.

"Cole..."

Another band of gray snaked up and wound around Robert's neck.

Raven tugged on Cole's uninjured arm. "You can't hurt him."

Cole shrugged her off. "No. I can't kill him. There's a distinction. The important question is whether the doctor understands the significance of the difference."

The band around Robert's neck tightened. The doctor's eyes bulged.

"You will heal this shifter and you will do it now," Cole repeated. "If you call security, you'll never live to see them arrive. If you refuse, you won't leave the hospital breathing."

Well, then.

Robert trembled.

As worried as Raven was that the police would somehow barge into the room at any moment and arrest them all, seeing Robert this scared was very, very satisfying.

What was happening to her? When Robert first left, she considered finding him and taking a run at him with Jean Claude, or accepting Bear's offer to "rough him up," but in the end, common sense and human decency prevailed. Yet here she was, revelling in Robert's near strangulation.

Well, no one's perfect.

"Do you understand?" Cole asked.

Robert nodded.

The shadows instantly withdrew, and the normal too-bright fluorescent lighting of the room returned.

Nurse Jordan leaned toward her and stage whispered, "That was awesome."

Raven agreed.

Chapter Twelve

"Siblings: children of the same parents, each of whom is perfectly normal until they get together."

~Sam Levenson

Raven walked up the steps to her parents' home beside her brother. Human, clothed and exhausted, Mike now sported a bright-white cast to support the radius and ulna bones as they healed. The shifting had gone well, and the bones remained in place. They didn't require resetting and he shouldn't have difficulties the next time he shifted. If anything could be called a success tonight, that was it.

Mike had apparently craved a night run in fox form after doing some work for Dad—something he'd probably second guess in the future. That thought alone infuriated Raven.

The early dawn light cast long shadows down the stairs. Dew clung to the air, and birds chirped to greet the day. Most of them would head south soon. No sign of the goat.

The Lord of Shadows and Vanquisher of Slimy Exes trailed behind them. Keenly aware of his presence, Raven reached the landing and held her breath. She reached for the door handle.

The front door flew open and Elizabeth Crawford stood on the other side with narrowed blue eyes and crossed arms. Her tan Capri pants with a pastel blue blouse, and red hair pulled into a smooth ponytail fit perfectly with her refined image. No one would guess at her wild past; instead, they saw a human resources manager who rocked a pantsuit and the evil eye.

"What in the Underworld?" Mom demanded. Her lean frame tensed. Her gaze adopted that shrewd-mom-look where Raven swore she read minds and gleaned all her secrets.

Raven knew how it appeared. She wore dirty and ripped clothes. Her hair had clumped together with unknown goo, and she'd scraped her hands badly. Instead of her normal healthy glow, the colour from her face had drained and she resembled an extra from a post-apocalyptic movie. Raven was exhausted and smelled of rotten food. But her appearance wasn't what shocked or concerned their mother. Her baby boy stood beside Raven, bruised, scraped and bandaged.

"Get in," Mom hissed. Her tone made it clear not to argue.

Cole's hand pressed into Raven's back. He took a step back into the shadows, away from the impending tsunami of a mother bear's rage.

Mom's head snapped to Cole. Her gaze narrowed again. She raised a stiff index finger and jabbed it in the air toward the Lord of Shadows. "You, too."

Raven startled. Mom would've noticed his eyes and felt his potent Underworld energy. Apparently, Mommy Dearest didn't give a wit about who or what he was.

Her mom's previous days as a party animal actually aided her in her current role as a manager, wife and mother. At least according to her. Mom read people, well. Extremely well. Some would say disturbingly so. Her mom understood what made people tick and could exploit their weaknesses ruthlessly if she chose to do so. Whatever she gleaned from Cole's expression empowered her to boss the dark fae lord around.

Mom's glower encompassed all three of them on the landing. "Inside, now."

They stepped into the home and the savoury smell of juicy bacon greeted her. Home. No matter how long she lived on her own, stepping into the warmth and smell of this house put her at ease. Raven inhaled deeply and kicked off her shoes without untying the laces.

"Animal," Cole whispered in her ear. He took a seat on the padded bench by the door and clinically untied and removed his boots.

Raven stared at the well-behaving assassin for a second before turning to Mom. "Bacon and eggs?"

Mom stopped glaring at Cole and turned to her. "Everything's better with bacon."

With one last glare at Cole, Mom gathered Mike in her arms and squeezed.

"Mom!" he wheezed, eyes bulging.

"Don't you ever scare me like that again," she whispered.

Mike's expression softened and he sank into the hug, wrapping his one good arm around her.

Dad thumped down the stairs. He wore his usual attire—crisply ironed khaki pants and a polo shirt. He owned about four or five pairs of the same pants in slightly different shades and eight or nine shirts in the same style, different colours. Raven had snuck into her parents' bedroom once with Juni when they were younger. The identical clothes, pressed and hung evenly spaced in the closet, had horrified them. They ran from the room screaming. Raven swore to never venture into her parents' room again.

"About time you got here," Dad said. His gaze settled on Cole, who stood between the group and the door. His steps faltered. "And you brought a guest." His tone remained chipper, but his shoulders tensed.

Cole stood and held his hand out to Dad. "Sir."

Dad's gaze snapped between Cole's hand and face. "You're the one who kidnapped my daughter."

How'd Dad figure that out so quickly? She must've

described Cole well. Her cheeks warmed. The Lord of Shadows certainly made a lasting impression on her and his face certainly played a recurring role in her dreams.

The fae lord rocked back on his heels. His white teeth flashed. "And returned her unharmed."

Mom sucked in a breath, squeezed Mike harder, and glared at Cole over his shoulder.

Mike wheezed. Poor little fox.

Cole remained relaxed, arm extended, and waited. His gaze cut to Raven and his smile broadened. Did the memory of abducting her make him feel all warm and fuzzy inside?

"Dad," Raven said.

Dad grumbled and reluctantly shook Cole's outreached hand. Thankfully, neither seemed inclined to do the over-compensating man-squeeze, tug-a-war handshake some men tried to do.

Cole placed his boots neatly beside Raven's haphazardly strewn flip flops on the mat.

"This way," Raven said and led him down the hall to the kitchen and dining room.

Juni sat at the dining table, her hair somewhat tamed. With cheeks puffed out like a greedy chipmunk, she'd stuffed her mouth full of bacon. When Juni spotted Raven, she froze mid-chomp. She lowered her fork and gave Raven a nervous smile— thankfully, with her mouth closed.

Yeah, that's right. We both know who tipped off Mom and Dad. Juni never stood a chance, really. Their dad was a PI. He could ferret out a secret better than, well, a ferret. At least Raven didn't have to lend one of her only nice outfits anymore.

Cole stepped up beside Raven at the foot of the table.

Juni's eyes widened when her gaze landed on their guest. Her mouth dropped open. "Whoa."

Dad's gaze snapped between his youngest daughter and Cole. He pursed his lips and his expression darkened.

"There's bacon, Dad," Raven said.

"Your mother's idea," Dad spoke with a dry tone.

"Everything's better with bacon." Juni stuffed more in her mouth but kept watching Cole with large, round eyes. At her rate, there'd be no bacon left by the time they sat down. She paused to scan Raven again. "What's up with your hair?"

Raven patted down the curling frizz. "Apparently, dark fae energy provides extra body."

Juni stopped gnawing on food and her gaze riveted to Cole. She connected the dots and swallowed the mouthful of bacon. "How come your hair didn't curl around Bear, then?"

Raven shrugged. "I must be impervious to his energy somehow."

"You going to tell us what's going on, Rayray?" Dad interrupted their conversation.

Mike pulled out of their mother's arms. "Dad, chill. Let's eat before Juni takes all the bacon."

"You snooze, you lose," Juni said. She spoke through

another mouthful of food, so it came out garbled. They'd heard her utter those words enough, though, that they didn't require an interpreter.

"Personally, I prefer sausage," Raven said.

Cole paused on his way to the table and looked over his shoulder at her. His lips twitched.

Heat flooded her face. "Breakfast sausage." Pervert.

Cole shook his head and chuckled.

"There's sausage in the oven." Juni may have spoken to Raven, but her gaze had remained trained on Cole. She cleared her throat. "Are you going to introduce us?"

"This is Cole. Cole, this is my family. My mother Elizabeth, my father Terry, and my sister Juniper. Obviously, you already know Mike."

Cole nodded at each person as she pointed and named them.

"Cole?" Juni's face scrunched up with a skeptical look only a fifteen-year-old girl could pull off.

"Beul na h-Oidhche gu Camhanaich," he said.

Juni gagged.

Raven turned to her sister.

Juni swallowed. Her face paled. "The Lord of Shadows?"

Mom tensed beside Raven. Dad's eyes narrowed.

"We're learning about you in school."

Geez. Maybe Raven should've paid more attention in class. She didn't recall learning anything about Beul na h-Oidhche gu Camhanaich.

"Nothing but good things, I hope." Cole winked

and pulled out a chair. He turned to Raven. "I told you there'd be a chapter on me,"

"There's a whole section," Juni piped up. "It covers the Shadow Realm, the creation of the Assassin's Guild, alliances with other courts and how Fm in the Shadow Realm pulls from both the dark and light realms, making it not only unique, but arguably more potent in Other energy than the other domains."

A slight smile tugged at Cole's lips and he sat down without comment.

Juni picked up her plate and scurried to take the seat beside him. She moved the unused dishes out of her way and dropped her plate on the placemat. Raven hadn't seen her sister move that fast since the sample shoe sale downtown last year. Raven had watched her sister dodge and weave around other shopping hopefuls and shoe enthusiasts, throwing an elbow or two in the fray to get a mean pair of designer boots at a non-designer price. If Raven had less monstrous feet that fit the sample sizes, she would've joined the fray. Instead, she was relegated to the sidelines to act as a chaperone and cheerleader.

Juni eyed their guest with the same pining look she'd cast at those boots a year ago.

Raven rolled her eyes and sat beside Mike. She slid into the worn dining chair and leaned back into the cushion. She closed her eyes for a second and took a deep breath of savoury breakfast goodness surrounded by the din and clatter of her family around the table. Home.

"Honey, dear," Mom said.

Raven's eyes pinged open.

"When was the last time you spoke to Megan?" Mom asked. "I ran into her today. She didn't have the kids with her. Poor thing looked exhausted. I remember those days. She probably needs some adult conversation."

Raven's stomach dropped. She was a bad friend. She'd meant to visit her bestie sooner rather than later, but life kept getting in the way. And now her brother was missing, dark fae lords kept popping up like prairie dogs, and Mike got injured. "I'll go see her."

"You better." Mom nodded. "You don't have many friends."

"Geez, Mom!"

"Well..." Mom looked away and her gaze resettled on Cole. Now two of the three Crawford women stared at the fae lord.

Dad grumbled and sat down at the end of the table with a thump. He looked ready to leap up and pounce at any moment. He'd once said he didn't need to get a shotgun to protect his daughters from men; that he raised them to be independent and good judges of character; that he trusted them to make good decisions. Right now, he looked as though he regretted those words.

Juni wrinkled her nose and scowled. "What's that smell?"

Cole laughed, his deep voice rumbling and stirring all sorts of feels deep within her.

Raven sighed. "It's me."

Juni snorted. "You smell worse than Mike's room."

"Hey!" Mike looked up from his food to scowl.

Juni giggled. "You smell like a trash bag."

"Raven, dear," Mom said. "Do you want to shower before eating? Or borrow some clean clothes perhaps?"

"Absolutely not." Raven folded her arms in front of her chest. "There'll be nothing left."

"I could set something aside," Mom said.

"I fell for that once. Never again." Raven said.

"You do smell..." Dad grimaced.

"Ripe," Mike finished.

"Well, tough. I had to endure you going through puberty." She jabbed a finger at her brother. "And both of you crapping your diapers." She waved her finger at her siblings.

Mike shrugged. "I'm used to it."

Cole nodded. "Me, too. Fully acclimatized."

"Gross." Juni's mouth turned down.

Raven's mom pulled out a pan full of sausage goodness from the oven and placed it in front of Raven on a trivet. The tubes of sweating fat sizzled and spat. Raven's mouth watered.

"Fine, but eat fast," Mom continued. "I don't want to get used to that smell."

Raven bit back a laugh. Her mom might complain about the smell, yet, she let Mike live in the cesspool he called a bedroom.

"Okay, what gives? I bring home your pride and joy, bruised and broken, and you feed me breakfast sausage without hosing me off first. Are you trying to fatten me up for the slaughter or are you working some other angle?"

"No angle." Mom huffed and took a seat. "You're *all* my pride and joy."

Raven and Juni rolled their eyes.

Her sister reached for more bacon, and Mike slapped her hand away before plucking some meat from the plate for himself. After the brief food-induced interlude, Raven's sister resumed her unsubtle admiration of Cole.

"Is it true you pulled the shadows from dark and light to create the Realm of Shadow? To spite your father?" Juni asked. She somehow managed to blink dramatically about fifty times during her questions. "Did you kill him as the textbook suggests? No one's seen him since the creation of the Shadow Realm, and the experts think you used his life force to form the realm somehow."

"Juni! You can't just ask someone if they murdered their father at the dinner table," Mom said.

"Yeah," Raven said. "If he used his father's death magic to fuel the creation of a separate realm that's his own—" Wait, what?

"Is it true you're the Patron Fae of Assassins and have your own personal army of killers?" Juni interrupted, leaning in.

What else would an army consist of? Raven scrunched her face. Cole's presence had somehow turned her intelligent sister dumb. Yet, her teenaged sister knew more about their guest than she did. What did that say about Raven?

She slumped in her chair and scowled. That lovely thought knocked the wind right out of her sails.

Cole shifted in his seat to create more distance from Juni. He glanced at Raven.

"Please, oh, Great One." She leaned forward and rested her chin on her laced fingers. "Tell us more."

"I will tell you anything you wish to know," he said.

Liar. He told her earlier knowledge was power. Like he'd hand it over now for—

"For a price," Cole finished.

Raven snorted.

Dad cleared his throat. "How about one of you, and I don't care who, tells us what in the Underworld is going on? For free."

Juni pointed a fork at their father. "Technically, you're paying them with bacon."

Raven leaned back, grateful for a legitimate reason to break eye contact from Cole's smouldering gaze. Did someone raise the temperature in the room? She glanced at the oven. Nope. Mom hadn't forgotten to close the door or turn off an element.

Mike put his fork down and started talking.

While half listening to Mike's explanation, Raven grabbed her fork and reached forward to stab a couple of sausages. She loaded them on her plate, skipping the scrambled eggs, bacon and toast. She'd essentially ran a marathon last night. She deserved sausage. The hot juices exploded in her mouth with the first bite.

Mmmmm.

Mom folded her arms across her chest while her youngest daughter gorged on bacon and continued to ogle their guest.

Raven pretended to listen raptly as Mike recounted the tale from his point of view, but really, she watched the Lord of Shadows as well, but unlike her sister, she managed to watch him more covertly. At least, she hoped she was more subtle.

She glanced at her sister again. A red blotch on Juni's neck, right by the collar of her T-shirt stared back.

"Is that a hickey?" Raven blurted out.

Juni choked on her food. She swallowed with a loud gulp and slapped a hand against her neck. The conversation at the table stopped and everyone turned to Juni.

"No!" she burst out.

"Then what is it?"

"I..." Her gaze darted back and forth. "I..."

Raven folded her arms.

Juni's shoulders sagged. "I don't know."

Mike reached across the table and pulled Juni's hand away. "Looks like a rash."

"A rash." Mom pushed away from the table so abruptly, her chair tipped backward. She tittered before she caught herself on the edge of the table. With absolutely no shame, Mom launched off her chair and scuttled over to her youngest daughter.

Juni shied away.

Mom ignored Juni's attempt to swat her away, grabbed her head and leaned in close. "This looks like it could get nasty."

"Mom!" Juni's face turned bright red.

Cole pushed his chair back, so her mom's ass wasn't right in his face.

"It could be a heat rash," Raven suggested.

"Or it could be contagious," Mom said.

"Or it could be a reaction to the new laundry detergent," Mike suggested.

"We need to get this looked at right away. Maybe the walk-in is open," Mom said.

"Now, now." Dad leaned back in his chair. "Let's not make any *rash* decisions."

Raven choked on her sausage.

Mike reached over and gave their dad a high-five. They started laughing.

Cole used their distraction to shovel more bacon onto his plate, gaze darting between Juni, the bacon monster, and his food.

Mom straightened and folded her arms. "This isn't funny."

"Oh, I disagree." Mike chomped off the end of a bacon strip.

Mom pursed her lips and looked around the table. The only other person not laughing, or smiling was Juni. If she turned any redder, she'd combust.

"If it looks worse tomorrow, we'll get her into the doctor's office," Dad said.

Mom grumbled but walked back to her seat.

"I want more details about tonight's events, but I'll get those later." Dad's eyes narrowed at Raven.

Great. What he meant was he planned to interrogate her, PI-style.

"Fine," she said. "Maybe you can tell me why there was a goat in the backyard."

Dad straightened in his chair, lips twisting into a snarl. "Mrs. Humphreys."

"That crazy old bat has a goat?" Raven asked. "I didn't think she was capable of caring for anything other than herself." Their crazy, bigoted neighbour, not Tarzan.

"It's Dad's spite goat," Juni said.

"His what?"

"His spite goat," her sister repeated as if she made perfect sense.

Raven turned back to Dad. "Please explain."

"Mrs. Humphreys complained to council again about the 'pests' coming to and from the house," he said.

By pests, Mrs. Humphreys referred to her family running around in their fox forms.

"She's always done that. She's a bigot and probably belongs to a Regulator chapter." Raven cringed when she said the name of the anti-supernatural group that loathed anything and anyone with special abilities. "How was this different?"

Dad threw his fork down on his plate. "I'm tired of it! I researched the city bylaws and there's nothing in it saying we can't keep small farm animals on the premises."

She choked on her coffee.

Mike reached over and slapped her on the back. Hard.

Raven cleared her throat. "So, you bought a goat and named him Spite?"

"Don't be silly. His name is Pepe," Dad said.

Of course, it was.

"And we borrowed him from a friend in Mission." Dad turned to her brother. "So, what are you learning right now in school, Mike?"

Apparently, they were done discussing Dad's spite goat. Really, there wasn't much more to discuss. Dad topped the polls when it came to passive aggressive retaliation.

Raven shook her head and turned to Mike. "Yeah, what are you learning? Besides how to be annoying?" Raven asked.

Mike smirked. He'd already finished explaining tonight's events up until they ran into Doctor Douche. Frankly, their parents didn't need to hear that part of the story. Instead of describing the cowardice of Robert, and Cole's subsequent threats, he told a story about how his classmates created a pickup line test bank to try out on their female cohorts. They planned to run a series of controlled experiments to give each pickup line a success rating.

Cole leaned back with a small smile, gaze dancing between her family members as they talked. Did he have family meals like this one? Gatherings? Reunions?

Or did he bond with his father, Erebus, in a war room while planning some dark fae invasion? Maybe *the* dark fae invasion.

She knew so little of the man sitting across from her. What she did know was her skin heated every time his attention rested on her, and she swore something in his dark gaze softened in return.

Chapter Thirteen

*"If you like people who do stupid shit all the time,
become a parent."*

~Kelly Oxford

Raven stepped into her apartment. The early morning light created a glowing, rectangular halo around the blackout curtains hanging in front of her living room window. Despite scrubbing the place from the dented baseboard to the cracked ceiling, she failed to remove the small, one-bedroom apartment's musty smell. The walls sweated brown oil during the summer and anytime she showered, indicating years of chain smoking from the previous owners. Now, she associated the smell with her home.

Her small, stinky home, devoid of asshats.

Raven shucked off her shoes, using her toes on one foot to pry the shoe from the heel of her other foot. She rarely untied her shoes properly to take them off. Next, came the socks. She peeled the sweat-soaked fabric from her feet and held them at arm's length.

Ew.

Her feet were something else that smelled no matter how diligently she cleaned them. She was meant to live a life in flip flops...for everyone's sake. Another reason why she should travel to a tropical paradise.

From her entranceway, she threw the sweat-soaked socks into the laundry hamper and tossed her keys toward the bowl that sat on the corner table by the front door.

The keys hit the table's surface and slid to the edge. They clattered to the floor.

Ugh. Just perfect. Her keys acted as a reminder of how messed up the last twenty-four hours had been. A little how-do-you-like-that to top off the day. And technically, the day had just started.

After plucking the keys from the worn linoleum, she repositioned the bowl to the center of the table where she liked it, instead of pushed against the wall.

With heavy limbs, she plodded to her small "apartment-sized" couch and flopped into the cushions. Her dry eyes itched from leaving her contacts in for too long. She used her legs to move the ottoman back to its usual spot and propped her feet up. The worn ottoman, soft and supple, cushioned her aching feet. A long sigh escaped her lips and sleep tugged heavily on her eyelids. She should probably shower and clean the mystery goop out of her hair, but the idea of peeling off the rest of her clothes was exhausting all on its own.

She reached out to grab the remote. It wasn't there.

She froze. The hairs on her arms and the back of her neck stood up. The heavy clunking of her fridge and the steady buzzing sound she'd long ago associated with her building prevented absolute silence.

The remote sat on the other arm of the couch. She never sat there. Her skin prickled. Her scalp itched.

The key bowl. The ottoman. The remote.

Each as individual anomalies wouldn't create any suspicion, but together...

Someone had been in her place.

Her breath lodged in her throat. The lingering taste of breakfast sausages in her mouth turned sour.

Should she call Cole? He promised protection. But what if he'd been the one in her place. She shivered. Sure, he'd spent the evening and this morning with her and her family, but he had plenty of opportunity to do this—whatever this was—beforehand. For all she knew, he was leafing through her photo albums when she called to agree to his deal. Argh.

If it wasn't Cole though...who'd been here? Bane? Some lackey? How long had they hung out among her trinkets and dirty laundry pile? When did they leave?

Raven froze.

Someone could still be in her place.

A ripple of unease slithered down her spine and

churned her gut. Raven had somehow managed to land in a twisted cat and mouse game and she sure wasn't the cat.

Raven surged up from her spot on the couch and scanned the apartment. Was anything taken? Or had the mysterious culprit searched her dilapidated home and left? Nothing else seemed out of place, and her computer—her one possession worth more than fifty bucks at a thrift store—sat on the kitchen table right where she'd left it. So probably not theft. A scouting mission for information on Bear seemed more likely. Now she had to confirm whether the person or persons were still here.

At least with a small apartment, there were few places to hide. She didn't even have a closet in her bedroom. Her mattress sat directly on the laminate flooring because she sold her headboard and frame months ago to make rent, and she'd pushed the mattress right up against the wall to free up space. No monsters could lurk under her bed here. One look in her room confirmed it was empty. She grabbed a large kitchen knife and tiptoed to the bathroom. The door loomed before her—somehow larger and certainly more ominous than before. Her heart thudded in her ears. She reached out and wrapped her hand around the smooth, cold surface of the doorknob. Her muscles tensed. She glanced down at the shiny blade. Then the door. Then the blade again.

What was she thinking? She had no idea how to fight, let alone wield a knife effectively in a brawl.

She'd likely end up sticking the pointy end in her own thigh.

Raven swallowed the groan threatening to escape her lungs and returned the knife to its block in the kitchen.

She opened the one functioning window to her stuffy apartment. No screen. The morning air of late summer rushed in. She resisted the urge to stand there and breathe. Instead, she retrieved her robe from the bedroom. Her feet slapped against the floor. Aside from the bedroom, the entire place had thin linoleum that curled up at the baseboards.

Raven might have mediocre fighting skills—whatever she retained from years of growing up with tough-love brothers and a hooligan for a little sister—but she excelled in fleeing. Sure, she tried to avoid shifting, and flying from her own place, but she wouldn't risk her life to avoid either of those things.

Raven peeled off her clothes and wrapped her short robe around her. The fuzzy towel-like material had long ago lost its softness and rubbed her skin like a rough over-sized cat tongue. Some might question her choice to confront a B&E criminal practically naked, but the supernatural community rarely made sense. Clothes were cumbersome in a shift and could cause one or more of her birds to become entangled. She couldn't afford to lose any more than she already had.

Raven left the robe untied and padded back to the bathroom. With a deep breath, she wrenched open the door. The simple three-piece washroom greeted her—

empty.

Relief washed through her veins. Raven sank to the floor and laughed. What did she do now? Stay in a place she knew had been compromised? Go back to her parents' place and put them at more risk? Call Cole and ask him to relieve her stress levels with some epic, dark fae lord sexual healing?

Mmmmm. Option number three, please.

Her phone buzzed in her room. Raven took several deep breaths before scrambling to her feet to find the device. It sat on her bed's cloud-like comforter. A picture of Raven and Megan splashed across the screen. They'd snapped the picture a couple of years ago after sneaking into some random white-trash music event at the community hall. Their scrunched-up idiotic faces showed exactly how intoxicated they'd been.

Raven smiled and hit the green circle. "Hey babe, what's up?"

"Oh, thank goodness, I thought you were dead." Megan's voice, normally on the lower, huskier side, came out high pitched and theatrical.

Raven snorted, shaking off the tension from her apartment search. A few minutes ago, she'd certainly felt as though her life was at risk. "And a phone call would save me?"

"Well, it's all I've got. Take it or leave it."

"I'm pretty sure you still have chocolate bars and potato chips hoarded behind the flour bag in the pantry. I'll take those, instead."

"Back off my stash, woman."

"Do you still hide from your kids in there?" Raven held the phone between her shoulder and cheek and walked back to the front door to double check the locks. She shifted the corner table to sit in front of the door.

"Are you working out?"

"No, why?"

"You're grunting."

"Am not." She clamped her mouth shut and shimmied the table a little more. Grunting. Psshhht. She was a perfect specimen of the female form. And now, if someone picked her locks again, the door would knock over the table and alert her. "Stop deflecting and answer the question."

"No, just the one. Theo isn't old enough to follow me and beg for treats yet."

Raven plodded to the bathroom and washed her hands while she clamped the phone between her ear and shoulder again. Next, she removed her contacts, which were dry and stuck to her eyeballs. Raven grimaced and pried them out.

Ahhhhh. Much better.

She squeezed some eye drops in. The cool liquid coated her eyes and stung before easing the scratchy, tired feeling away. She'd put in a new set of contacts tomorrow morning, but for the rest of today, at least, she'd have some relief.

Raven smiled at the image of Megan hiding from her kids in her pantry while stuffing her face with junk food. "It's only a matter of time before Theo figures it out, too."

"I'm aware," Megan said, dryly.

"My mom said she ran into you." Raven gathered her arsenal of supplies for a thorough scrub and placed them on the edge of the tub.

"Yeah. First time I've escaped the house alone since Theo's birth."

A pit dropped in her stomach. "Oh, Megan, I'm so sorry."

"Why? It was awesome."

"No, I'm a bad friend. I haven't been over in a while or watched the kids for you."

Megan sighed dramatically. "There's only one thing you can do to make it up to me."

"Anything."

"Come over for coffee."

"Done." She didn't want to stay here, anyway. "I just need to scrub off some grime first."

Megan's throaty laugh vibrated her phone. "I can't wait for that story."

Two soul-deep, brown eyes gazed at Raven with doe-like adoration. The sweet smell of baby powder surrounded him like an invisible shield. Panic spread through her core as she clutched the squishy infant in her hands. If his head kept bobbling, would it fall off?

"Should I support his neck more?" she bellowed in the direction of the kitchen. A visit with one of her best friends was long overdue. They only lived thirty minutes apart, yet, their lives seemed to send them in different directions. Despite the long gaps between hanging out, though, they always picked up where they'd left off as if no time had passed.

Megan chuckled from the other room. "Not anymore. He's six months."

"Are you sure?" Raven eyed the cooing baby. A small stream of drool ran down his chin. For once, Raven wasn't in her serving uniform or drenched in sweat. Instead, she was clean—at least relatively—and comfortable, wearing her favourite maxi dress. She generally preferred active wear. Pretty things like dresses and purses quickly became liabilities in her life or lost during a shift. Of course, Theodore made sure to spit up and drool on her within the first five minutes of her visit. Instead of smelling like her coconut body wash, she now reeked of spoiled milk.

"He's a baby, not antique china You're fine."

Megan's son, aka trouble wrapped in cuteness, whipped his head in the direction of his mom's voice. When she walked into the room with two mugs filled with steamy, heaven-scented coffee, he flapped his arms and lurched forward.

"Whoa!"

One minute, he contently sat on Raven's lap like an edible doughboy, and the next, he attempted to launch from her lap like some baby hatchling off for his first flight.

"Not happening, buddy." Raven knew all about

flying, and how to fail at it. "So how are things going?"

"Oh, well, the usual. The highlight of my week was going to the grocery store by myself. That was a vacation." Megan placed the mugs down and sighed. She reached out with both hands. Theo gurgled and cooed, throwing all his weight toward his mom.

"Here." Raven gladly handed the little cherub over. She didn't hate babies. Quite the opposite. The memories of holding her younger siblings and helping Mom with them when they were little ignited fuzzy warmth inside her. But she'd been a kid and that was a long time ago. Now that she was older and more knowledgeable about how messed up the real world was, other people's babies made her nervous. These babies came into the world, good and new. She didn't worry about dropping them so much as tainting them with whatever unfortunate curse plagued her own life. That other parents, such as her friend, trusted her to hold their pride and joy and keep them safe, always surprised her. She could barely take care of herself.

Megan rolled her eyes and took the squealing infant from Raven. She sat down in the armchair beside Raven and bounced her son on her knee. Raven hadn't seen her friend in anything other than a simple shirt paired with either yoga or sweatpants in the last year. She wasn't judging Megan, she envied her.

Exhaustion clung to Raven's limbs from running around all night and braving her mother's wrath this morning. She sank into the couch and sighed. Her phone vibrated in her mini purse. She reached over, fished it out, and accepted the call from Mike. "What's up?"

"Just checking in. I ran background checks on Cole and Luke Bane."

"And?"

"Nothing."

"Nothing?" Raven frowned.

Megan glanced over and her eyebrows furrowed.

"Well, nothing traceable in the Mortal Realm like land titles, financial institutions, business dealings or criminal records. Now, if you want historical accounts, dark fae lord based smutty fan fiction or research papers on the Other Realms, including their positions, dealings and personas in the Underworld, I can email you an extensive reading list."

"I'll pass."

"Okay."

"No wait," she said, quickly, before he hung up. "Maybe just a basic summary on their positions and powers in the Underworld."

"And the smut?"

She chewed her lip.

"Thought so." Mike laughed. "I'll send the links." Her brother hung up before she had a chance to scowl at her screen and punch the red dot.

"He's pretty cute, isn't he?"

"Mike? God no, but hopefully he'll find someone who loves him and all his quirks." She chucked the phone back in her purse.

"I meant my baby." Her friend's tone was dry.

"Oh yeah. Totally. Not bad for crotch fruit," Raven mumbled into her coffee. The crisp-flavoured, hot liquid ran down her throat. The heat of the mug warmed her hands. Megan was a trustworthy friend. It was never too hot for coffee at her house, either.

Megan smiled down at her son before sitting him on the floor in front of a bunch of colourful plastic containers. "Did you just refer to my beloved child as crotch fruit?"

"Don't act offended. Until you jumped on this baby-making bandwagon, you were just as horrified with the idea of having children. Besides, didn't your own husband refer to your lady business as a train wreck when you gave birth?"

Megan frowned. "I did not appreciate his analogies for my *lady business*."

Raven snorted.

"He's not all bad." Megan's gaze grew distant, and a whimsical look replaced the disgust.

Oh, gag. "They're all bad."

Megan refocused and studied Raven. After a second or two, she reached for her mug and took a long drink. The steam fogged up her glasses. "Not all men are assholes, Raven."

"You're right." Raven mirrored her friend and drank some more coffee. Megan made it just the way she liked it—enough milk to make it beige. "Your husband, my dad and my brothers aren't so bad."

"Actually, I'd argue that Bear is an asshole," Megan said.

"Just because things didn't work out between—"

Megan clutched her mug in one hand and held out the other. "This has nothing to do with that. You warned me I'd end up as another notch in his belt, and I thought I'd be different. You were right, I was wrong. I'll admit, getting dumped by him hurt but that was a long time ago. I'm happily married now. I have two kids. I'm not angry at Bear anymore. At least not for myself."

Raven scrunched up her lips and stared at the top of her coffee mug. "For who?"

"You," Megan said. "Bear's an asshole because of how he treats you and your family."

Raven's hands tightened on the mug. *Well, crap.* She'd expected Megan to list a number of Bear's well-known faults and exploits. Raven hadn't anticipated Megan pointing in her direction.

A loud bang made them both jump. Even Theo paused in his gleeful squealing.

"I'm okay!" Megan's oldest son's voice yelled down the stairs.

Her friend rolled her eyes. "Honestly. I had no idea children were so hell bent to greet death until I birthed them."

Raven grunted.

The bright summer sunshine streamed in from a nearby window, illuminating Megan's grave expression. "Seriously, though. Bear's distanced himself from the family. Don't pretend his absence doesn't cut you. I see the pain in your face. Little by little, he pulls farther away. And little by little, he breaks your heart. The shine in your skin and the light in your eyes are gone."

Raven grumbled. Okay, so she wasn't going to win a skin modeling campaign anytime soon.

"Don't try to tell me it's only exhaustion from work and the stress of your debt."

Raven clamped her mouth shut. *There goes the witty retort.*

Megan continued. "And Bear treats the man who loved and raised him as his own with cold disdain, or indifference at best, acting as if your family shunned him instead of the other way around. He also takes the very jobs your dad refuses to consider due to ethical or moral reasons. He's trying to make a point and spite your dad. A giant fuck you to the very people who love him."

Raven set the mug down. Megan had excellent points. She couldn't deny any of the things she said. Her friend knew her family well, but Megan didn't know everything. As a non-supernatural being, or a "reg," Raven and Bear kept specifics regarding their abilities to a minimum. Not because they didn't trust her, but because she had no natural defence if someone came looking for the twins one day. They had no idea who their biological father was, but from the way their mom acted, they didn't want to risk Megan's life and take a chance. They heavily guarded their secrets. Megan didn't know what made Bear the way he was. "He has his reasons."

Odin's nutsack. That sounded lame, even to her.

Megan's oldest son squealed something unintelligible upstairs. More thumping. A giant bang.

"I'm okay!" he yelled again with less enthusiasm and after a longer pause.

Megan shook her head and picked up her youngest to bounce on her knee. "I think the only person Bear cares for is you."

"He cared about you, too."

Megan glared at her.

"As much as he could, at least," Raven quickly added.

"He didn't like me enough to whisk me away to his secret hook-up place, and I was one of the 'luckier' ones who he actually referred to as his girlfriend and kept around for longer than a week," Megan said, matter of fact.

"Excuse me, what?"

"Well, we probably only lasted as long as we did because he took some time trying to figure out how to dump his twin's best friend." Megan shrugged.

"You're giving him too much credit, and yourself too little. I think you scared the crap out of him, or his feelings for you did." Raven thumbed the handle of her mug. "But that's not what I was asking about. What did you mean when you said his secret hook-up place?"

"What do you mean, what do I mean?"

"Did he have a special place he took his lady friends? Like a make-out spot on Burnaby Mountain, or something else?"

Megan put her coffee down and looked at Raven oddly.

"What?"

"I can't believe he didn't tell you."

"Tell me what?" Raven loved her friend, but she might throttle her if she didn't spit it out soon.

"He had some sort of hideaway. A 'special place' to get away from all the 'noise.'" Her friend used air quotes and dropped her voice to imitate Bear and the way he spoke. That was why they were friends.

"I only know about the place because he slipped and mentioned it once to Marcus in front of me," Megan continued. "Must've forgotten I was there."

Marcus had been Bear's best friend since they were three and discovered they both shared the same love for farting and jumping off any object they could climb. The three of them grew up together. "A special place?"

Megan nodded. "Probably to escape the horde of disgruntled women who follow him everywhere."

"He's not that bad," Raven said. Special place? What special place?

Megan picked up her coffee and took another sip. "If you say so."

Was Bear's special place a safe house? She'd have to dig into that later. If Bear had a safe house, he could be hiding there. *Good thinking, Brainiac.*

Her gaze snagged on a brochure resting on the nearby desk. She stood up and plucked the glossy folded paper from the smooth surface, "Regulators?"

Megan sighed somewhere behind her. "It's a group of regs who meet once a month."

"I know who Regulators are," Raven snapped, maybe a little too harshly. Of course, she knew about the group of regs who hated anyone with an ounce of fae blood. She took a deep breath and tried for a softer tone. "What do you discuss when you meet?"

"What don't regs have to talk about?"

Raven flipped the pamphlet open and skimmed through the material. "They want to rebuild the barrier?"

"Don't you? We need to do something to keep the Others from our realm and away from our children." Megan's usually soft voice grew harder.

Raven's heart pulsed as if stabbed. "You sound like a politician."

Megan grunted.

"Next, you'll claim they're taking all our jobs." Raven dropped the pamphlet on the desk as if it suddenly burst into flame and turned to her friend.

"Not our jobs, our lives." Megan pursed her lips. "This isn't about separating us from another country, Raven. This is about separating the sheep from the wolves. It's about protecting us from a magical realm full of power-thirsty despots."

"Despots? You mean people like me?" Her spine straightened and her skin itched.

Megan recoiled. "Of course not You're not one of them. I'm not talking about shifters or witches or any of the supernaturals who coexisted relatively peacefully with regs prior to the barrier getting ripped down."

"Things aren't that bad." Raven bit her tongue. Maybe they should've told Megan more about themselves. Maybe she'd view the situation differently if she knew Bear and Raven were part Other, as well.

Nausea rolled in her gut.

Or maybe Megan would treat them differently instead. Did Raven want to find out the truth? Her throat tightened. Maybe she should tell Megan now. Admit to years of lies and see if their friendship could withstand Megan's hatred toward the Others and Raven's duplicity.

"Look around you, Raven. They nearly wiped us out. They damaged our cities and towns. Their wars, and our wars with them, ravaged the ecosystem and we're still scrambling to rebuild. How long before they knock us back down? They let us thrive just enough to prevent a rebellion but keep us desperate for their presence and help at the same time."

Raven cringed. Maybe she'd tell Megan later. Raven couldn't face losing a friend right now if Megan turned out to hate Raven's nature more than she loved her as a person. Instead, Raven said, "Odin put a stop to the wars."

"Odin's done shit." Megan slammed down her mug. "People think he saved the regs, but all he's done is successfully contain the humans in a tidy pen for future minion duty."

Raven's mouth dropped open.

"I have two children, Raven. Two beautiful babies

without any special powers besides their inherent awesomeness. What kind of future will they have? All that stands between them and servitude is the word of a narcissistic warmonger who sits on a throne of skulls. They have to have a way to defend themselves."

Raven stood speechless. What could she possibly say to assuage Megan's realistic worries as a mother? She'd visited her friend to catch up, provide company and have a selfish moment of friendship without fixating on her current problems. Instead, she felt hollow with no idea how to fix anything currently combusting in her life and the lives of those she cared about.

"I see your point," she said when she could think of nothing else to break the silence. She saw Megan's point, all right. She saw the point as the sharp tip of a sword aimed at her heart. She swallowed her uneased and pushed the troublesome thoughts away. "How are your parents?"

Chapter Fourteen

"I don't mean to brag, but I just broke my personal record for the longest consecutive time lived."
　　　　　~Raven, every day, trying to stay positive

Water dripped from Raven's still wet hair and the short robe stuck to her damp skin. After her visit with Megan, she ran some errands to let her heart mend and her brain run through options. Since Mike's background checks came up empty for Cole and Luke aside from what the textbooks said, she needed to figure out her next move.

She stepped out of her bathroom, and a cloud of steam flowed from the tiny room with her, billowing out to the rest of her small apartment. Heat still tingled her skin and the tension from her limbs had long since fled, leaving her languid and a little boneless. She smiled and continued to dry her long hair with the towel. In the shower, her thoughts had repeatedly drifted to Cole. If he was with her, would he touch her here? Would he stroke her like this? Kiss her with passion? Explore her body with his tongue? She'd remained warm with devious thoughts of the Lord of Shadows long after the hot water ran cold. Even now, standing outside her bathroom door in a thin robe, the heat danced along her skin.

The steam cleared, snaking out the open window into the dark night. The shadow of a large man stood in the middle of her apartment.

Raven gasped. The towel dropped to the floor with a splat.

Cole?

Her heart rate picked up and new heat spread through her body. Had she gasped his name in the shower? Had he heard?

Her cheeks warmed. Her lips parted.

Did he visit to make her wicked dreams come true?

The remaining steam cleared, and the man turned around to face her. The lone light from the kitchen illuminated his face.

Not Cole.

Luke.

Her stomach sank.

Luke Bane.

She pulled her worn robe tight around her.

Bane, Lord of War. In her apartment. Here. Now.

The heat raced from her skin, replaced with prickling ice. "What are you doing here?"

Luke's gaze travelled up her body. His smirk spread. "I think that's obvious."

"Excuse me?"

Luke let out a long exasperated sigh, as if to say, "Mortals are so tiresome."

She waited.

"You chose the wrong fae lord to work with. I'm here to remedy the situation."

She rocked back on her heels. "You want to work with me?"

Bane scoffed. "Not at all."

Moisture trailed down her face and neck from her wet hair. A small puddle of water pooled at her feet. She'd intended to dry off and get dressed, not stand around talking in circles with a dark fae lord. At least she hadn't peed herself. Yet.

"It's late. I'm tired. Just tell me what you want."

"You're coming with me."

"No, thanks."

"That wasn't a request."

"Just because you want something, doesn't mean you get it."

Bane's smirk twisted into a cruel smile. "I'm the Lord of War. I always get what I want."

Raven glanced over her shoulder. Her front door was two lunge-worthy steps away. Bane was three in the other direction but had considerably longer legs than her, and undoubtedly faster reflexes. He'd grab her before she cleared the front door. Once someone placed their hands on her, it made it more difficult to shift. Somehow, physical skin-on-skin contact, especially with an Other, disrupted her own dark energy.

Her skin prickled. Why would Bane want her? The same reason he tried to nab Mike with the trap? A bargaining chip?

Raven's decision to work with Cole might turn out to be a mistake but going with Bane would be disastrous.

Like he gave her a choice.

"Abduction isn't going to make me want to help you," she clarified.

"I waited until you finished your lengthy cleaning ritual. I could've barged in, you know."

She opened her mouth to thank him and stopped. She clamped her mouth shut. Had she really almost thanked the Lord of War for waiting to kidnap her? Idiot! Grandma Lu would be pulling her gray hair out right now.

Anger suffused her skin. She balled her hands into fists.

Calm down. Think.

Bane took a threatening step forward.

The window over his right shoulder was open wide enough for clearance.

"Stop looking around. You won't find any escape routes." Bane took another step forward, placing himself within slapping distance. One step away, now. "This will go easier for you if you don't fight."

Instead of replying, Raven untied the sash to her bathrobe, letting it fall open.

Bane straightened. A dark eyebrow rose. "Seduction will not get you out of this."

"No," she agreed, calling the corvid energy to her. "But it will get me out of here."

Bane's eyes narrowed. He lunged forward.

Raven's power snapped in place. Her mind fractured and her body split into multiple birds.

Bane's hands snatched at empty air.

She drove the birds toward the open window. One bird dive-bombed Luke and took a swipe at his face. He growled and smacked the bird away.

Pain lanced through her collective mind—like someone snapped an elastic band against her brain. The birds faltered but evaded Luke's follow-up strike. They flew out the window and into the night, all of them. She hadn't lost a bird. Phew.

She settled the group in the tree outside her apartment and waited. The summer evening air washed over the birds. They gripped the rough bark so hard with their talons, the wood groaned and splintered. Minutes later, Bane strode from her building. He stopped at the base of the tree and looked up, his dark Other gaze two black pools in the night.

She turned all her birds' beady eyes to him. How many would she lose if she attacked his pretty face? She couldn't defeat him in any way but scratching him up would feel nice.

Instead of looking shocked or thunderous as expected, the Lord of War appeared thoughtful. A small smile tugged at his cruel lips, and his eyes crinkled.

Unease flittered through the conspiracy of ravens.

"An interesting development," Bane crooned.

She croaked a bird equivalent of "Fuck you."

His gaze laughed at her. If he didn't understand raven-speech, he still somehow grasped the intent. "Until we meet again, little raven."

He threw a glowing disc at the ground. The air snapped as the power formed a portal. A blast of dark energy rushed past her. Within a minute, Bane disappeared to who-cared-where and the normal non-fae vibe of her neighbourhood returned.

What should she do now? She glanced at her apartment's window. Bane left it open. With a single thought, she directed the birds back to her home. Bane's unwelcomed visit obliterated the lingering effects of her hot shower and any enjoyment she'd gained from the twenty-minute guilt-free me-time. That alone was reason enough to hate him.

She shifted to human and pulled on long, baggy pajama pants, and a T-shirt. She found her phone and hit Cole's contact information. She gripped the smooth device and held its cool surface close to her ear. Her hand shook a little. The call went to voicemail.

"Camhanaich." His rich seductive voice preceded a loud, annoying beep.

"It's Raven. Bane tried to kidnap me in my apartment and failed. Call me."

She hung up and waited. What if he didn't call back? What would she do? Where would she go?

The dead bolt on her apartment's door stared back at her. Useless. It hadn't stopped Bane from gaining entry to her place the first time, she doubted it would be triumphant a second time. Bane could evade her measly defenses, and now he knew her little magic trick. The next time he came for her, he'd be prepared, and she'd be screwed.

Should she go to her parents? Yes. Cole promised to protect them, so she should be safe there. One location was easier to protect than two, but it also created a giant all-encompassing target composed of her entire family.

Her phone rang in her hand. She jumped and dropped it.

"Odin's scrotum!" she cursed. Swiftly scooping the phone from the floor, Cole's name appeared across the undamaged screen. She sighed. She couldn't afford a new phone.

She answered. "Hello?"

"I'm coming over."

Before she could reply, Cole hung up. Raven kept the phone to her ear and listened to the dial tone. Yeah, right. Like a magical voice would suddenly start explaining stuff to her over the airways. Her brain scrambled.

The shadows around her darkened, pooling

together. They lowered from the corners of the room and moved to the center where they twisted together. The bands kept streaming and twisting, like the ribbons from some demented May-Pole celebration. The tall shadowy pyre continued to grow until Cole materialized in her living room, large and imposing.

Raven breathed out. Wow.

Cole strode toward her, dark jeans clinging to powerful thighs, shirt stretched across his strong chest.

She gulped. Her nipples tightened, her shirt now rough against the sensitive skin.

Crap! She should've thrown on a sweatshirt or something. Better to drip sweat than let her bra-less state show Cole how his mere presence made her nipples ping. Her arm muscles twitched to fold across her chest.

Cole's gaze scanned her apartment, and then her. "You're unharmed."

"Physically, yes."

He tilted his head. "Did he hurt you psychologically, somehow?"

Her shoulders slumped. "No. I'm just freaking out. I'm not safe in my own home and I don't know why Bane wants me."

Cole's gaze darkened and roamed her body again. Unlike his calculating scan earlier, he took his time, letting his attention linger. "I have an idea."

"I don't get that vibe from him.' Nope. The Lord of War wasn't interested in playing hide the bologna with her...thank Odin!

"No?"

"No."

His jaw unclenched and his lips twitched. "What vibe do you get from me?"

Predatory.

She clamped her mouth shut. If he chose to actively seduce her, she'd resist for a solid two seconds before melting into a puddle of need.

His gaze drifted to her lips. He took another step forward, within kissing distance.

Her lungs constricted. Her stomach tightened. "You're supposed to protect me," she blurted.

Cole straightened. "No, you asked me to protect your family." He looked around the apartment. His attention snagged on something. His dark brows pinched in. He took a step toward her couch. There, on the armrest, lay a perfect glistening feather.

Raven gulped.

He plucked the feather from where it rested. His breath sucked in and he squeezed his eyes shut. When they reopened, the irises had bled out to cover the whites of his eyes. "Not a fox shifter like your family, then..."

He never thought she was a fox shifter. She'd bet her last pair of pumps on that. He knew she was part Other the moment they met and asked her to take her contacts out, but the feather must've confirmed his suspicions. Whatever information he gleaned from it had affected him enough to make his eyes change. And for someone that exuded confidence and control, that said more than any words he uttered.

She clenched her teeth and pulled her shoulders back. "You need to provide protection for me."

His eyebrows shot up. "You don't seem to need protection."

He must've drawn that conclusion from the lack of blood and guts splattered across the walls, but Raven had no way to prevent Bane from returning. Her stellar wits and fleeing skills would only get her so far. "I disagree."

"Oh, don't worry." His smouldering gaze held all sorts of suggestions. "I plan to keep a closer eye on you."

"Promises, promises."

"It wouldn't be advantageous for Bane to gain you as leverage." He continued to twirl the feather between his fingers.

"How do I get a hold of you if I don't have a phone, or you're in the Other Realms?"

"Summoning is simple." He leaned in, dousing her with his mysterious forest scent. His voice rumbled. He ran the feather down her nose. "Just say my name."

Her thighs tensed. "Just your name?"

He nodded and reached out with his free hand to gather a strand of her still-damp hair. He ran it between two of his fingers, staring hard, as if mesmerized. "My full fae name."

"That's it?" She held her hand out for the feather.

He shook his head. "While drawing your blood or the blood of another."

Said blood drained from her face. "Just draw and quarter myself while screaming your name." She snapped her fingers. "Easy."

He chuckled. "Although the idea of you screaming my name is...delicious." He paused and let her hair slip from his fingers. "It's unnecessary. And although you need more blood than a pinprick or scratch, drawing and quartering is excessive. There'd be nothing left for me to protect once I arrive."

"Wouldn't it be annoying and a little too easy for your name to be the key ingredient for a summoning? Like, anyone could do it and you'd be zinging all over the Mortal Realm to answer calls." She ran her hands down the thin cotton of her pajama pants. Anything to keep from reaching out and touching Cole.

"Not really. For instance, right now, the thirteen-year-old, pimple-faced brat across the road is dabbling in the occult. He's using my name like a bad song stuck on repeat because he wants to be a *badass assassin* and thinks I can somehow transform him. He's even learned to add the blood component." He tucked the feather into the waist of his jeans, flashing a muscular torso.

She licked her lips.

He pulled his T-shirt over to cover the feather and pin it in place.

"Blood component?" she asked. This conversation needed to get back on track before her mind went right off the rails and into the gutter.

"Every spell has a price. For a summoning to be

heard, you must feed your voice, and the chow of choice is your life essence."

"Blood."

He nodded. "Blood."

Yup, no amount of repeating this fact made it lose the ick factor. "Don't you have to go to him, then? He's bleeding and crying your name."

Cole smirked. "No. Even this close, the tug is weak. He lacks any true power or the ability to compel me. I probably only feel it because I am so close in proximity." He paused. "Summoning me might be easy but controlling me isn't. I don't need to answer a summons. Think of it as an invasive type of phone call. And if I do answer, I'm not some demon caged in a witch's circle on a full moon. Most people fear my retribution too much to summon me callously. I could choose to show up and make your neighbour's life miserable or I could stay here with much better company."

Her cheeks warmed.

He stepped in closer. So close the warmth of his body pressed against her skin. The gentle draft of his breath fanned her cheek. If she stuck out her tongue, she'd learn whether he tasted as good as he looked.

"You on the other hand," he said. "My name on your lips is a siren's call I couldn't resist."

The shadow bands reached forward and ran along her skin. Cole's large, capable hands cradled her face and his lips pressed against hers, hot and lush. His tongue slipped in and stroked hers. Time slowed along with her heart and the room disappeared. Only Cole and his mouth on hers chased away any lingering fear from Bane's visit. She melted into his lips and he gathered her in his strong, protective arms. His hands gripped her while shadows explored her body. Feather light, wisps of promised pleasure, they moved along and teased her skin.

Cole deepened the kiss and pulled her into his body, hard where she was soft. He tasted of dark promises and scandalous nights. His chest pressed against her breasts. All the while, his shadows continued to move and explore. Emboldened, their touch increased their pressure.

Raven's head spun. Her limbs grew limp, her heart melted. Her hands clutched the soft fabric of his shirt. Cole offered unhindered passion and pleasure in his arms.

The arms of a stranger.

Raven stiffened. She knew almost nothing about this man. He might still plot to kill her own brother.

Heck, even when she knew someone, she still managed to get burned.

Cole withdrew, still holding her in his arms, his gaze searched hers. His lips twitched. "You think entirely too much, Einin."

"What should I do, then?" she whispered, still catching her breath.

"Feel." He rubbed her arms.

Oh, how she wanted to. How she wanted to throw caution to the curb and slap her naked body against his.

How she wanted to forget all her troubles and let Cole fill her mind with pleasure.

Cole's gaze softened. He leaned forward and delivered a quick kiss before releasing her. The skin prickled where his shadows left her. She felt their absence keenly.

"Go to sleep, Einin. I'll take the couch."

She looked over at the apartment-sized abomination she purchased second-hand online. "You're going to sleep on that?"

His gaze smouldered. "I would rather sleep on, or with, something else."

Heat flooded her skin.

He leaned in. "But not even my self-control is that good. I only take what's freely given."

"Uhhh..."

He shifted away from her, leaving cool air where heat had once been. "What's the plan for tomorrow?"

Her brain clunked to switch gears. Her body was still slapping itself for missing out on great sex. What was wrong with her?

He raised an eyebrow.

"Going to question an old friend."

"Yours or Bear's?"

She hesitated. "Both." *I think.*

Chapter Fifteen

"I'm not an early bird or a night owl. I am some form of permanently exhausted pigeon."
        ~Unknown, but obviously Raven's kindred spirit

Raven and Cole stepped into the air-conditioned working area of Marcus Automotive, a concrete room adrift in car fumes. The cool air hit her bare arms and legs. The caustic, yet oddly comforting, mix of grease, gas, diesel and oil overwhelmed her senses. With a few deep breaths, the familiar smell washed over her. Marcus had always loved cars. She'd grown up playing in his dad's garage while he tinkered with his latest project.

Mr. Lamont had passed away five years ago. She'd

attended his funeral, and Marcus Lamont had cried on her shoulder.

Air-powered tools punctuated the tune of sparse voices, drills, clanking metal and the traffic from Boundary Street a few blocks over.

Marcus had inherited his dad's shop. They'd found the old man's body in this room beside a dilapidated jeep. They said his heart just gave out.

Raven walked toward a pickup truck with its hood popped open. Her flip flops slapped the concrete floor. "Hey, Marcus."

Every week, the trolls opened access on the Lion's Gate Bridge. No fees, no favours, no death threats. The troll bridge toll-free Fridays. Last year, Bear had everyone over for a barbeque, including Marcus. She hadn't seen him since.

The man under the hood straightened and moved to the side of the truck. Grease streaked his face and painted his nails and fingertips black. Stubble accentuated the chiseled lines on his face. He'd grown out his dark brown hair since the last time she saw him. It fell in front of his face. He used his grease-stained hands to push it back.

"Raven." A smile spread across his face, white teeth contrasting with his tan skin and grime. "You still driving that piece of shit?"

"Don't talk about Jean Claude like that."

"He needs a checkup. You're way overdue for a service." He leaned against the side of the truck. "It's almost as though you're avoiding me."

"What? No." Okay, she totally was. She couldn't afford to pay for the service, and she wouldn't let Marcus work for free, which is what he'd offer if he knew how bad things were financially for her. Just to prove him otherwise, she walked over and gave him a hug.

His arms hesitated for a second before closing around her. He was warm, solid and smelled like car oil. He let her go when she pulled away and stepped back. His gaze shifted to Cole. His smile faltered. "Not a social call, I take it?"

"Not really. I tried to call." An elderly woman had answered his old cell phone number and Raven ended up talking to the woman about the weather and how fast technology changed these days for over half an hour. She'd also called the shop, but some rude technician hung up on her.

"Changed my cell provider a while ago. New number."

"Ah."

They stared at each other.

"Do you know where Bear is?" she asked.

He grabbed a nearby rag and wiped his hands. "I had a few guys come into the shop yesterday and ask the exact same thing. What's going on?"

The constant staccato of machinery lightened. She glanced around the shop. Some of the other mechanics had straightened and now watched Raven and Cole. The few she recognized nodded at her and went back to work. The rest continued to stare. "Can we talk in your office?"

He nodded. "Sure."

Raven followed Marcus to the back room. He still looked good in jeans. Cole trailed behind, a dark, looming hulk of a man as her shadow. At least, he hadn't tried to butt in or take over the conversation. When they reached his office, Marcus closed the door behind them.

Stuffy, his office appeared as the dumping ground for all things paper. An uncovered light bulb with low wattage dangled from the ceiling. Dust lined the frames of a family photo and his automotive service technician red seal certificate. Grease smudges decorated the walls. A small fan whirled in the corner, making a little dent in the heat and teasing the corners of the papers. The room smelled like a combination of car oil and male sweat.

Marcus stood a couple feet from Cole. The men sized each other up. Neither seemed impressed with what they saw.

Marcus' eyes narrowed. "Who's your...friend?"

"Marcus, this is Cole. Cole, Marcus." She waved her hands at each of them.

They nodded at each other. Neither offered a hand to shake. Marcus pulled his gaze from the Lord of Shadows and focused on her. His eyebrows relaxed and the creases around his eyes smoothed away. "Why didn't you call the shop?"

"I did. Some guy hung up on me."

Marcus' gaze darkened. "Who?"

"Brian, maybe?"

Marcus nodded, his expression closed off. "I'll deal with it."

"Thanks."

A paused stretched into awkward silence.

"What's going on, Wenny?"

Only Marcus called her that. Well, only Marcus called her that and lived. She'd take up martial arts to kill anyone else who dared. Cole's head snapped to her. His shoulders tensed.

"Bear's in trouble," she said.

Marcus frowned. "What else is new?"

"Real trouble, Marcus."

He hesitated. With another glance at Cole, he walked around his desk and sat. He waved at the other two empty plastic patio chairs, circa 1990.

Raven plunked down. The chair wobbled but held. Her bare skin slid along the smooth surface until it stuck. The coffee she'd consumed hours ago had turned her mouth stale. She dug into her purse and pulled out some gum. The vanilla mint flavour danced along her taste buds. She glanced over her shoulder and held up the gum package. Cole, maintaining his position by the door with folded arms, shook his head.

She turned to Marcus and he shook his head as well. She put the gum away.

"Does this trouble of Bear's have anything to do with your dark fae entourage?" Marcus asked.

She didn't bother asking him how he knew Cole was dark fae instead of light. The man dripped midnight liaisons from his pores.

"We're working together."

"Uh-huh." His lip curled like the times Bear offered to trade him their mom's leftover meatloaf for lunch. "Can't trust the fae, Wenny."

Cole growled.

Marcus ignored him.

"I'm fae, Marcus." Raven reminded him. Her phone buzzed in her pocket.

"Half fae." The tension released from Marcus' shoulders and he sat back. "And you're different."

Raven dug her phone out and read the text from Mike: *Need you at home. NE.*

NE stood for non-emergency. Raven sighed. Last time Mike needed her to help with computer research, she had to sit by one of his computers with code scrolling up the screen while he went to the bathroom. If he used her for a potty break again, cast or no cast, she'd hurt him.

Cole stepped forward. "Can you describe the men who came by yesterday?"

Marcus scowled. For a moment, he looked as though he'd refuse to answer. His gaze flicked to Raven.

She nodded.

Marcus' lips flattened into a firm line. "Dark fae, like you. Hired thugs, most likely. Didn't like being told no and didn't want to leave."

"Yet, you and your establishment are unscathed from the altercation," Cole observed.

Marcus flashed his teeth at the fae lord. He flipped

his hand in the air and made the dust in the room dance. Despite acting like an alpha werewolf, ready to dominate and piss on things, Marcus was a witch, or a warlock, as he preferred to be called. He wasn't super powerful, but witches and warlocks excelled in protecting their hearth, regardless of personal strength. She'd be surprised if Marcus considered anywhere other than this shop his home.

Cole straightened. His body tensed. The room dimmed. The lone light bulb flickered.

"I'm not without resources." Marcus turned back to Raven. "How can I help?"

"Do you know where Bear is?"

"No. I haven't spoken to him in about a week or so."

"Do you know about his secret hideaway? The one he liked to take girls to?"

Marcus's eyes widened. "He dated women, not girls. Not that he took them there. How do you know about his hideaway? He wanted to keep it a secret, even from you."

Shock pierced her body.

"He worried you'd tell the rest of the family."

A heavy pit sank to the bottom of her stomach. Bear hadn't trusted her. She slumped in her seat. "I'd never betray him."

"That's what I told him. It was a weak excuse. In truth, I think he didn't want to burden you with information that someone might come searching for." Marcus leaned forward. "Bear knew the dangers of the jobs he took and felt the payouts were worth the risk. I know you didn't approve of his work, but he wasn't an idiot. He still took precautions."

Sounded like Bear. "Do you know where his safe house is?"

Marcus shook his head. "No. He never told me." He glanced up at Cole. "My advice?"

"Of course."

"If he's in real trouble, bad enough to make him run to his safe house, leave him there. He'll emerge when he's ready. You don't want to bring trouble to his door." His gaze flicked to the Lord of Shadows again.

Subtle, Marcus. Real subtle.

Cole grunted and stepped forward.

The air shimmered as Marcus stood and pulled power to him. The light in the room dimmed again as the shadows pooled around Cole. Raven bolted from her seat. Her skin ripped from the plastic. The back of her thighs stung from being wrenched from the plastic chair.

With one step, she placed herself between the two men. "Don't."

Marcus grumbled.

Cole scowled.

The lighting and air returned to normal.

"We'll show ourselves out." Raven grabbed Cole's arm and pulled him toward the door. "Thanks for your help, Marcus. It was good to see you again."

"It's been too long." Marcus' hands clenched. "I wish it was under different circumstances."

"Me too." She shoved Cole out the door and left

Marcus in the office. They walked quickly out of the shop without saying a word. The heat from the summer's day blasted her face.

"How long has your brother's best friend been in love with you?" Cole asked as they walked toward Jean Claude.

Raven stumbled. "Marcus? No. He's not in love with me. Not in that way."

"Didn't appear that way to me."

Raven sighed. "He thinks of me as a sister. A little sister, even though I'm actually older than him by three months." And two days, but who's counting?

"What I saw was not brotherly love." He wrenched the passenger side door open. It creaked. Loudly.

"Can we not talk about this? Marcus' feelings aren't involved in this case."

"Touchy subject?"

"Awkward subject." Raven jumped into the driver's side and sucked in a breath. The hot seat burned her legs. She shut the door and turned the car on. She may as well head over to her parents' house now and find out what Mike needed. Jean Claude grunted his disapproval.

Cole leaned down to speak through the open door. "Why?"

"He's my twin brother's best friend. We grew up together. He's like family."

"How long have you been in love with him?" Cole slid into the passenger seat, making the interior of her small car seem smaller in an instant. He wrenched the door closed and turned to her. "Are you still in love with him?"

"What? No." Not anymore, at least. That ship had sailed long ago.

Cole scowled, his look full of unspoken criticism.

Raven furiously rolled down the window. They hadn't been gone long, but Jean Claude still managed to turn into a sauna. "Okay. I might've had a small infatuation with him when we were in high school. That was a long time ago."

Cole raised a dark brow and waited, saying nothing.

Her chest tightened, squeezing her lungs. "We kissed at a weekend party once. That's it. I thought we were going to be a thing, but by the time Monday rolled around, I arrived at school to learn he was dating Mandy Penner."

"Who's Mandy Penner?"

"My rival in pretty much everything. It stung, but I got over it." And she had, but the bitter sting of jealousy still struck when she thought of it. She really hated Mandy Penner. The tension in her chest released, leaving a harsh burning sensation.

"He obviously didn't."

Raven glanced over her shoulder and checked her mirrors to ensure the lane was clear, turned the wheel and punched the gas. Jean Claude groaned and clunked but did as she commanded. "That's a long time to carry a torch for someone."

"Carry a torch?" He tilted his head.

"Yeah, you know..."

"No. No I don't."

"To have feelings for someone you're not with."

"I see."

"Besides, he had two black eyes and walked with a limp for the week following the party."

"You?"

Raven laughed. "No. I'm not the scrapper in the family. Bear is. I think my brother found out about our moment and they fought over it. Whatever feelings we may have had for each other, we both let it go. Bear means more to us than we do to each other."

Cole grunted.

"What?"

"Your brother sounds like a selfish prick."

Her throat closed up and a heavy pit fell in her stomach. She swallowed a couple of times before speaking. "My best friend called him something similar yesterday."

"And?"

Raven shrugged. "And I get it. I see how you both came to that conclusion, but I don't think he's a prick or a jerk. He's my brother." In hindsight, Bear probably did them all a favour. They were too young. Had Raven and Marcus dated in high school, they probably would've had a messy, painful break-up that would've destroyed Marcus' friendship with Raven and with Bear.

"If he loves you half as much as you obviously love him, he'd care about your happiness, too," Cole said.

The light ahead turned red. She stepped on the

brake and peered over at Cole. "Are you advocating for a Raven-Marcus hook up? Our couple name could be Marven, or Ravus. It would be spectacular."

"Your couple name?" He shook his head. "No. But your brother shouldn't have intervened."

"So, you're saying you'd be okay with your best friend making a move on your sister? Assuming you have one, of course."

"A friend?"

"A sister." She paused. "Well, both, actually." She didn't know anything about the shadow man who sat beside her. Most of the documents Mike sent over didn't cover his personal life, and the fanfiction couldn't be trusted.

The light turned green and she stomped on the gas. The car lurched forward. She normally didn't drive aggressively, but the faster she pushed Jean Claude, the more the car forced air through the open windows.

"I'd probably drive my dagger through the man's chest," Cole said, answering her question.

She smirked. "Who's the selfish prick, now?"

Cole clamped his mouth shut and glared.

Raven waited, but he didn't appear to have a reply. "So...you have a sister?"

Cole shook his head and looked away. Silence filled the car as she drove along the cracked and uneven streets of North Burnaby. Well, okay, then. Apparently, sharing time was over.

"Your real name isn't Raven, is it? Just like Bear is a nickname."

Raven glanced over at Cole. Technically, Bear's real name was Bjorn, but no one called him that, especially not Raven. Before they arrived in the world with mops of black hair and black eyes, their mom had believed their father was a dark-haired swede. Mom had named Raven's twin brother Bjorn, a Swedish name meaning "Bear," as a shout-out to their "Scandinavian" father. Mom now referred to this man as the sperm donor. They couldn't get mad at her either, because she wasn't wrong. Their biological father had never been in their lives.

Bear and Raven were a product of their mom's wild days. The sperm donor, whatever his name was, probably had no clue they existed, and all they knew about him was his apparent ethnicity, and "god-like" appearance.

Nice, Mom. Real nice.

And just like Bear, Raven also had a "real name," though she never used it. Young, pregnant and alone, Elizabeth Crawford had attempted to pay homage to their Scandinavian father and her own heritage. Branwen was a Welsh name, meaning "beautiful raven." Of course, Bear and Raven had ruined Mom's efforts by simultaneously choosing to use the simpler translations as names. Their mom hadn't been impressed. She still gnashed her teeth about it.

"Raven?" Cole said.

"No, it's not."

"What is your real name?"

She pursed her lips. He probably already knew. He

was the Patron Fae of Assassins, for Odin's sack. He probably had minions bringing him dossiers full of information on her and her family. Maybe he needed her to admit to her full legal name for him to wield some crazy Other World mumbo jumbo sorcery crap on her.

"You know my full fae name. It seems only fair you tell me yours."

His statement held no tease, or heat, only manipulation. His words seemed oddly reminiscent of a childhood memory—when Gary Gerrard tricked her into showing him her private parts when they were eight. They'd laid in wait in some grassy ditch in a neighbourhood-wide kid's game of some sort.

Gary had turned to Raven, and said, "I'll show you mine if you show me yours."

Both eight and friends since birth, she'd giggled at the idea. "No!"

"Okay," he said. They returned to peering over the ditch edge, looking out for the other team. The grass had been thick and lush, filling her nose with its fresh scent.

"Hey, Raven?" Gary said.

"Yeah?" She'd turned to look at him and there it was. Little boy penis. He'd proudly displayed it, thrusting his hips out, and placing his hands on his hips. Maybe it would've been impressive or shocking to someone else, but Raven had a twin brother. Her childhood was filled with little boy penis.

"I showed you mine." Gary beamed. "Now you

have to show me yours."

Raven's cheeks heated. To this day, she was ashamed to admit she'd fallen for a fellow eight year old's manipulation.

Bear and Marcus had found out and beat the snot out of Gary the next day. Broke his front tooth and everything. Neither set of parents had disciplined the boys when they discovered the reason. Raven had the worst punishment—a sit down discussion with dear old Mom about the birds and the bees and not caving into pressure.

Raven cringed.

Cole wasn't eight, and she wasn't so naïve anymore. The Lord of Shadows had already proven he respected a woman's boundaries, so that wasn't the concern, but information was power, and Cole had enough over her, both in abilities and knowledge.

"Raven?"

She shook her head and shifted Jean Claude into park. "We're here."

Chapter Sixteen

"I like failure. It's one thing I'm good at."

~Raven, trying to stay positive

The rusty doors to Jean Claude Grand Am screeched as they stepped out of the car into the hot sun. The air conditioning no longer worked in JC, but with the windows down it had been slightly cooler while driving. Now, the mid-afternoon sun beat down on them and radiated in waves off the cooked concrete. Her skin grew warm and sweat pebbled on her nose and forehead. She couldn't find a free parking spot near her parents' place. Unfamiliar cars lined the streets. Mrs. Humphreys, the cranky neighbour with a penchant for hating anything different from herself, must be having some sort of pensioners' shindig. Raven had to park a few blocks away at the nearby shops.

Two ravens perched on a nearby power line and tilted their beady-eyed heads at her. Cole joined Raven on the sidewalk as if meeting her in the park for a leisurely stroll. He glanced at the birds and paused. His brows furrowed as if he tried to silently answer a question.

Did he know what she was? He'd seen the feather, but did he know the extent of her abilities?

While she panted in a tank top and jean shorts, Cole appeared cool, calm and completely unaffected by the heat wave even though he wore enough black to turn a Goth green with envy.

"Aren't you warm?"

Cole looked away from the birds and turned to her with a pale face showing no signs of perspiration. "Not at all."

"Do you ever get hot?" She spat her gum out in the trash as they passed. Her mouth no longer tasted of stale coffee, but the gum had lost its fresh vanilla mint flavour.

He leaned in. "I make things hot, Einin."

Whoo boy, could he ever. Raven froze with her hand halfway to her face. It had risen as if animated on its own to fan her flushed cheeks. She readjusted her purse strap.

"Tell me." Cole stepped in. "Why does your pulse race every time I come near?"

"You're the Patron Fae of Assassins." Her heart thumped against her breastbone. Odin's sack. He'd asked something similar in the hospital. He was onto her. He'd kissed her last night and although she'd eventually pushed him away, she'd kissed him back like her soul depended on it.

Cole smirked. "Why do your cheeks flush a beautiful rose colour?"

"Your wardrobe makes me feel woefully underdressed." Heat crept up her neck and spread across her face, and it had nothing to do with the afternoon sun or Cole's outfit. Why did he have to stand so close?

"And your eyes?"

"What about my eyes?" They tingled as if they had a mind of their own and were delighted to have Cole's attention.

"Why do they bleed out with the darkness of the Underworld and roam over me with hunger?"

"Uh..." Crap! She hadn't realized her eyes did that. Her contacts only covered so much. If her Otherness bled out to the whites of her eyes when she was...Odin's nutsack! He must've known every time she'd wanted to dry hump him She groaned. She needed to find Bear's hidey hole to curl up in and die from mortification.

Cole closed the distance between them. Only an inch separated his muscle-packed body from hers. The heat from his skin stroked hers, begging to be touched, to be explored.

"Why do you melt in my arms and let me steal your breath with my kiss?"

Well, crap. He knew she was attracted to him. She actively participated in those bone-melting kisses. She was an adult. So was he. Why did she try to deny it?

Her throat tightened. "You're an attractive piece of man flesh. I can't help how my body responds to you."

"Man flesh?" His gaze smouldered and flicked to her lips.

"Cole," she warned.

"Yes?" He leaned down. His intoxicating forest scent caressed her.

Raven closed her eyes, expecting the lush sensation of his mouth on hers. His arms closed around her torso and wrenched her to the side.

"Wha—?" Her eyes snapped open.

A large ball of fire flew past her face, the heat scalding her cheeks. Two seconds ago, they'd stood directly in its path ready to tongue wrestle. A fuzzy sensation gripped her scalp. Her muscles tensed. Cole flung her to the nearby alley. Her arms flailed and she slammed into the brick wall. Her vision blurred. She wobbled on her legs.

"Stay here," Cole said.

His shadows wove around her body like a cloak. The now-familiar film slid over her vision. Three dark fae in medieval-esque clothes, probably the latest fashion in the Underworld fae circles, fanned out to approach Cole. In broad daylight, mere blocks from her parents' house. Odin's shrivelled twig and berries.

Cole pulled back his shoulders and relaxed his legs. He probably smirked at his opponents, but all Raven could admire was how his jet-black hair shone under the sunlight. Sure, Cole was tall, dark and dangerous, but everyone had weaknesses, right? Instead of admiring how his wide shoulders pulled at his shirt when he moved or how fabulous his ass looked in those pants, she should be concerned about his welfare.

One fae, wearing a red-lined cloak, rotated his hands as if coddling an invisible ball while whispering something absurd, like "my precious." Fire sparked between his hands and grew. The dark fae's eyes changed from black to dancing fire. He flung the ball at Cole. It sizzled through the air, almost too fast to track. Raven's breath caught in her throat.

Cole stepped to the side.

The fireball whizzed past him and smashed against the wall beside Raven. She squeaked and jumped. A cold sensation clamped around her stomach, clutching her gut with its icy grip. The smell of scorched rock burst in the air.

The second fae quickly drew throwing daggers from his belt. His skin pulsed with a bluish gray glow, and his smile revealed jagged teeth as his hands darted out. Silver flashed in the air under the sunlight. Time slowed. Raven's heart convulsed.

Cole leaned to the side.

The daggers embedded in the wall, already scorched from the fireball. Dark liquid dripped from the metal down the bricks. Raven's lip trembled.

Cole stepped to the side to avoid another fireball.

Like the last one, the fire exploded against the wall. Heat blasted the side of her face. Raven gulped. Would the shadow shield thingy protect her from a fireball?

The third fae raised his hands out to the side. Air rushed by him. The gust ruffled Cole's hair and clothes and pushed against her body, pressing her against the wall. The wind increased in strength.

A fire fae, wind fae and who-knew-what fae. Hopefully, not a weapon warper. They didn't begin with any elaborate speeches or showy maneuvers. They attacked, which meant they were likely mercenaries. Raven squirmed against the brick.

Cole held his position, slipping from side to side to dodge fireballs and knives.

When their initial attacks failed, the dark fae advanced in unison with no spoken words and no change of emotion. Their stone faces remained trained on the one man capable of getting Raven out of this mess.

Maybe she should run? Would Cole's shadows continue to cloak her if she escaped?

As if flicking on an internal switch from passive to active, Cole moved. He snaked across the pavement and closed the distance to the other fae with fluid grace. Like liquefied shadow, he continued to dodge their attacks.

Metal flashed in the air. The brick crunched as two knives sank into the wall about a foot from Raven's head. She straightened and swallowed. Maybe "stay here" wasn't such a good idea.

Her feet grew roots into the pavement and her limbs froze.

Cole slipped around the weapon fae and delivered staggering blows to the kidneys before completing some sort of judo throw. The first fae to attack continued to fling fireballs at Cole, but he'd started to back away from the Lord of Shadows. Cole advanced, picking up speed, spinning, leaning, ducking around whatever the fae threw at him. In a breath, he appeared behind the fire fae, reached out and snapped his neck in one swift move. The dark fae crumpled to the ground.

The wind fae continued to direct blasts of air at Cole, but the Lord of Shadows was too quick. He continued to duck in and out of shadows, striking at the fae. A knife materialized in Cole's hand. With lightning fast reflexes, he plunged the knife into the fae's chest.

Raven gasped.

The wind fae's eyes widened. He clutched at his chest and sank to the ground.

She stepped forward.

A ninja star flew through the air. Cole slipped to the side, narrowly escaping the sharp edges. The weapon fae staggered to his feet and the two squared off. Cole smiled. They feinted and dodged. Like trying to hold water with a bare hand, Cole slipped through and around every attack the other dark fae threw. It became clear in a few shuddered breaths Cole could've incapacitated the fae at any time of his choosing.

Sweat dripped down the other dark fae's face as he continued his failing assault.

"Cole!"

He winked before shadow jumping to place himself behind the weapon fae. He kicked his opponent's legs out from under him.

"What?" His porcelain pale face showed no exertion. No rose-tinted cheeks or sweat. Instead, his smooth skin glowed with evanescent light under the midday heat of the summer sun.

"You're not a cat." She meant to scold him about playing with their attacker but blurted out the cat comment instead. She smacked her palm against her forehead.

Cole sighed and straightened. The weapon fae staggered to his feet and scowled. Hands clenched, he snarled at the Lord of Shadows. His gaze darted in Raven's direction. His shoulders tensed and he drew another dagger. He flicked his wrist and the metal flashed through the air until it struck the brick one foot to the left of Raven's stomach. Raven trembled. The weapon warper's eyes narrowed, but he didn't focus on her exact location, so Cole's shadow veil prevailed. Good thing, too. He'd probably skewer her if he could locate her. Raven took a large step to the right. Maybe she should keep her mouth shut for once.

Cole turned to face the other fae. Instead of engaging in another fight, he stood eerily still as dark bands shot out from the alley and from the fae's own shadow. They wove around the weapon fae's neck, wrists and ankles before flinging him against the alley wall opposite of Raven.

Oh goody. Front row seats to Underworld torture. If only she had some popcorn.

Cole's shadow bands continued to hold the man in place.

The weapon fae's eyes widened. "Camhanaich."

Cole nodded and walked over to Raven. His shadow veil slipped away, and he ran a finger down her cheek, his fingertip hot against her skin.

The other fae's face paled and his shoulders dropped. "We didn't know."

Cole nodded without turning toward the other fae. Instead, his gaze flicked to the two daggers embedded in the wall by her head and near her stomach. His jaw clenched. "Were your orders to kill or capture the girl?"

Um, excuse me. This girl is a grown ass woman, thank you very much. Raven bit her tongue. Now was not the time.

The weapon fae swallowed. "Capture the girl if possible, kill if not. Eliminate any witnesses."

"Who holds your contract?"

"Anonymous. As are all jobs through the guild."

Definitely mercenaries then.

"Timeline?"

"Open."

"Payment?" Cole asked.

"Upon completion."

"Amount?"

"Three thousand gold."

Cole's shoulders relaxed. With one more finger stroke against her cheek, he turned to the attacker.

"I didn't know, my lord."

Cole nodded. "I'm allowing you to live for two reasons. One, you're mine now." He flicked up his fingers to emphasize his points. "And two, you will go back to the guild and tell them Raven Crawford and her family are under my protection."

The weapon fae's eyes bulged out of his skull. His head snapped in her direction.

"Anyone who takes that contract will be destroyed. I will show no mercy next time."

The other fae dipped his chin. "The guild will pull it."

"They better." Cole released the shadows, and the fae dropped to his feet. "Or I will destroy them as well."

The weapon fae's gaze slid to Raven, again.

"Leave."

The man nodded before throwing a portal disc at the ground. Cole used his shadows to fling the dead bodies of the other two fae through the portal after the lone survivor. Once the portal snapped shut, taking the disc with it, Raven breathed again.

"Holy fuck," she whispered.

Cole turned. "There's nothing holy about fucking."

"It's an expression."

He frowned.

"So, those were fae mercenaries?"

"Yes," he said. "We won't have to worry about them anymore."

"Why not? Won't the person behind the contract just raise their price?" Three thousand was a lot of money. Not enough for her to turn herself in but enough to pause.

Cole picked up her purse and handed it to her. His shadow reached out and smoothed the bumps on her arms. "He or she could, but the guild won't post it."

"Why not? Shouldn't they be impartial?" Mental note: Add researching the Underworld's Assassin's Guild to the "To Do List." She took the purse from Cole and slung the thin strap over her shoulder.

Cole chuckled. "Unless it concerns me."

"What makes you so special?"

Cole let out an exasperated sigh and turned toward her parents' house. "I made the guild. I can unmake it."

A shiver raced along her spine. Okay. Move research up the list. Right under finding out everything she could about the mysterious man walking beside her, especially anything explaining this moth-to-the-flame attraction. She'd met attractive men before, but none of them caused her to become a complete bumbling idiot in their presence. "Who's protecting my family exactly?"

"I'm the Patron Fae of Assassins," he said as if it answered everything. And it did in an ominous way.

She remained frozen in place. Of course, she knew he held that title. She knew he was deadly. She knew he commanded assassins. But the true meaning of his title and its implications finally sank in, smacking a few brain cells on the way down. What had she done? Had she made the right choice?

He glanced over his shoulder. "They're guarded well."

"We're meters from my parents' house right now. Why didn't these guards come to help? Where are they?"

"One, they're supposed to remain undetected. I'd be extremely disappointed if you spotted them." Cole smirked. "Two, they didn't help because I didn't need it. Abandoning their positions to unnecessarily offer aid would leave your family vulnerable. If this was meant as a diversion, the puppet master pulling the strings would've achieved what he or she wanted."

"Do you think Bane sent them?"

"Bane? No. Not his style. He'd never send someone in his place if there was a chance for a fight."

Raven jogged to catch up. Her flip flops slapped against her feet and the sidewalk. "If we no longer have to worry about mercenaries or assassins, why do you look like you just swallowed week-old sushi?"

Cole opened the gate to her parents' place and stood to the side so she could go first.

"Thanks." She brushed past him, inhaling his earthy scent.

He nodded and followed. "Now that I've taken the paid, anonymous option away, whomever was behind this attack will have to come at us with his or her own court or house."

Pepe lifted his head from munching grass and bleated at them with his mouth half full.

"Hey, Pepe." Guess Dad was still pissed at the neighbour. She mulled over what Cole said about the possibility of an impending fae attack. "And the fae coming at us with their own house is worse?"

"It can be."

Chapter Seventeen

"Research is what I'm doing when I don't know what I'm doing."

~*Wenher von Braun*

Raven sat precariously between a pile of questionably smelling clothes and an empty pizza box. Her lips twisted into a frown. Cole had walked her to the front door of her parents' place and after a toe-curling kiss, disappeared into his shadows.

"You could clear a space for yourself." Mike winked and turned back to his computer. He sat in the expensive office chair Mom and Dad got him last Christmas, wearing athletic shorts and a white tank top. He looked like he planned to go to the gym, but still managed somehow to sit with the authority of a Supreme Court judge. Raven had entered his kingdom.

"I'm not touching anything in this sin bin without a hazmat suit." She'd already sat here longer than she wanted, briefing Mike on all that she'd learned so far.

Mike scowled. "Yet, you let Romeo kiss you goodbye."

"Were you spying on me?" Ew.

"You two thumped down the walkway like an inexperienced marching band. I looked outside and the two of you were playing tonsil tennis. Trust me. That's the last thing I wanted to see. Not even industrial-strength soap can clean the image out of my mind."

Her face flamed. She glanced at the window. Although shut, Mike had pulled up the blinds. Natural afternoon sunlight streamed in. "What in the Mortal Realm does this have to do with the filth you insist on living in? When are you going to stop marking your territory with your stench? Pretty soon Mom and Dad are going to invest in door seals and install them to contain the stink."

"You sound like Mom."

She glared.

Mike spun around. "Because out of the two situations—sitting in my room of questionable sanitation or snogging the Lord of Darkness—"

"Shadows."

"Whatever."

She folded her arms.

"The latter is infinitely more hazardous to your health."

She eyed the pizza box and toed the magazine with a naked chick draped over the hood of a truck. "I'm not so sure."

Please, don't let there be a black light. Ignorance was bliss in some cases.

Mike shrugged.

"Why am I here? Why couldn't we talk someplace else, or on the phone, or better yet, just texted each other so we could avoid all this person-to-person interaction and skipped all the old-school social etiquette stuff?"

"Etiquette?" Mike chuckled. "I don't think you've practiced that, like, ever."

She flashed her middle finger at his back.

"Saw that." Mike smirked at his computer screen. "You're here, young Padawan, because we're going to hack into our brother dearest's email account."

"You think we can discover where he is from his email?" Bear wouldn't be that stupid.

"No. Bear's not that dumb," Mike said.

"Then?" Maybe she should invest in a cattle prod. She could use it for conversations with Mike, and Megan...and people in general. She'd give them a little zap when they took too long to get to the point.

Raven rubbed her bare arms. Her parents had invested in an air conditioner for the three weeks in summer it got hot enough in the Lower Mainland to need one. Sitting in Mike's room with her tank top and short shorts left her cold and her lungs dry. She relished the cool sensation when she first walked into the house from the summer heat but not now. Maybe she should raid Juni's room for a sweater.

"Once we have access to his email, we're going to reset his password for his online banking."

Raven's mouth dropped open. "We're hacking a bank? You look like you're about to go for a run, not commit a crime."

"We're not really hacking. I'm not attacking their code."

"Sounds like a technicality. It's still fraud."

"Sounds like you don't want to find Bear."

She pursed her lips and sat back. Her bare shoulders hit the wall and she jerked forward. Mike's room. Touch nothing. Or at least, touch as little as possible. She crossed her arms and hugged herself. "Dad can't find out."

Mike rolled his eyes. "Obviously."

"Why do you need me here? Besides dragging me down as an accomplice."

"The bank requires Bear to answer personal security questions when he resets his password or logs in from a new location. In this case, we're doing both. His email also requires security questions for password resets."

Raven grumbled.

"What is it?"

"I can barely remember the answers for my own account." She flapped her hand at one of the screens. "I mean, I know the answer, usually, but not how I originally typed it in. Like did I use capitals, spaces or pronouns? How am I supposed to know what Bear's answers are?"

"Relax." Mike turned to face her. His gaze softened. "If we don't get in, we're no worse off than before. It's worth a try, though, right?"

Her shoulders sagged. "Right."

"Besides, if this fails, I can always attack the bank's code."

Raven groaned. The sunlight from outside transformed into streams of gold and red. The room darkened.

Mike flicked on his desk lamp. Along with his bedroom light, his room was illuminated enough to qualify as a maximum-security prison. Her brother swiveled back to his computers. "Ready?"

"Hit me with it."

"Pet."

"Fucking hell spawn."

"K-i-s-s-a." Mike spoke as he typed. "Favourite beach?"

What in the Underworld? There were tons of beaches in the area, and Bear visited a lot of them, in addition to going surfing on the island. "Tofino?"

"That's a town, not a beach."

"Long Beach?"

Clickety-click-click. Mike shook his head.

"Chesterman?"

"Nope. Maybe try one of significance?"

"Rathtrevor?" She named the beach from the picture they both had framed. The sprawling white sand beach on the east coast of Vancouver Island was the only beach they had a shared memory of. But that was so long ago. She'd never been back since the end of high school. Neither had Bear as far as she knew.

"Bingo. Good work. One more. Oldest sister."

Raven snorted.

Mike hit enter and grunted. "Didn't work."

"Branwen."

Mike groaned. "Of course." He typed again. "Okay, we're in his email. Now for the bank." Mike shifted to look at another screen while his fingers tap danced along the keyboard.

Raven stood and navigated around the hordes of clothing to look out Mike's window. The sun had set, casting the world in shades of gray as the light slipped behind the trees. Her parents' yard, now cast in darkness, echoed memories of her past. She'd run around this patch of grass yelling, squealing, playing and laughing with her siblings. With Bear. Her heart ached.

Pepe's bell jingled as he meandered around the grass. Did he ever stop eating?

A shadow moved along the edge of the property near the neighbour's trees. Her breathing stopped. She leaned forward. There it was again.

Her heart pounded. She pulled out her phone and hit Cole's contact information.

He picked up on the third ring. "Camhanaich."

"There are suspicious shadows moving around my front yard. Is that you?"

"No. Is it the goat?"

"No," she hissed. Did he think she was that stupid? Someone was out there. Or something. Her hand trembled on the phone.

"Where?"

"Southeast corner of my parents' property. By the trees."

"Just a second." He mumbled in the background.

Who the heck was he talking to? Her phone buzzed with a little static and warmed against her cheek.

"That's one of my guys."

Raven let out a long breath and her heart stopped racing. He said he'd be angry if she managed to spot one of his guys...but here they were. "Don't peck his eyes out."

Without saying goodbye, the Lord of Shadows hung up on her.

She stared at her phone's screen. Yup. He definitely ended the call. Who was he with? A lady friend? A servant? Someone else he was interrogating as a part of the investigation. Ugh... She needed to calm her tits. She had no claim over the dark fae lord. He owed her nothing except protection and not killing her twin when they found him. She needed to keep that straight in her brain. His delicious mouth moving along hers while his shadows caressed her skin didn't change the facts.

Yet, if she closed her eyes, she could feel his hands

on her body and taste him on her tongue.

"You need to stop staring out the window like a distraught Rapunzel."

She turned to glare at her brother, but he remained focused on his computer screens.

"By the way, do you know what Einin means?" he asked, still clicking and typing away. He selected the "Forgot My Password" option on the bank's login screen.

"No." She'd meant to look up the name Cole kept calling her, but she didn't know how to spell it. She ran her hands up and down her thighs a couple of times to warm them up. Ugh. She needed to shave.

"It's Irish for 'little bird.'"

Her skin warmed. Her face twitched, itching to break out into a wide smile. He'd called her that before he discovered her feather. She forced her mouth back to normal, or her "resting bitch face" as Juni called it. She couldn't let Mike see her grinning like a giddy teenager. While one part of her brain wanted to dance and ride off into the sunset on a rainbow unicorn, the other part scolded her. Grandma Lu would have a fit right about now if she saw her eldest granddaughter swooning over a pet name given by a serial killer for hire. So, what if the Patron Fae of Assassins called her little bird in another language. It wasn't exactly a term of endearment, right? "Wait. Don't the Irish speak English?"

"Yes. It's an Irish name, silly. But for the record, when you say Irish as a language, it means Irish

Gaelic."

"You're such a know-it-all."

"Guess what else I know?"

She rolled her eyes and waited.

"Beul na h-Oidhche gu Camhanaich means 'Mouth of the Night to First Light.'"

After she got over being impressed and a tad jealous from Mike's ability to not only find the correct spelling of the fae name, but pronounce it with relative ease, she mulled over Cole's true name. "So, his name literally means from dusk to dawn?"

Mike smirked. He paused and leaned forward, his nose inches from the screen. He chuckled.

"What?"

"Same questions. At least so far. Looks like Bear's just as bad at remembering the answers to security questions as you are."

"We can't all be evil geniuses like you."

Mike shrugged. Even with his cast, her brother's fingers flew across his keyboard as he leaned forward and squinted at his screen. He made a little grunt and head bob every time he hit enter and got to the next question. Kind of cute in a total nerdy gamer way.

Mike straightened, his mouth twisted down in a deformed frown.

"What is it?" She hated talking to Mike when he was on the computer—nothing but incomplete sentences, long pauses and troubled facial expressions.

His mouth gaped open, but no words came out. Instead, he leaned to the side and reached out to turn his screen toward her.

Biological Father.

Raven's stomach dropped. "We don't know his name."

"But we all know he was a stud."

Raven groaned. *Thanks, Mom.*

"Maybe Bear found out?" Mike suggested.

"How? Mom's refused to tell us. I don't see her telling Bear and not me."

"Would he keep the information from you if he found out some other way?"

"I'd like to think he wouldn't." Raven's stomach twisted. "But I'm finding out I didn't know my twin as well as I thought I did."

Mike reached out and squeezed her arm. "Not telling you about his safe house was probably for your own protection."

She scowled at him.

"Think about it. You can't confess what you don't know."

"I can still be tortured for it." She picked at her tank top.

"I didn't say his system was perfect."

She stared at Mike's computer screen. His cursor flashed, mocking her lack of knowledge, taunting her. Stupid mother fucking computer.

Raven stilled. Wait a minute...

Mike pushed his shoulders back and laced his fingers together to stretch them out. Apparently, he was limbering up to initiate his bank hacking attack plan.

"Motherfucker," she said.

"He's still our brother, Rayray."

"No, dummy. Try 'Motherfucker' as the answer."

Mike shook his head and typed it in. The hourglass popped up in the middle of the screen. A few seconds later, a message confirmed an email to reset the password had been sent. Mike laughed.

"Motherfucker," he wheezed.

"Bear's always been very matter-of-fact."

Mike's laughter deepened. He bent over and slapped his knee.

"Calm down. It's not *that* funny." Geez, he laughed like Dad.

Mike straightened and wiped at the tears forming in the corner of his eyes. "I disagree."

"Need I remind you of Bear's impending doom?"

Mike grunted and his serious gamer face slid over his expression. Five minutes later, after resetting the password from the email, Mike confirmed no recent bank activity, put the accounts on hold, made new security questions, and added a password hint that said, "Call home."

"If he resurfaces, he'll have to go to the bank or see us." Mike sat back with a smug smile. "Despite how he might feel about the family, I'd like to think he'd prefer us to the sheep in suits."

Her brother's features pinched in and his shoulders slumped. He looked away and straightened in his chair.

"Mike." Raven scanned his face. She recognized the

hurt in his expression; she saw it in the mirror often enough. "His distance has nothing to do with you."

Her brother grunted again, but his gaze cut away too quickly.

She reached out and squeezed his hand. "You know that, right?"

"Yeah, sure."

Sometimes, she forgot her little brother was only nineteen, and still so new to the whole adulting thing. "I'm serious, Mike. He has some daddy issues, and some..." Her brain scrambled for the right phrase.

"Insecurities?" Mike offered.

"Not quite the word I was looking for, but yeah. We're all shifters, he's not. He wanted to run in the woods with Dad and make him proud and make him worthy of the man who raised us."

Mike frowned.

"Bear believes his abilities deprive him of this."

He nodded. "I get it. Kind of."

The pain continued to punch at her younger brother's features, but she let it go. No amount of words would ease his heart right now. At least none of the words she had to offer.

She needed to find Bear to save his life, but also to get him to fix this fracture he created in their family. Find Bear, yell at Bear, fix family. Simple. "I don't suppose Brother Bear had a regular rental payment come out in addition to his apartment?"

"Too traceable. The big lug isn't that dense." He clicked on history. His gaze narrowed as he scanned the chequing account's activities. Everyone was a little dumb in comparison to Mike. "Hold on."

"What?" She leaned forward.

"No rent, but a regular cash withdrawal near the end of each month."

"Same amount?"

"No. But always over nine hundred dollars."

She tapped her chin. "Can't be a nice place, then."

"It's a safe house. Not a luxury inn."

She nodded. "So, this just confirms he has it but not where."

Mike continued to click with his mouse and tap away on his keyboard, his lips twisted into an evil grin. "He used the same teller machine."

Raven snapped her fingers. "Of course. He wouldn't want to hold that much cash for long. He probably withdrew it on his way to pay the landlord."

"I agree. This bank machine is close to his safe house."

"Can you find out where it is?"

"Can I..." Mike rolled his eyes. He clicked a few more things and suddenly a map of the Lower Mainland popped up on his screen. "This is the machine he withdrew cash from." Mike tapped the little red icon on the screen. "These are the neighbouring bank machines from the same institution. Bear's pragmatic and tight-fisted. He wouldn't use another bank's machine and accrue extra service charges unless he had to." *Tap, tap, tap.* "Assuming the machine he used is the closest to the safe house that means..."

"He has to be somewhere here." She circled the area surrounding the bank machine with her finger. She squinted at the map. "Commercial and Broadway. East Van."

Mike nodded. "And right by a train stop."

"There's too many apartments and rentals there. It will take forever to go through them all. Unless..." She smiled at her brother. "We just follow your nose."

Mike glanced down at his cast and shook his arm at her. "I'm kind of out of commission."

"You won't need to shift."

"In East Van? To follow a week-old trail amongst junkies, patchouli-drenched hippies, the homeless, and hipsters? Yes. Yes, I will."

She sighed. Her shoulders dropped.

"You could take Dad."

"Are you kidding me? And have World War III when he and Bear inevitably start arguing?"

Mike laughed.

"I'm not sure I even want to go." She sank down on Mike's bed again. The comforter puffed out around her and released a cloud of funk. She should've remained standing.

"What do you mean?"

"Something Marcus said."

Mike let out an exasperated sigh and rolled his hand out as if to say, "Out with it."

Like he should talk.

Mike waited.

"He implied I might be causing more harm than good if I searched for Bear. I'd basically hand him over to the person he stole from. Maybe."

"So, you have to decide between going to Bear's safe house and risking Cole will go back on his word and destroy our brother, or not going to Bear's safe house and risking someone else finding him first or that he's in need of your help."

"It's quite the predicament."

"Actually, you have a dilemma. A predicament is a problem with no apparent solution. A dilemma is a problem with two or more undesirable solutions."

Raven rolled her eyes.

"What?"

"I hope you're learning more at school than how to piss people off."

"This is important stuff."

"How? How is it important? When are you ever going to use this crap?" she asked.

"I'm using it right now."

"Ugh!" She picked up his pillow and threw it at him.

Mike laughed and batted the pillow out of the way. When he straightened, his expression sobered. "What are you going to do?"

"Cole swore a fae oath. The other option has too much unknown to it. I'm going, and I need a little fox to help me."

Mike groaned. "You know what that means?"

"I'm not sure I can afford this." Raven's stomach

dropped. She popped open Mike's bedroom door and hollered down the hall. "Juni!"

Chapter Eighteen

"To keep your secret is wisdom; to expect others to keep it is folly."

~William Samuel Johnson

Raven clutched her sister in fox form to her chest as she stared at the bank machine across the street. She ran her hands through Juni's soft, dense fur before turning to the dark fae lord beside her. "You'll transport my sister back as soon as we locate Bear's safe house?"

Cole peered down at her and nodded. The summer sun shone against his ink-black hair. "And you promise not to try to squirrel your brother somewhere else to hide him while I'm gone. It won't take long."

"Of course. We have a deal."

"We have a sworn oath."

"Whatever." She swallowed. She'd love to shield Bear from whatever came his way, but she needed Juni safe and Cole already promised, with a fae oath, not to harm her brother. She couldn't go back on their deal.

Raven set her sister down on the pavement and clicked the leash to her pink rhinestone studded collar. If her sister wanted to run off, that was fine with Raven. More than fine, because Juni would inevitably run back to Raven when she realized she couldn't get into the house without shifting and had no clothes or phone.

The collar and leash were strictly for show to appease the Fish and Wildlife officers, bylaw officials, and those generally scared of anything furry running around on four legs.

"Inhumane!" Some hippie yelled at them from across the street.

"You are the animal!" the hippie woman's friend with dreads bellowed.

Cole turned to glare at them. Their eyes bugged and they looked away, suddenly very fixated on the beading of their guitar straps. Raven didn't think they'd be so brave if they were on the same side of the street.

Pffft. Not the first time someone called Raven an animal. When Mike was seven, he had a police helmet he felt invincible in. He'd jump off the roof and Raven would cheer him on along with Bear. Mom lost it, screeching at them and calling them animals. Mike had collected himself off the lawn and stepped away from the deep indents his heels made on impact. After he brushed off the dirt on his shirt, he pulled his shoulders back and calmly informed Mom, with a straight face, they were all animals, including her. She sent them to their rooms without bedtime stories.

Technically, Mike was correct. *Homo sapiens* and *Vulpes vulpes*, or red foxes, both fell under the Kingdom Animalia.

The urge to shout back and correct the entitled hippies across the street today with her superior knowledge of taxonomy bubbled up her throat. She shut her mouth and clenched her jaw. She might not be book smart like her brother, but she had street smarts. Getting into a bickering match with two hippies on Commercial Drive was not an effective use of her time. Instead, she followed her sister with Cole in tow as Juni pranced along the dirty sidewalk.

When they reached the security door to the ATM, her sister sniffed the pavement. She snorted, shook her head and whined.

"Suck it up, buttercup. We need to find Bear."

A woman standing nearby jumped. Her eyes widened and her mouth turned down.

Woman, this is none of your business. Raven stared back until she looked away.

Juni shook her coat and snuffled around in circles.

Cole leaned in. "Are you sure this will work?"

Raven ignored him and pulled the hem of her blue tank top down to her hips again. The stupid shirt insisted on rolling up. She should've worn a different one. She kept giving this shirt chances to make her look good, and it kept failing. She sighed. The tank top had such potential.

Juni scraped her sharp claws along the concrete. Her ears pinged forward and she lurched ahead. The leash snapped straight and tugged at Raven's hand.

"This way." Raven followed her sister as she flounced down the sidewalk, looking more like a well-coifed Shiba Inu than an actual fox.

Pedestrians shied away from their small party. Not because of her or Juni, but because Cole walked beside her, full of menace. He'd be great at a concert or riot. He parted hordes of people faster than she parted her hair. They couldn't get away from him fast enough.

Raven didn't want to run or hide from Cole. Instead, she resisted the tangible need to haul him to a private room and do all sorts of naughty things with him. Along with all that danger emanating from his pores, he somehow embodied carnal pleasure.

Raven had never been into mixing those two things—danger and lust. She hated watching horror movies and refused to go on any scary rides at the amusement park. She never understood why someone would not only want to get the crap scared out of them, but willingly pay for the experience.

Now she got it. Oh, did she get it. Cole hailed from a place known for its blurred lines and ruthless consequences. Raven read her sister's textbooks. Along with other powerful dark fae, Cole created the Shadow

Realm by pulling from the essence of the Underworld and the Realm of Light, or ROL. Somehow, the domain of shadows acted like a buffer between the Mortal Realm and the Other Realms, like the annoying middle child inserting themselves into a fight they had nothing to do with.

The Shadow Realm existed between the spaces of the other domains and all who wanted entry to another realm had to pass through it either by their own magic or a portal.

"Who rules the Realm of Shadows?"

"The Queen of Corvids." Cole glanced at her sideways.

Huh. Good name. "Why don't you control the shadows?" He was powerful enough to occupy a position of power and he helped create the realm.

Cole smirked. In answer, the shadows from the nearby buildings and alleys pooled around her feet and flowed up her body to cover her like a blanket. "I do."

Raven shivered. "You know that's not what I was asking. Why don't you rule the Realm of Shadows?"

Cole let the shadows slipped away. "If I ruled, I would no longer exist within the shadows."

Huh. She bobbed her head as if his words made sense. They didn't.

The sidewalk darkened again, and gray bands wound around Cole until they flowed over him like a cascading cape. She mulled over his explanation some more. Maybe he did make sense. Kind of. If he ruled, he couldn't hide. He'd be in the spotlight. The textbook explanation of the Shadow Realm played over her neurons. "You exist between the spaces."

A salacious smile spread across Cole's face.

Oh God. How'd he turn her words into a sexual innuendo with a flash of his straight, white teeth? Heat flooded her body and warmed her core. Illicit images of him existing in her space flashed through her mind like a porn feed stuck on shuffle.

"Are you feeling all right?" Cole asked.

"Of course. Why?"

"Your face is flushed."

Juni snorted and bolted forward, pulling on the leash.

Good timing. Raven quickened her pace to keep up and avoid choking her sister. As much as Juni pushed her buttons and stole her clothes, Raven would never harm her.

They turned off Commercial and sped along some side streets before coming to a stop in front of a small apartment building. The old construction had a central main floor and two balconies on the second and third floor facing the street. Raven had once rented an apartment in a similar building off Hastings. There'd be balconies on the backside as well, facing the alleyway. This building probably housed eight units in total—four on each floor—with the lobby, laundry and mailboxes on the main level and storage in the basement.

The tenant listings didn't offer any names, just unit numbers, but if Raven had to select an affordable safe house in the middle of the urban jungle, this building would do. With large trees lining the walkway, the main entrance remained cloaked with branches and shadows, and the low number of tenants ensured few witnesses.

"Good spot," Cole observed.

"Hey, any word about our request for an audience with Odin?" Raven asked.

Cole shook his head. "These things really do take time. I should hear something in the next few days."

Juni whined and sat down. Her ears pinged back.

"What is it, Juni?" Raven tugged her tank top down again.

Juni rubbed her snout with one paw and whined again.

"Something smell bad?" Raven asked.

Her sister nodded.

Unease twisted Raven's stomach into a knot. Bear better be okay. If he wasn't, she'd peck out the eyes of whomever harmed him.

Then again, if Bear was okay and made all of them worry for no stinking reason, she'd make him wish he was at least injured in some way.

The building's glass door to the lobby stared back at her. "Glenshire Manor" in fake-gold, old-fashioned italicized letters adorned the glass. The sterile, unfurnished lobby waited on the other side. Raven reached out and tugged on the door handle. Locked. Midday on a weekday made it unlikely an inattentive tenant would conveniently meander out of the building at any moment and leave the door open so a group of strangers could slip in—one of which was an imposing dark fae lord.

"After you." Cole made a sweeping wave with his hand toward the door.

"Can't you use your shadowy parlour tricks to get us in?"

He raised a brow.

She tugged down her tank top again.

"I could, but I like watching you work," he said.

Juni snorted.

Raven grunted and turned back to the door. She pulled her lock pick and tension wrench from the back pocket of her cut-off jean shorts and squatted down in front of the lock.

Raven had wrongly assumed it would take Bear days or weeks to teach her how to break into a house, but minutes after he gave her instructions, she successfully picked her first lock. In that moment, she realized what a sham safety really was. People in the Mortal Realm bought into the image of security, but it was all an illusion.

Raven quickly inserted the tension wrench into the bottom part of the keyhole. With gentle pressure applied in the direction the key turned, Raven kept the tension wrench in pace and inserted her pick into the top of the lock. Raking the pick back and forth, she pushed down on the pins each time she pulled back with the pick. In less than a minute, she set all the pins. The lock clicked. Raven stepped back and Cole opened the door.

He leaned in. "Like I said, I like watching you work."

Despite the shadowed entrance, her quick lock-picking skills and Cole shielding her actions with his drool-worthy body, they had to act fast before anyone noticed her less-than-legal actions. They stepped into the building. The stale lobby air rushed out to greet them.

"Smells off," Cole said.

Raven agreed, but she couldn't pinpoint how. Something metallic, maybe.

Juni pulled the leash toward the stairs. With each step, the tension wrapping around Raven's heart intensified.

The stale air grew thicker as they climbed to the third floor. Cole swung the fire door open and led them to the hallway. The lights flickered above, and one fixture hung from the ceiling. The apartment door at the end of the hall sat ajar, a long crack running from the base almost the entire way to the top. A dark red handprint wrapped around the trim.

"Is that—?"

"Blood?" Cole stepped toward the apartment. "Yes. Maybe you should wait here."

"Just because I'm not some warrior woman, doesn't mean I'm weak," she growled and stared at the door down the hall.

He rose an eyebrow. "What does it mean, then?"

What did it mean? Good question. "It means I lack

hand-eye coordination and physical stamina. Now shut up, and—"

"Take your sister home?"

She remained stiff legged and unmoving near the doors to the staircase. Her banter reflected little of the turmoil swirling within her like a Cat 5 hurricane making landfall on an unprepared coastline. Cole hesitated before striding back to where she stood with confident steps. Without a word, he picked up Juni and gently cradled her sister in his arms. The little fox sighed contently and snuggled into his chest.

Normally, Raven would make some snarky comment but not today. Not right now. The second after she registered Cole's actions, her attention whipped back to her brother's broken door, and remained riveted on the bloody handprint, large enough to be her brother's.

"It will be okay." Cole plucked Juni's leash from her hands. "Wait here, and we'll go in together."

She nodded.

The shadows wrapped around Cole and Juni. When they disappeared, Raven stood alone under the hallway's flickering light. Her brother's door loomed ahead, beckoning and warning her all at once. The silence of the apartment called to her. An invisible and silent pull propelled her forward. The air buzzed.

Bear could be in there.

Bear could need help.

Footstep by footstep, she drew closer to the unknown awaiting her in her brother's safe house, and farther from relative safety.

He could be in there.

Raven swallowed and reached forward. She hesitated.

What condition would she find him in? He could be...

Raven forced air into her lungs and pushed her shoulders back. She stared at the doorknob. Some blood had dripped off the metal. Did she risk leaving fingerprints? The cops hadn't been here yet, or there'd be crime scene tape. The blood and broken door had to be recent, or the other apartments on this floor empty. No one with a conscience could walk by this place and not call the cops.

Then again, her brother wasn't known for keeping savoury company—with the exception of herself and Marcus, of course.

Bear could be in there.

With a deep breath, Raven nudged the door open with her toe. The hinges creaked. The unexpected sound ran along her spine like a demented demon from the Underworld. The main lights were off, but a small lamp with a crooked shade on a side table remained on. Aside from the fridge's constant whirring, the apartment sat silent, waiting. A turned over loveseat and crumpled rug lay beside the table. The couch doubled as a pull-out bed, and a large chunk of the mattress poked out. Limp sheets pooled on the floor. Either someone folded up the sofa in a haste, or someone gave it a good upheaval.

Blood spattered the fake-marble linoleum floor and stark white walls. No large pools, and not enough to indicate a serious injury, but a brutal fight took place in Bear's safe house. He could still be alive. Some of the tension cording her neck and shoulder muscles eased.

Raven crept around the bachelor suite and peeked inside the closet. Her heart rate picked up as she approached the bathroom. What was up with her and bathrooms? Like it was completely plausible the big bad guy would run and cower behind a toilet.

She slipped a tea towel from the oven door. The fluffy soft material indicated Bear purchased the towel recently. It hadn't been through a spin cycle yet. Raven used the towel to cover the bathroom's doorknob and prevent her fingerprints from transferring onto a surface in a soon-to-be active crime scene. With a deep breath, she opened the door. Empty. A full tube of toothpaste sat on the small space of counter beside the simple sink and next to a couple of toothbrushes.

Raven straightened and scanned the room for clues.

A couple of toothbrushes. She stepped into the small room and leaned in closer. Both green, so no hint regarding the gender of Bear's guest. The bristles still had their full colour and shape, and no toothpaste caked the handles.

The toilet roll was almost full, and the small shower stall dry. Bear hadn't been here long, but he came with someone else.

Raven stretched her neck, side to side, and left the bathroom. Aside from those two not-so-helpful tidbits, she had...

Nothing.

Her shoulders dropped and a long, pent-up breath escaped her lips.

Keep it together, Crawford. Bear still needs you.

Cole would return any minute now, and she wanted to get as much information as possible before he arrived.

The small bachelor pad had little room for anything and as a safe house, she doubted she'd find an itinerary of events and locations to help her solve this mystery. She searched anyway, padding around the small space, avoiding splotches of blood or leaving her fingerprints.

What was that?

Raven crouched down and plucked a long black feather from the ground. It had fallen partially behind the capsized sofa bed.

Raven or crow?

It was difficult to tell the difference, but the length and size indicated a raven as the source. Unlike some Others, she lacked the ability to "read" objects and know their source.

Was it one of hers? It looked like it, but she'd never been here. And as much as Bear loved her, he wouldn't hold on to one of her feathers as a keepsake. That would just be weird. They were close, but not *that* close.

Raven clutched the feather to her chest and glanced around. Cole was still with her sister, but he'd be back any minute. She stuffed the feather halfway down the leg of her shorts and pinned it in place with her waistband much like Cole had with her own feather. The shaft scratched against her outer thigh and the vanes tickled her ribs. She pulled down her tank top to cover the top half. The shirt better not roll up again. At least she hadn't bought into that new style of cut-offs where half her ass hung out beneath the hem. She'd have no way of hiding the feather with that kind of shorts.

Time to keep looking. Maybe she'd find more than the feather as a clue.

She found a trash can under the sink and dumped it out. As much as she loathed rifling through other people's garbage, the refuse often held valuable information. Empty food wrappers. No bandages.

A long blonde strand of hair lay coiled on the smooth linoleum floor. Raven reached over the garbage and plucked the strand from the surface to examine it closer. White. Not gray or blonde. Interesting. Was this transfer evidence? Hitching a ride on Bear's clothes from a recent date or did the white hair provide a clue to a guest or assailant?

The shadows in the room pooled around her. A silent slow-turning tornado of shadow formed a column of dark promises in front of her. When the shadows cleared, they revealed Cole. Even in ordinary "human" clothes—jeans, T-shirt and runners, he looked extraordinary, and not of this world. The jeans hugged all the right places and though she stood in her brother's blood spattered safe house, she still had to make a concerted effort not to admire how the denim bunched at his groin.

Sorry, Grandma Lu.

"I thought you were going to wait?" Cole folded his arms across his chest. The fabric stretched against his thick arm muscles. "Are you okay?"

"I'm fine. How's my sister?"

"A little shaken."

Raven snorted. A little shaken. No doubt her teenaged sister hoped for some strong, comforting arms to wrap around her.

"Other than her damsel in distress act, did she say anything about the scene?"

Cole glanced away and clenched his jaw. "She picked up something unexpected."

"Let me guess. Two different blood signatures?"

Cole's head whipped back to her. His muscles tensed.

"How did you know?" he asked.

She held up the long white hair. "This."

Cole narrowed his eyes and leaned forward. "That could've been left by an attacker." He glanced around the room again. "From the damage, there was probably more than one."

"Agreed. And the second blood signature could've been left by one of Bear's attackers as well, but he also had a guest."

"You sound sure."

"Two toothbrushes."

Cole rocked back on his heels. "I see. Anything

else?"

The feather burned against the smooth skin of her abdomen where the waistband of her pants pinned it in place. "Not really. I don't think they were here for long."

"What makes you say that?"

"The toothbrush bristles are barely worn—they're stiff with a full strip of colour in the middle, indicating minimal use. Bear has a heavy hand. He always applies too much pressure and the dentist has warned him repeatedly of the risk of receding gum lines."

"Receding gum lines?"

"You have your Underworld probs, we have mortal ones."

Cole shook his head and waved his hand in the air for her to continue.

"Also, there's a full pack of toilet paper, and the first roll is hardly used."

Cole laughed. "You used toilet paper usage to gauge their length of stay?"

"I have two brothers."

Cole's expression turned thoughtful. "Good point."

She nodded. Toilet paper and bathroom time was a serious matter when you lived with boys and men. "I don't think the attack happened too long ago, either. There's no crime scene tape, and the blood is dry, but not flaky. Let's do a final sweep and get out of here. With my luck, the neighbours will pick this moment to become good Samaritans and call this in. I don't want to be here when the cops arrive."

"Eager to return me to your frazzled sister to offer support?"

Raven groaned. She hoped Juni was coping and her reaction was simply an act. Despite her posturing and on-point attitude, Juni was only fifteen and she just tracked their brother to his bloody safe house.

Raven sighed. Maybe the emotional display wasn't theatrics to gain Cole's attention. Maybe Juni tried to buy Raven more time to investigate without Cole looming over her shoulder. Maybe Juni really was upset. Maybe Raven was an asshole. Her mouth grew dry and fuzzy. Stale. She needed a coffee or a strong drink.

The Lord of Shadows walked ahead of her, taking in the overturned and displaced furniture as he moved. He walked with deadly purpose—well-balanced, focused and fluid—each motion controlled, yet, smooth. When he twisted to move around objects, the corded muscles in his back popped out, nicely accentuated by the clingy cotton.

Raven pursed her lips. Yeah, her sister might be upset, but Raven would bet her last pair of intact heels, Juni had an act prepared for Cole. And she couldn't blame her.

Chapter Nineteen

"The customer is always right."
    ~No waitress, anywhere, ever. At least not seriously

urned out, Raven's sister was perfectly fine when she realized Cole didn't return with Raven. Juni greeted her sister with a scowl, spun on her heel and left Raven on the stoop. With no need to console, Raven left to get ready for her next night shift.

When the heavy, non-conditioned air of the diner hit her face upon arrival at Dan's Diner, she once again questioned her life choices. The shift so far was slow, but steadily staggered with enough losers to ensure Raven never got a break.

She eyed her brother's cast, already tinged brown from the diner's greasy atmosphere. Her black pants stuck to her sweaty legs, and her ugly, white blouse offered no cooling reprieve with its 100% polyester material. The heat from the kitchen hit her face with the smell of cooked meat and that slightly off smell she associated with Dan's Diner. "Should you be working?"

"I only need one good arm to flip burgers." He shrugged and to emphasize his point, flipped the burger patties sizzling on the grill. "Find anything at Bear's?"

"You first. What did you find with your research?" An advantage of having a tech-savvy brother included in-depth research with a side of hacking.

"The Claíomh Solais is often referred to as the Sword of Light, or the Shining Sword. In Irish mythology, it's depicted as a god-slaying weapon."

"A sword?"

He pointed his spatula at her. "A god-slaying sword."

Made sense why the dark fae wanted it.

"Well, maybe, a sword." Mike continued as he prepped more burger buns. "In other translations, it's a 'white glaive of light' and when going through some of the older references, the Claíomh Solais is merely described as a weapon, no mention of swords at all."

"Isn't a glaive the same thing as a sword?"

Mike grunted and used his spatula to transfer the hamburger patties to their waiting buns. After adding fries and a scoop of questionable pre-made coleslaw from a bucket, he slid the plates under the heat lamps. "Run this out to table ten and then we'll discuss the nuances of the English language."

"Brat." She pulled the plates from the pass-through service window and delivered them to the couple in the corner. The heat from the white plates burned the scratches on her hands from her "Raven versus the forest floor" kerfuffle and her leg muscles still ached from all the running.

Thankfully, the couple had stopped arguing about whatever they'd been fighting over, and now sat in tense, bitter silence.

A group of women entered the diner, their high pitched, excited voices mingled with the annoying bell on the door. They took one of the booths without a break in conversation. Their coiffed hair shone luxuriously under the artificial light. Raven changed course to deliver menus at the table. A ping of jealousy for their friendship and carefree outing stabbed at Raven's heart.

A blonde woman with bright blue eyes and perfectly shaped eyebrows looked up at her. "I'm vegan."

Raven's head jerked back and the specials she'd prepared to tell them about tumbled off her tongue. "Oh, okay."

"What do you recommend?"

Not eating here?

Raven didn't have a problem with vegans on a personal level and respected their choice, but as a waitress, vegans generally provided an additional pain in the ass she didn't need or want. She empathized with the difficulties they faced trying to eat out, but even if they weren't making off-menu orders, or extensively modifying existing dishes, a number of vegans insisted on sitting away from customers who consumed "animal carcasses." They also made sure their company, the server, and anyone else within a three-foot radius knew of their superior life choices.

The vegan continued to bat her long eye lashes at Raven.

"Um...we have some lettuce? I mean, salad." Raven clutched the pen in her hand. She groaned on the inside. She sucked at this. She'd long ago reached the apex of her serving career where caring and her need to earn money far exceeded her pride and contempt for the general public. Since then, she'd plunged downhill, having less and less fucks to give.

The vegan rolled her eyes. "Do you have separate deep fryers?"

"Our vat fat is contaminated with animal products."

She recoiled. Her friends flinched. "You know it's possible to designate one of your deep fryers for plant-based foods only, right?"

Raven bit back the words she wanted to say—you know this is a greasy spoon, twenty-four-hour diner, right? Instead, she forced a smile on her face, repeated her mental "be nice" mantra and said, "We serve predominantly pub-style food and cater to the more carnivorous members of society. This might go easier if you just tell me what you want, and I'll find a way to bring it to you."

The woman's nose and mouth scrunched up and she opened the menu without a word, holding it high enough to cover her face.

"Can I get any of you something to drink to start?" If anyone needed a cool drink right now, it was Raven.

"Um." One of the brunette customers glanced at her mute friends. "I think we'll take a look at our menus first."

"Sure thing." Raven maintained her fake smile and willed her legs to carry her away from the women. They planned to dash. Raven knew that shifty look customers got when they wanted to leave but didn't have the guts to tell the server they planned to eat elsewhere.

Raven turned to the woman sitting alone at a window table. With dark hair cascading down her back and dark slashes for eyebrows, her severe expression didn't invite anyone to join her. The sharp cast to the customer's features and drawn mouth gave Raven the impression she plotted the gory murder of everyone in the restaurant, including her less-than-talented waitress.

Raven shook herself and her over-the-top imagination. Maybe the mysterious woman just had a bad case of resting bitch face. Regardless, Raven's job meant she not only had to approach the customer but serve them.

Raven's skin tingled as she walked up to the table

for two and ice clamped up her spine. "See anything you like?"

The woman turned toward Raven. Her dark brown gaze studied Raven down her straight nose. "Not at all."

At least she was honest. Having two tables in a row balk at the menu, though, meant Raven's customer batting average took another dive.

"I'm sorry to hear that," Raven said through another fake smile. "Is there anything I can get you?"

The woman pursed her lips and continued to appraise Raven head to foot. "Not at this time." She pinched the corner of the laminated menu between her manicured forefinger and thumb and dangled it in the air as if it were actually a dead rat.

Raven plucked the menu from the snooty woman. "Have a nice day."

The woman smirked before sliding off her chair and walking out of the diner without a response or even a look back. Weird.

Well, this was Dan's Diner. Weird wasn't a side effect of awesome here. Nope. Here, it may as well be a requirement for service...like a shirt and shoes.

After delivering a bill to the elderly couple coming down from a gambling high, and the third round of refills to the burnouts at table three, she returned to the pass-through window behind the counter. While her back was turned, the table of women "snuck" out of the restaurant. She could've turned and called out to ask them questions. Watching them squirm would've been entertaining, but not tonight. She just didn't care.

From his spot by the grill, Mike glanced over his shoulder and laughed. "Nice scowl."

"Okay, little fox. Continue with the lecture. Teach me, oh, wise-one."

He straightened from the grill and turned to her. "No lecture. Just a hunch. The author of the original reference, or at least the oldest reference I could find, was a poet, not a historian."

She tapped her fingers along the smooth counter. Mike would eventually get to the point, given the time. Whether she had the patience to wait him out was the more important question.

"I think, in this instance, glaive is a metaphor for something else," he said.

"Not an analogy?"

Mike rolled his eyes. "Did you *pass* English in high school? An analogy compares one thing to another, and a metaphor is one of the figures of speech you can use to make that comparison."

"So, we're both right?"

Mike let out a long, loud, suffering sigh. She loved to push his buttons. Maybe she should call the metaphor a simile next, and watch his face go red.

"Anyway, I think glaive is a *metaphor*," Mike grumbled.

"For what?" She pulled the collar of her blouse in and out to send air rushing under her shirt in an attempt to cool down.

"A weapon of some sort."

"So, now we're looking for a weapon of light...instead of looking for a weapon of light?"

Mike's dimple deepened as he lost his pensive expression and grinned. "Exactly."

Raven groaned.

"What did you find?" Mike asked.

She hadn't had time to explain what happened at Bear's apartment. He'd been in class all day and they didn't carpool to work together. She'd texted the basics but had to wait for lulls during their shift to go into detail. "A feather. Probably one of mine. I'll need you to sniff it later."

"Why would your feather be at a place you've never been?" Mike crossed his arms, the broken one in the cast over the healthy one. "A lot of supernaturals are associated with crows."

"Ravens."

"Whatever. The Morrigan, Odin, Valkyries, Lloth, Athena, Apollo—"

"Me."

Mike shrugged. "But one thing's for sure."

"What's that?" She pinched the plastic-like material of her pants at the thighs and pulled. The polyester blend peeled from her skin with a wet suction-like slurping sound. Well. That wasn't attractive *at all*.

"Most of those I listed are associated with the Underworld."

"And death." She poured herself a coffee.

"Sort of. Makes sense, though."

"How so?" She peeled open the lids on three

creamers and dumped the contents into her coffee. Sure, she was overheated, but coffee made everything better.

"The Claíomh Solais is from the Shadow Realm."

"I thought you said it was a weapon of light?" A drop of sweat ran down the side of her face. How did Mike stand by the grills all shift? She grabbed a spoon and stirred her coffee.

"Since when did anything or anyone from the Other Realms make sense?"

"True."

"Cole is also from the Shadow Realm..."

"Mike..."

"What?"

She pointed her spoon at Mike. Some coffee dripped onto the counter. "We've already been over this."

"You can't trust him, Rayray."

"I don't. I trust that he will keep his sealed promise, as he's fae." She fanned her body with her blouse again.

"Why do you think he made this agreement?" Mike narrowed his eyes. "I know why you did, but why would he bother when he could just follow you around like a perverted shadow?"

Raven took a sip of coffee and winced. Dan used an inexpensive blend. Despite smelling great, the coffee was sharper than she preferred. She took another long sip and thought about what Mike said. The same question had plagued Raven's mind and she didn't like the answer. "I think he's using me."

Mike grunted and gave me his "I told you so" stare-down. *My little brother.* He was a genius, but that didn't mean he knew everything.

"I think he's using me as bait, just like Bane wanted to use me as a trade. Frankly, I prefer Cole's method, and in the end, who cares? He gave our family much needed protection and promised not to harm Bear."

"No. He promised not to kill him."

"No. The agreement was he will protect our family to the best of his abilities. He promised not to harm Bear when we find him, and in return I work with him, not for him." She drank more coffee, enjoying the heat as it slid down her throat. It still tasted awful.

Mike frowned.

"You were there!"

"I was in pain," Mike grumbled.

She folded her arms. He had a point. His arm had been broken and he was recovering from the trauma of getting caught in a leg-hold.

"You're thinking too much with..." Mike waved his hand at her.

"With what?"

"You know." He waved again, directing the finger wave at the center of her body.

She inhaled the sweet coffee scent and arched a brow over the rim of her too-small, white diner mug. "Are you trying to point at my crotch?"

Mike's cheeks turned a deep shade of red. His silence answered for him.

Raven jabbed her index finger at the air between

them. "Listen—"

The door to the diner swung open, jingling the bell, and Cole walked in. The deep forest scent unique to him—the smell she'd come to associate with the shadowy transition between day and night, dark, salacious promises, and something oddly reminiscent of her childhood—rushed in with the stench of a late summer night in North Burnaby.

Tonight, he looked every bit an assassin, with tall boots, pants, breastplate and gauntlets made of supple black leather and sword belts criss-crossed low at his waist. A dark cloak flowed behind him like one of the shadows he controlled. Black Other eyes pierced the room and left little doubt to his origin. Fierce authority radiated from his solid form. Customers cowered in their booths. The young couple by the door flattened against the wall to stay out of his way.

Her knees wobbled. She reached out and grabbed the counter edge. Her cheap blouse suddenly felt limp and her pants a size too tight. Crap! Her hair had so much grease embedded in the strands it looked wet. Why couldn't he visit at the beginning of her shift when she looked relatively fresh? She must resemble a reject from a 1950s greaser movie. The urge to check her reflection surged up. She swallowed and tightened her grip on the counter.

Mike groaned and turned back to his grill.

Cole stopped at the counter in front of her. His dark gaze locked on hers. Focused. Intense.

What she wouldn't give to keep that pointed

attention on her, that look of unwavering intent? She gulped, not liking the answer.

Anything.

One crook of his finger and a promise of his affection, even for a night, and she'd stumble over her own feet to reach for him. She wouldn't even pause to wipe the drool from her chin.

A slow smile spread across his gorgeous, striking face. "Good evening, Einin."

"Hi." He called her little bird again. It took every ounce of control not to swoon.

His smile grew.

"Uh...why are you here? It's certainly not for the food." And sadly, probably not to hook up with a sweaty waitress.

"Certainly not." His black eyes sparkled. "Your request with Odin has been granted."

Chapter Twenty

*"I'm looking for a concealer that will hide my
exhaustion from the last ten years."*
    ~Raven, at the department store make-up counter

The knock on her apartment door sent Raven's heart into a thudding mess. With a deep breath, she stepped forward, flipped the deadbolt and opened the door.

"Good evening, Einin." Cole stood tall and regal wearing a dubious amount of leather. His intimidating presence radiated wicked potency and made her ovaries ache. If she reached out, would he push her away, or pull her close?

She didn't think he could top the look he had when

he'd barged into the diner last night to announce her audience had been granted. She was wrong. Very, very wrong. With black armour, he vibrated with violent purpose. Instead of polished metal to shine under the austere lighting of her apartment building, the protective metal of his breastplate, gauntlets and tall boots muted the light with their matte black finish. He looked like a living shadow.

A long black cloak hung from metal shoulder pieces and descended to his heels. It billowed silently behind him as he stepped into her apartment. His ensemble matched his features and look, letting him blend perfectly with the looming shadows that clung to his presence like a dark cloud. Only his pale skin glowed in the darkness.

When he walked into her apartment, his boots, which covered his legs to just above his kneecaps with the plated matte metal, hit the ground silently.

Lethal.

Raven gulped. "Hi."

"Are you ready?"

"To visit the Allfather? No, of course not." She bent to pull her black riding boots over her dark jeans. Not exactly summer attire, but she wanted to look more respectful than cut-off jean shorts allowed.

"What do you know about Odin?"

"Not much. Big bad fae lord who's so powerful his eyes glow bright blue instead of black."

Cole's expression turned thoughtful. "I wouldn't say they glow, but they are bright. And only one eye is bright blue. He's blind in the other eye, so it's white with hints of blue."

Okay, then. Raven pulled on her second boot and straightened. "He surrounds himself with an army of loyal undead soldiers and prevented regs from utter annihilation when the barrier came down by creating some rules and exerting his considerable power to enforce them."

Cole nodded. "Odin keeps the warriors, or *einherjar*, in Valhalla, but not out of the tender warmness of his heart. He wants a large army to support him when Ragnarok comes."

"And when will that be?"

Cole shrugged. "Some thought the barrier coming down was a sign of the apocalypse, but the regs turned out to be..." Cole frowned.

"Humans without any power?"

"Pretty much. Some say Ragnarok is a delusional story existing only in Odin's mind.'

"They say that?"

Cole chuckled. "Not to his face."

Raven stood and straightened. Her heart continued to beat spastically. She was going to meet the Allfather with the Lord of Shadows by her side. Her. A waitress from Burnaby. She wasn't even a good waitress. The last few days had really turned her already shitty life upside down.

And she liked it.

Raven licked her lips.

Apparently, inherent danger and the promise of

utter demise was preferable to the night shift at Dan's Diner.

Shocking.

Cole's gaze softened as he watched her. He stepped forward and she flinched.

"If we're going to see Odin, we need to go now," he said. "Arriving late or standing him up aren't options I'd advise."

She squeezed her hands into fists and nodded.

He wrapped his strong arms around her and pulled her in. The shadows wrapped around them like a cocoon.

"We'll have to make a series of transports to get to his main gate," he whispered in her ear. "It won't be as fast as going to the Shadow Realm."

She nodded against his hard chest and inhaled his intoxicating scent. "Why don't you tell me more about Odin?"

She sensed more than saw him smile. He held her close. The apartment around them disappeared as they slipped into shadow.

Cole's deep voice rumbled against her ear as he explained Odin's history and his domain. She already knew a lot of what Cole told her from searching the internet and Mike's research. She didn't stop him from talking though. Doing so would involve breathing and she'd held her breath from the moment he arrived on her doorstep looking like the Lord of Sin.

She had other reasons for letting him speak, of course.

One, she loved the sound of his voice too much. Two, she didn't want to disrupt him cocooning her in his warmth and heady scent. And three, she'd discovered long ago, letting people assume her ignorance paid off in unexpected ways. Their demeanor and the information they provided told Raven more about them as a person.

Raven learned much from Cole's deep voice whispering in her ear. He clearly wanted her informed and provided pertinent details in a no-nonsense manner that lacked any condescension. She didn't interrupt once. She did, however, visualize ripping his clothes off and jumping on his naked body.

After a series of dizzying portals, the shadows slipped away and left them at the bottom of stone steps.

Raven stepped back and Cole's arms tensed before releasing her. The red moons of the Underworld bathed her in warm light and illuminated the stonework in front of her. Two oversized wolves sat at the top of the stairs under an archway. Clinking glass, shattering plates, loud shouts and laughter from Odin's Hall stampeded down the steps toward them.

She turned back to Cole. "Why not plunk us into the middle of the hall and save us the intimidating entrance and walk?"

"His main hall is shielded."

"So, you can't?"

Cole smiled.

Oh, he could. "Then why not?"

"It's considered a rude and aggressive move some

would interpret as an act of war. I have no wish to anger the Allfather just for convenience and a flashy entrance."

And who would want to start a war with the dark fae lord who made his reputation based on it?

"Let's go." He hooked her arm around his and walked toward the steps.

She could remain frozen and force Cole to drag her up the stones, but she somehow managed to regain control of her body to walk beside him. She wanted to meet Odin on her own two feet with whatever pride she had left.

Raven's muscles twitched as she tried to ignore the hunk of man beside her. His shadows draped around them, almost in a comforting manner, though she doubted he meant it that way. With one move, she could reach out and lick him—taste his smooth skin, nip at his ears, run her teeth along his rippling muscles, suck on... She shook her head.

Cole Camhanaich, the Mouth of the Night to First Light, escorted her through Odin's hall of fallen warriors. Battered shields lined the walls and swords hung overhead as rafters. The air, laden with the smell of metal, wood and earth, drifted by on swaths of heat. A gold roof reflected the light from the fire pits. If Raven's stomach hadn't busied itself by twisting into knots, she would've enjoyed the sight. Maybe. Imminent death had a way of ruining the moment.

Feasting tables filled with battle-worn fighters lined the aisle. The warriors, some handsome, some not, all with the eerie, slightly off aura that often adhered to the once dead, sat on the edge of seats made from breastplates of victims. At least, that's where she assumed they came from. The fighters sat in stiff silence—their boisterous partying paused the moment Cole and Raven stepped past the wolves guarding the gates and walked through the entrance.

"Easy." Cole leaned down to whisper in her ear, "They can sense your nerves."

The wolves trotted past them and loped ahead through Odin's hall. When they reached the bottom steps of a dais at the end of the aisle, Raven and Cole stopped. Without their footsteps marking their progress, silence settled over the room. The two wolves bounded up the steps and flopped down to lay by the feet of the lone man sitting on a large throne made of skulls. A pair of ravens perched on the man's broad shoulders snapped their heads in her direction. Black beady eyes scanned her, assessing, judging, and who-new-what-ing. The weight of their attention unwavering. Her skin tingled. The dark energy inside her twisted as if it had a mind of its own and wanted out to play.

Where the heck were the exits?

Odin had wrapped his long, blood-red cloak around him, hiding whatever body armour he wore underneath. He resembled a buff Santa Claus...after he fell off the sleigh, banged a few strippers, pumped a shitload of iron straight into his veins, and fought for the wrong side in a turf war, but somehow survived to tell the tale. Okay, maybe he didn't look like jolly-old Nick at all, but he had a long gray beard. A long scar ran from the middle of his forehead, over his white eye, to mid-cheek.

Her stomach twisted into an even tighter knot, and she cursed Bear for getting her into this hot mess. The black feather she'd retrieved from her brother's safe house burned against her skin. She'd secured it with the waistband of her jeans before covering the feather with her blouse. Mike had sniffed it earlier—wasn't hers.

Odin turned his ice blue and white gaze to Cole and nodded. "Beul na h-Oidhche gu Camhanaich, son of Erebus, welcome to my hall. What is the purpose of your visit? Are you here on Lloth's behalf?"

Lloth? Who was that? Raven eyed Cole, but he kept his attention forward. Guess Odin represented more of a threat than her curiosity. Fair enough.

"I'm here as an escort." Cole's voice rumbled with ease as he flicked a hand in her direction, his body language casual.

Odin's steely gaze narrowed as he assessed Raven. Her sister's textbooks said Odin was one of the few beings from the Underworld with blue eyes. The "experts" said the distinction was probably due to his superior power.

Odin's scarred lip snarled up. "And who are you?"

She cleared her throat. "My name is Raven." She dug out Odin's card from her pocket and held it up. "You sent this calling card to my brother."

"Your brother." Odin sneered. "Not you."

"Please. My brother has gone missing, and this is my only clue."

Odin scoffed and leaned back in his thrown. His fingers taped along the armrest. "What is your brother's name?"

"Bear."

"Never heard of him."

"His real name is Bjorn." Bjorn was a common Scandinavian name, but Cole had explained how Odin rarely gifted a calling card to anyone. "Bjorn Crawford."

Odin stilled. His fingers stopped tapping. Slowly, he leaned forward and squinted. "He never said he had a sister. Twin?"

Unease flittered along her skin. That was a freakishly good guess. She looked nothing like her brother. And why had Odin suddenly become so interested? Obviously, he recognized her brother's name, but what did that mean? Should she prepare for imminent smiting? At least she'd stuffed the last donut from her dad's office in her mouth. The sugary sweetness still coated her mouth.

She swallowed and met the war god's gaze. "Yes."

Odin straightened in his throne. He turned to one raven on his shoulder, then the other. "Huginn. Muninn."

The enormous black birds launched from Odin's shoulders in unison. With heavy beats of their wings, they rose above the king. Huginn and Muninn, Odin's spies.

Raven froze. What were they going to do? Spy her to death?

At least twice the size of regular ravens, the birds swooped down the stairs toward her. A strangled cry erupted from her mouth. Before they reached her, they careened into each other with a loud croak that shook the hall. The metal shields rattled, the swords clanked. Some of the warriors cursed.

The air shimmered and in place of two birds, a large, intimidating man stood in their place. Clad in black armour similar to Cole's, his dark Other gaze swept the room as he slowly descended the stairs with the grace of a vicious warrior. A long flowing cloak made of raven feathers trailed behind him and slipped down the stone surface of each step.

"Huginn and Muninn. Thought and Memory. My greatest creation." Odin's voice boomed from behind the immense warrior.

Raven stood transfixed at the approaching warrior. He looked oddly familiar. Something about his jawline.

"They are forged from my own essence—blood of my blood," Odin continued.

The giant man stopped in front of Raven and peered down at her, dark brows furrowed, black gaze blazing.

"And so too, are you, it seems," Odin said.

Huh?

Chapter Twenty-One

"What's done in darkness always comes to light."

~Unknown

U

nderstanding slapped Raven across the face like a cold, dead fish. Harsh and rank. Now she saw it. The familiar jawline, the broad shoulders and straight nose. The Huginn-Muninn-combo eerily resembled her twin brother, she should've made the connection sooner.

"Daddy?" Her mouth fell open and she gawked at Odin. Surely not. Surely, she'd have some more badass skills if she was the child of Odin.

The God of War shook his head and nodded at Huginn Muninn standing in front of her. Oh. She closed her mouth and peered up at the intimidating warrior. The warriors in Odin's hall faded in the background. "You're my biological father?"

Cole stiffened beside her, his expression alert. Shadows gathered around them, pulled from the summer night.

"You have grown into a beautiful, young woman, just like we knew you would, little raven." The man tilted his head and blinked his dark Other eyes. The scent of a densely wooded glen rolled off his body. Not just his face hit the familiarity button in her brain, his smell did, too. But how? He had to get close enough for her to capture his scent.

"You watched me," she said. Her mind reeled. What did this mean? Odin was her grandfather? Two mythical birds who combined to form one giant warrior were her father? How was that even possible? "You watched us."

He nodded. "An easy task, given your abilities and that of your brother's."

What's two more ravens sitting in a tree? His explanation made sense. Should she be creeped out? Odin's spies had, well, spied on her. Oddly, her skin didn't itch or tingle. Instead, she grew warm, and had to suppress the urge to leap forward and hug her biological father. Then she remembered how alone they'd been before Mom met Dad.

"Did you spy on my mother, too?" The question came out more accusatory than she intended.

Huginn Muninn tilted his head, much like a bird

would. "Sometimes."

"You have your share of women." Odin bellowed from somewhere behind Huginn Muninn. "What made this one so special?"

"She was wild," Huginn Muninn said. "She was unapologetic." This time, Huginn Muninn spoke with a slightly deeper voice.

"She was the most beautiful thing we'd ever seen." A two-toned voice erupted from her biological father's mouth, as if two people spoke at once.

Huginn Muninn nodded to himself.

Raven rubbed her arms. Okay, now she was a little creeped out. Instead of one individual splitting a single consciousness into multiple birds, Huginn Muninn appeared to have two distinct personalities that fused into one being. Was her biological father two birds who shifted into a human, or a human with multiple personalities who shifted into two birds?

Did it really matter?

Odin growled from his throne. "I ordered you to terminate your woman when..." He clamped his mouth shut and his gaze slid to Raven.

He didn't need to finish the sentence, but she did it for him anyway. "When you discovered she was pregnant." Asshole.

Odin grumbled, but he didn't look away. Instead, he leaned back in his throne and folded his arms across his considerable chest, expression defiant, body language challenging. Right, like she'd screech out a war cry and launch herself at the father of all warriors. She liked her head where it was, thanks.

Huginn Muninn turned to his, their, father. "You ordered us to kill her if she ever stepped into the Underworld again. She didn't."

Odin's glare turned cold. "Don't tell me you couldn't figure out a way to lure her into the Other Realms."

A twinkle sparkled in Huginn Muninn's gaze as he looked back to Raven. That look told her everything she needed to know. If he wasn't capable of loving her mother, he at least genuinely cared for her.

"That wasn't your order," Huginn Muninn said.

The reason for her mother's hatred of the Other Realms now made sense. She didn't hate Others at all. She feared them. As if she knew what fate awaited her the moment she exited a portal to the Underworld. As if Huginn Muninn warned her.

Mom forbade Bear and Raven from entering the Other Realms, too. Maybe she feared her children would face the same fate.

Cold prickled Raven's skin.

That's why Mom urged them to hide their nature. Pieces of her past clicked into place like a demented jigsaw puzzle. A lot of weird stuff from her childhood suddenly made sense.

"You defied me?" Odin growled.

"Not technically."

Huginn Muninn's lips turned into a brief smile. He shifted to place his body slightly in front of Raven, partially blocking the heat and light from the fire pits.

Their crackling broke the stiff silence in the hall.

Odin narrowed his eyes. "You would fight me now?"

"No, Father." Huginn Muninn bowed his head.

"But you wish to protect your daughter, as you would your son?"

"Yes," he hissed with the dual tone. "We have never asked for anything, Father. We have nothing of our own. Except this. Except her. And him."

Raven's heart swelled. Huginn Muninn would never replace Dad, but the protective look her way, and his defiance in the face of the Allfather, she'd find no enemy in her biological father, or rather, fathers.

How did that even work? What was the correct pronoun for this situation?

"Very well." Odin grunted. "Their mortal lives are insignificant, but they carry my blood, and they have the potential to pass it on."

Cole's posture relaxed and the shadows pooling by his feet withdrew.

Odin stood in one smooth move, defying his wizened appearance. The red cloak fell away, revealing its tattered and shredded condition, and the dented armour with scorch marks he wore beneath. In a previous battle, probably many generations before her existence, something ferocious with long claws had swiped Odin's midsection in an attempt to disembowel him. Obviously, the god's opponent was unsuccessful, but it had left some pretty wicked claw marks on the armour as a memory. Did Odin thumb the jagged edges when he reminisced about the good old days? Did the slashed metal bring a soft smile to his face, or a scowl?

Odin stomped down the stairs before her. His armour creaked with each step and his cloak whispered against the stone floor.

Huginn Muninn and Cole tensed.

"If she is to carry my blood and name, she should carry it well." Odin closed the distance. "There is no weakness in my line, and there must be no weakness in her."

Huginn Muninn hesitated briefly before moving aside. Odin stopped in front of her. Up close, the deep scars running down his face became more evident. Calling him grandpa right now would be a mistake. She clamped her mouth shut and bit her tongue.

"Your brother is known as an unscrupulous thief, with few redeeming qualities. I'd planned to dispose of him when he answered my summons," Odin said. "Turns out, he has one quality worth sparing his life. It is fortunate you appeared in his place."

Huginn Muninn's head snapped back and his brow furrowed. He curled his hands into fists behind his creator's back.

Why on earth would he spare Bear because of her? As much as she'd like to believe she had a winning personality that opened doors, experience told her that wasn't true. Her life was far from rainbows and unicorn poop.

"So, you didn't send Bear to steal something?"

"I am a war god with legions of fighters at my

disposal. I don't steal." He leaned in, his meaty breath hitting her face. "I take."

Raven's legs shook. "Noted."

With fighter-fast reflexes, he reached out and grasped her face with one calloused hand. His thumb dug into one cheek while his rough fingers sank into the other. His hand smelled of iron, leather, and steak. Well-done steak.

Shadows surged up and surrounded them in a silent threat.

"Easy, Lord of Shadows," Odin murmured.

Raven's breath caught. Her heart hammered and she focused on his good eye. Her awareness shrank until only Odin's image consumed her vision. His ice blue eye bore into her—intense and powerful. She tried to look away but couldn't. He said she was safe, right? She bit her tongue and tasted blood. The blue from his gaze expanded and sank into her skin. She grew cold and her skin clammy. Her heart slowed down as her blood froze. Like the water at her favourite beach, the cold continued to sink in until something sparked. Deep within her core, a light flickered, sputtered and then blazed molten hot. Like an internal explosion, the heat blasted outward, shattering the icicles forming on her soul from Odin's touch.

Odin snatched his hand back. His mouth compressed into a thin line.

Was this when the smiting happened?

After a tense minute that lingered for decades, Odin nodded. "You're worthy..."

His terse comment snapped her awareness back to the present.

"...Enough."

Cole and Huginn Muninn stood wide-eyed beside her, almost as if frozen by the same potent energy mojo crap Odin had soaked her in. The shadows retreated.

The Allfather spun on his heel and walked back up the steps to his throne without another comment.

Um, okay. Were they done?

Cole reached out and nudge her elbow. He lifted his chin toward the exit.

Guess so.

Odin's abrupt dismissal left Huginn Muninn to escort Raven and Cole to the gates. They turned without a word and walked back the way they came, past silent, watchful warriors. Raven stopped at the threshold.

The eerie red moons of the Otherworld glowed like fiery orbs in the dark summer night, cascading the group in streams of dark gold. The sweet-smelling trees lined the foreboding entrance to the hall and loomed ahead of them. Two torches crackled and lit the landing in a soft glow. The heat pressed against Raven's face.

She turned to her biological father. "So, *both* of you are my father, or just one of you, or...?"

"We are two halves to the same coin."

She rolled her eyes. "Yeah, yeah, yeah. I get it. You're Ben to his Jerry, Mac to his Cheese, Yin to his Yang."

Huginn Muninn arched his eyebrow and paused to briefly turn to Cole.

He shrugged.

Her father sighed. "I'm not sure you do."

What did that even mean? "Geez, can Others be less cryptic?"

Huginn Muninn shook his, their, whatever, head. Ugh, pronouns were so restrictive.

"So just to confirm, neither you nor Odin hired, kidnapped or harmed my brother Bear in any way? And you never met him, aside from watching us as children?"

"That is correct. If we discover his location, we'll send word."

Raven pulled the black feather from her waistband.

Cole jerked back.

Huginn Muninn narrowed his eyes and leaned in. His nostrils flared.

"Did you drop this when you searched Bear's hiding spot?"

Cole tensed.

"We did not search your brother's place or any hiding spot. We delivered the card to his apartment, only." Apparently, Odin's camp remained unaware of Bear's safe house.

"Then how'd this get there?"

Huginn Muninn frowned. Their cape billowed around their large body. "That feather is not ours."

"Whose is it then?"

Her father leaned in. "You should ask your escort."

Raven spun to glare at Cole. Odin had asked if Cole came to his court on behalf of...Lily...Lilith...Lithe... No. Lloth. Her mind flickered with memories. Mike had said something about Lloth. What was it? Something vague about the name pinged her high school memories, but her recollections from that time had long ago weakened, bumped out by other life experiences. Something about Lloth and the Underworld. Too obscure, and unimportant in the moment, her mind discarded the information.

Before she could demand answers from anyone, Huginn Muninn spread his arms wide. Her father burst into two large ravens. They beat their wings and flew away into the night. Waves of heated air hit her face.

Her skin prickled as all the hairs rose. That must be what she looked like when she transformed.

Cole leaned down. "Like father like daughter."

She jabbed a stiff finger into his hard chest. *Ouch.* "You better give me some answers."

"As should you. We had a deal, Raven. No secrets. You shouldn't have kept the feather from me."

She opened her mouth to explain, but Cole shook his head.

"Not here." He reached forward and enveloped her in his arms. The light dimmed. Raven squeaked as the world dissolved and Cole transported them through shadow, flooding her with warmth and his earthy scent. The darkness coating her bled away revealing her dimly lit apartment. She turned in Cole's arms. He hadn't let go. Eyes as dark as his shouldn't change colour, but they did. Much like the varying depths of shadow, his eerie gaze ebbed and flowed with different shades of black, gray and silver. Deep and rich, light and cold.

Right now, staring into the seemingly bottomless pits, they darkened into an abyss. Drawing her in, daring her to follow. His arms tensed. His hands clenched at her back, digging in a little.

She licked her lips. Memories of his mouth on hers plagued her mind. She could still taste him.

His gaze broke from hers and flicked down to her mouth. He leaned in. The clunking of the refrigerator softened. The whir of her laptop faded. The room around them disappeared.

"Am I interrupting?" A voice intruded. Her dream-like state shattered. The smug tone in Luke's voice sent fear ripping up her spine as she jumped out of Cole's arms.

Cole grunted and reached for her.

Too late.

Before his hand closed around her arm, a bright light erupted in the room.

Cole vanished.

A dark shroud in a room of light, Luke stepped in close and gripped her bicep. His fingers clamped down hard. His Other nature seeped into her skin and dampened her energy. Like smothering a flame, his power acted like a giant shovel full of gravel. Bane clutched a glowing orb in his other hand. The heady scent of blood and steel surrounded them. Pain lanced down her arm to her fingers. Her eyes hurt. The shocking white blaze radiated from the artifact held inches from her.

"Absolute light," Luke explained. "Not as good as the Claíomh Solais, of course, but it will buy me a minute or two." He tugged Raven close.

She stumbled into his large frame. Her face smacked against the soft fabric of his shirt. The gentle scent of his cologne conflicted with what was happening. She tugged at her ravens, but the dark energy sputtered and choked out like Jean Claude's failing engine.

"And a minute is all I need."

"Not something you often hear men bragging about."

Luke glared at her. He dropped the glowing orb and used his free hand to pull out a small red disc. He threw it at the ground. Another portal snapped in place. He stepped into the fuzzy red light to the Other Realms and hauled her with him.

Chapter Twenty-Two

*"Lincoln was not great because he was born in a cabin,
but because he got out of it."*

~James Truslow Adams

R aven blinked repeatedly. Slowly, the distorted vision of the room grew less fuzzy. Her ears rang from the sensory overload, and the room buzzed. Or maybe that was her. The dark energy inside her pulsed, demanding release. Feathers flapped and fluttered in her belly.

She shook her head. Fluffy hair brushed against her cheek.

Two couches by a roaring fire greeted her with clarity. The pine finish of the walls and earthy smell in the air suggested a log cabin. Though the drapes were pulled shut, the surge in her dark energy, and its continued twisting suggested Luke had scurried her off to one of the Other Realms. A portal didn't affect time, so though she travelled to a different realm, it mirrored hers. It was still summer and still night.

The vise-like grip on her arm unclamped. Her dark energy surged up, pressing against her skin. She gasped. No. She couldn't shift right now. Not without more information. Where would she flee? She wrestled with the potent corvid essence and pushed it back down. The birds settled a little but croaked with displeasure. Shifting right now served no purpose and placed her in the bodies of smaller, more vulnerable creatures. She needed an escape plan first.

Luke stepped away from her and waved his beefy arm at one of the sofas. His cologne with subtle hints of sandalwood washed over her. Bad guys shouldn't smell good. It was confusing. He didn't tempt her in any way, but nothing about an abduction should be pleasant.

Bane made a gracious wave with his hand at the cabin's interior. "I advise against attempting your little shifting display. The doors and windows are spelled to remain shut. You need a portal to get in and out."

Her Other energy relaxed a little more. She folded her arms and gave the Lord of War her best fall-down-and-die stare.

He chuckled. "Suit yourself."

He took two giant steps before sprawling on one of the couches. He propped his feet on the ottoman. No mud or grime splattered onto the furniture. His military boots appeared immaculately clean. Maybe the Lord of War didn't get his hands or boots dirty. His arms spanned the backrest. "He won't reach you here, you know. He can't save you."

"You Others need to stop abducting women."

Luke sneered. "Did Cole try that?"

She pursed her lips.

Luke's cruel mouth snarled up in what would probably be a smirk on a mere mortal. On him, it was something else, something more, but certainly condescending. "Did he realize he could catch more bees with honey?"

She shuffled her feet.

"Or did you give him a taste of your honey...honey?"

Her cheeks heated. "You're disgusting."

Luke barked out a laugh. "I'm the Lord of War. People often assume battles can only be fought through fists and bloodshed." He settled into the couch. "I've found more pleasant ways over the years to wage war."

She blanched. "Is that why you brought me here? To pick a fight in some sick, twisted way?"

Luke's gaze sparkled and his mouth twisted into a cruel smirk again. Obviously, he found her question greatly amusing. "No. Sorry to disappoint."

She relaxed a little and uncrossed her arms. Of course, he found it amusing. He probably never had to worry about his safety or protecting his "honour."

He stood. His new jeans crinkled and failed to move

as fluidly as he did. Instead of walking to her, he moved to the roaring fire. He faced the crackling flames and gave her a view of his broad shoulders and back, apparently, unconcerned about placing himself in a vulnerable position. He clasped his hands behind his back. "You're not my type."

He probably preferred glamazons who'd pop her head off like an unwanted zit. Relief washed through her. The last thing she needed in her already complicated and sucky life was an amorous, blood-thirsty warrior with no respect for boundaries. "Then why am I here? Besides your need to ridicule a mortal to bide your time."

Luke spun around. His dark, Other gaze flickered with its own fire while the lighting in the room cast the rest of him in shadow. Empty shadow. Heat continued to pump from the fire in waves.

"Bjorn Crawford has something I want. Something I paid him to retrieve. He refuses to deliver, so now I have something he wants."

"Bear and I are hardly besties." She spat out the words without any heat—anything to cover her reeling mind. Bane had paid Bear to steal the Claíomh Solais. All this time, she thought the Claíomh Solais was stolen from him. She ran through her previous conversations with the Lord of War. He didn't lie, but he talked his way around the truth with expert finesse. He always said it was stolen. Son of a banshee. He let her and Dad assume the item belonged to him. Now, Bane confirmed Cole spoke the truth. The Claíomh

Solais belonged to the Shadow Lord. Whatever that meant.

Bane said something in return.

"What?"

"You're his soulmate," he repeated. "He'll come for you. You're probably the only thing he values more than what he stole."

"Cole?" Her heart skipped a beat.

Bane laughed. A deep, bellowing sound communicating his amusement and mockery at the same time.

Heat burned her face.

Bane finished laughing. "No. Bjorn."

"Um, eww. He's my brother. You should fire the person you get your information from because you're grossly misinformed."

"I disagree. I find myself perfectly informed."

"Then you're just gross."

Luke's gaze darkened in the flickering firelight. "Watch yourself."

"Why? You're not the Lord of Torture, are you? You want what my brother has. I hardly doubt you'd damage your best trading chip."

"That's where you're wrong. I need you alive, but what condition you're delivered in is not a given." He cocked his head as if he could hear her teeth chattering or her knees wobbling.

Maybe he could. What the fuck was she thinking? Why antagonize the warmonger? Without using a drop of his power, he could snap her in half with his bare hands before she could say, "Ouch."

"You obviously have no experience with war," he said.

"Not true."

He raised a dark eyebrow.

"I'm a pretty vicious armchair warrior when it comes to social media fights."

He crossed his arms. The soft fabric of his shirt stretched.

Instead of causing her to fall into a drooling frenzy of hot need, like the sight of Cole's muscles did, Bane's imposing figure only incited fear. A lot of fear. A whole barrel full. Her throat grew dry. "Seriously. Just point me toward an antivaxxer and watch me go."

He frowned. "Did I accidentally hit your head when I brought you over?"

"No." She scratched her temple.

"So, you're normally this idiotic?"

"Just biding my time." The sweet taste of donut had faded from her mouth, along with the memory of Cole's tongue playing with hers. Her stomach rumbled. Bane couldn't dispose of her now. Not on an empty stomach with a stale taste in her mouth. That would be cruel.

"What about companionable silence?"

"That implies we're companions."

He took a menacing step toward her. "How about just silence, then?"

"No deal. How am I to trick you into revealing your diabolical master plan?"

"Is that what this is?"

"Maybe?"

"I've already told you my 'diabolical master plan.'"

She pursed her lips. He had. Literally two minutes ago, he'd explained how he planned to hold her in exchange for the Claíomh Solais. She needed time to process. Like a kid who just jumped off the merry-go-round, her head spun, and she struggled to focus on what was in front of her. She knew one thing. She couldn't allow Bear to exchange the Claíomh Solais for her. Even if Luke kept his word and she went home safe, Bear wouldn't receive the same assurances. The Lord of War didn't seem like the forgiving type. She needed to get out of here and that meant help from Cole. She pursed her lips.

"Or are you trying to distract me, hoping Camhanaich will somehow save you?" Luke's voice cut through her thoughts.

Nailed it. She swallowed and refused to look away from Luke's knowing gaze.

"There's no need to stall. He can't reach you here and I have no plans to torture you...yet. Keep up that incoherent babbling and things might change."

"How do you know Bear refuses to deliver?" The awful scene at his safe house flashed through her vision. She shivered.

"What are you suggesting?"

"Maybe someone took Bear before he could bring you the Claíomh Solais."

Luke dropped his head back and barked out more

laughter. The sound rumbled deep from his chest and filled the cozy room. Instead of putting her at ease, his laughter amped up the flight part of her fight or flight response. Prey drive fully engaged, she wanted out. Her leg muscles twitched. Her energy surged again, begging for release. She scanned the room for potential exits. Theoretically, she only needed one bird to escape alive.

Bane's laughter died down. "He seemed perfectly fine and in complete control when he told me to, and I quote, 'Fuck off. You'll never get the Claíomh Solais.'"

Raven's shoulders drooped. He must've talked to Bear before whatever happened in his safe house...happened. What in the Underworld, Bear? The more she attempted to dig her brother out of trouble, the deeper he burrowed. Like a fucking clam on crack.

Everything about this situation confused her.

"Why would he do that?" she asked. "He's never reneged on a contract before."

"Reneged is an incorrect word choice as it implies renegotiation. Your brother made no effort to reach a new agreement."

"But why?"

"He found the Claíomh Solais." He spoke his statement as if it was the only explanation needed. Maybe she *had* bonked her head when he brought her over because that made no sense.

"What exactly is the Claíomh Solais?"

Luke chuckled.

Her hands twitched. Raven wasn't normally a violent person, but an insane urge to punch the Lord of War in the gut consumed her. Her muscles tensed. Yeah, like that would end well. Memories of her trying to tackle Bear while he held her at arm's reach surfaced and drowned her with humiliation and a much needed reminder of her incompetence as a fighter against a bigger, stronger opponent.

With his laughing fit over, Luke's attention fixed on her. "Ah, my silly girl. You ask the wrong question."

She frowned.

"Not what, but who."

Chapter Twenty-Three

"Me: I want to travel.
Bank Account: Like...to the backyard?"
~Unknown, but also Raven's internal dialogue

Raven slammed the cutlery drawer shut. The contents jangled. "Seriously?"

Luke didn't own a single sharp object in the entire cabin where he imprisoned her. After he dropped his Claíomh Solais bombshell and refused to elaborate, he'd left to "run an errand." Her mind reeled, sifting through old conversations in an attempt to make sense of this new information.

This is what she knew:

1) Bane didn't have any donuts in the cabin.

2) The Claíomh Solais was a person.
3) They were a weapon of some kind or could be used as one.
4) They *belonged* to Cole.

She struggled with point number four the most. How did one person belong to another? What exactly did "belonging" to Cole entail? Was the Claíomh Solais a slave? A weapon used at his command? That would squash any romantic feelings she held for him. Or was the Claíomh Solais something else to Cole? Something more? Maybe his kid? A child would explain Bear's instant protectiveness and refusal to make good on his deal with Luke, and it would explain Cole's determination to retrieve him or her.

She gulped.

Or, if the Claíomh Solais was female, was she Cole's lover? Wife?

Her stomach twisted. She needed to focus on getting out of Bane's Cabin of Doom, instead of asking questions she couldn't answer.

Escape first. Understanding later.

The moment Bane stepped out the door, she'd attempted to leave the glorified hut. As Luke promised, the entire place was spelled with a magical boundary. The only way in or out was with a portal disc.

Or a summoning.

At least she hoped summoning was an option. Bane had said the windows were spelled and she required a portal to get in and out, but he didn't say portals were the *only* way.

Raven needed to spill her blood. Cole had been quite clear about the requirement. Her teeth and nails weren't sharp enough, and the entire cabin was so well baby-proofed, Luke may as well have contained her in a padded jail cell. If only Megan's oldest son was around. He'd find something to cut himself within minutes.

The single random thought landed Raven in the Awful Person Category. Maybe she deserved to be imprisoned in Bane's creepy cabin. She didn't actually want her best friend's son detained with her and injured.

Outside the trees swayed, mocking her with their freedom on the other side of the sealed, unbreakable windows. Despite Luke's warning, she still pulled back the drapes and tried to wrench the double paned windows open. No luck. She tried throwing heavy objects at them as well, only to have them bounce back, crash to the floor, or in the case of the ottoman, hit her. She might've pulled a bicep as well, but if she got out of here and anyone asked, she'd deny everything.

Dark clouds rolled across the night sky and blotted out the two red suns. Luke had brought her to one of the Other Realms, but she didn't know which one. One within the Underworld, most likely. Beings from the Realms of Light rarely lowered themselves to cavort with mortals let alone allow dark fae lords to set up camp. The dark energy continued to pulse and twist inside her, more potent and stronger than before.

Someone had hung a vintage-styled plaque on the

wall that read, "Life is better at the cabin." Odin's blue balls. Had Bane lumbered in here, post war, in his bloodied armour with a small nail and hammer to hang this himself? Had he chuckled at the irony? Or had he whipped some poor fae servant to make the place "cozier" for his future prisoners? What else had the unfortunate employee been tasked with? What other supplies did Bane require for his friendly interrogations? Besides a medic.

Another idea crossed her mind and she raced to the simple, three piece bathroom. The air in the room was slightly cooler than the rest of the cabin and smelled of cleaner. Somehow, the idea of Luke Bane crouched by the toilet in his expensive suit to clean the base didn't ease her sense of impending doom.

Her reflection stared back at her. Mouth tense, brow furrowed and her normally poker straight hair cascading past her shoulders in waves.

Whelp. The curling hair confirmed it. She knew absolutely nothing about the Other Realms. Time to go.

She yanked open the cabinet under the sink and riffled through the contents.

Yes! A First Aid kit. She flung the red tin open. Gauze, bandages and tape...and childproof scissors.

Gah!

Raven dropped from her squatting position to the floor. Her butt hit the tiles with a smack. Her jeans stretched and the waistband dug into her stomach. Seriously? This guy thought of everything. The small windowless room with dull lighting closed in on her.

She held the blunt blade of the scissors to her fingertips.

The next few minutes proved just how well the "childproof" label was. With red, angry skin and a couple of developing bruises, Raven flung the scissors back into the cabinet and gave up. She'd managed to get a few tiny droplets of blood, but it wasn't enough.

She needed more than a sissy pinprick or scrape. Her ravens could attack each other, but most wounds healed when she shifted back to human, and she needed to draw blood and recite Cole's true name at the same time. A raven could mimic human speech, and she wasn't bad at it, but her human tongue stumbled over Cole's full name. Not that she practiced at night when she was alone, or anything.

Nope. That would be pathetic. She totally wouldn't...okay, she did. Every night.

Ugh. What was she going to do? She couldn't let Bear deliver the Claíomh Solais, whomever he or she was. It might save Raven, but she knew enough about Luke to realize Bear wouldn't walk away from the exchange alive. He'd tried to back out of a deal with the Lord of War, and that had consequences.

Bear had his faults, many faults, but none of those should carry a death sentence. Although not exactly altruistic, Bear wouldn't cross a client for just anything. He must've had a good reason. Justified or not, his death would tear a hole in her heart. She eyed her angry fingers and palms again. She'd do anything to keep Bear safe. She couldn't be under Luke's control to do that.

Raven drummed her fingers along the smooth bathroom tiles. The dark energy continued to swirl in her core, the essence she reached for when she shifted, thrummed in her veins. Each time she came to the Other Realms, it grew stronger, even if her visits were short-lived. After Odin's power blast, her awareness of her otherness had crystalized. The energy pulsed with each heartbeat.

Raven reached down and grasped the dark power. It swirled around her. Normally, it spiralled out and as the energy flowed through, her consciousness fractured into multiple ravens to operate like a hive mind.

Her brow furrowed. Little pebbles of sweat broke across her nose and slid down her face. Not this time. She needed one raven, and only one raven body part— something she'd never tried before. Would it even work?

As her power began its twisted ascent, she strained to keep the potency from breaking apart. Sweat ran down her back. Her head ached. The energy pushed against her guiding hold.

No! Stay.

She tensed and squeezed. The power grew and intensified, like a fast flowing river reaching a precipice. She attempted to contain and control the flow...with paddles too small for the job and no experience.

Her body hurt. Her heart throbbed as it thudded

hard and heavy. Just a little farther.

The energy ran into her right leg. Raven gasped. More power arrived, slamming into her foot. Pain lanced up her leg. She screeched.

Bear. Think of Bear.

The wind outside picked up, howling against the cabin in unison with her, mirroring her misery.

Her vision wavered. Her control slipped. No!

The agony eased. Instant relief flooded her body.

Scrambling, she gathered the power and directed it toward her foot again. The agony returned. She gritted her teeth. She clenched her jaw so hard a filling cracked. Pain exploded in her head. Blood coated her tongue. *Think of Bear.* She needed to get out of here to save him. Memories of her childhood with her twin surfaced. Bear pulling her pigtails. Raven pushing him down a deep ditch. Snowball fights. Car rides bickering. Playground tantrums. Bear hugging her after punching Thomas Lavé in the face for calling her "Plumpy Monkey." Her mind distanced from the pain, the intense ache washed over her.

As if she flicked a switch, the transformational energy took hold. Her boot ripped apart and the leg of her jeans tore as talons of a human-sized raven erupted from what was once her foot. Pale skin peeled back to reveal dark scales. The ghastly stench of raw flesh and magic hit her nose.

Raven panted and stared at her glistening black talons. The sight both beautiful and a hideous abomination.

Hopefully, she could reverse this.

Odin's shriveled scrotum! What if she couldn't reverse this? Her heart spasmed before pounding so hard, her ears thudded.

Deep breaths. Deep, deep breaths. Keep it together, Crawford. Think of Bear. Think of Bear. Her lungs ached.

Something metal clanked outside as the storm continued to gain momentum.

The air suddenly rushed out of the bathroom. The small room buzzed as a portal snapped in place in the living room.

"Oh, little Raven, where are you?" Luke crooned.

She didn't need to see his face to know he was smirking. Asshat. Had he returned with more kitschy plaques to hang? Maybe a singing fish?

Her skin prickled. With a grunt, she moved her still throbbing leg and ran one talon along the delicate skin of her other leg's calf. She winced as the sharp talon dug in and split her flesh. Blood ran out and splattered on the floor.

"Beul na h-Oidhche gu Camhanaich, I summon you," she whispered. Good thing she'd practiced his name, even if her reasons for doing so were embarrassing. Her cheeks grew warm.

Luke's heavy footsteps thumped around the living room. Then the kitchen.

"Raven?" he barked. He headed down the hall.

"In the bathroom. Go away." She slammed the door shut from her seated position and locked it before turning back to stare at her bleeding leg. "Beul na h-Oidhche gu Camhanaich, I summon you."

Luke growled outside the bathroom "Get out here now, or I'll break down the door."

Pretty sure at least part of that sentence was from a children's movie featuring a beast having a tantrum. Somehow the image of Bane as a beast prince didn't lighten the situation. Sweat ran down her face. Why hadn't Cole shown up yet? Could he hear her? Did she have to scream his name?

Luke thumped his fist on the door. The wood shook and the hinges rattled.

"Can't a girl pee?"

"Now!"

"Beul na h-Oidhche gu Camhanaich, I summon thee!" she cried.

Luke roared.

The shadows shifted. She scooted away from the shaking door and toward the growing darkness.

Luke rammed through the bathroom door. It splintered on contact. Wood fragments flew through the air. One sliced her cheek. He paused where the door once hung, his large muscular frame taking up the entire entrance. He looked down at her deformed leg. His eyes widened.

The shadows wrapped around her.

Metal flashed through the air as something passed her head toward Luke. Ninja stars, the metal reflecting the bathroom's dull light.

Luke grunted and stepped aside to avoid the

weapons. They sank into the soft wood of the door frame.

Before Cole whisked her away through shadows, she met Luke's angry gaze. The Lord of War stared back, furious, eyes glowing red as his tense body vibrated with malice. The promise of revenge in his dark expression was the last thing she saw before the shadows enveloped her.

Chapter Twenty-Four

"We're all searching for someone whose demons play well with ours."

~Meghan Coates

The shadows cleared like clouds parting to a bright, full moon, leaving Raven in Cole's warm embrace, in the middle of her small apartment. His arms tightened around her and his chest pressed against her back. Warm air swept against her neck with each breath he took. The sting from the cut on her cheek eased away. He ran the bridge of his nose against her ear, his satin lips brushed her skin. All the while, the gentle caress of his breath continued to massage her senses.

Tension flowed from her muscles. She grew languid in his arms. Her body molded to his own. As if stoking a flame deep within her, heat rose with each gentle touch, each a silent request for more.

Cole paused. "Has your foot sprouted talons?"

Warmth flooded her cheeks. She looked down. Her foot remained a large, grotesque deformity. She stiffened in his arms.

"Shhh." He ran his hands down her arms.

"I needed to draw blood." She gulped. "I...I couldn't find anything sharp."

Cole continued to stroke her arms. "Is this normal?"

"No."

"Have you tried—?"

"No." She sighed and forced the muscles in her shoulders and neck to relax. Her body slumped against Cole's. His strong arms tightened to support her, but his contact didn't disrupt her dark energy the way Bane's did. Instead, his own power pushed out and synched with her essence. Her head grew light and her vision swam, yet, she felt good. Really good. Like she'd done one too many strawberry liqueur shots in a row. Reaching inside, she found the dark potent energy of her ravens waiting and pulled hard.

When the chaotic call of the birds spiraled up, she embraced the power, riding it like a giant tidal wave. No longer fighting, or attempting to control and direct, she surrendered, merging with the darkness. Her body burst into multiple black bodies. Feathers flapped as her consciousness split between the birds. Like it normally did. Normal.

Thank the Banshee's left tit.

Cole stepped back and opened his arms, creating more room for the birds to spread their wings. His eyebrows shot up.

The corvids croaked and settled down and a calm familiarity swept through the group. They perched around the room, turning beady eyes to the dark wonder of Cole. In this form, his body wavered with the shadows, bending with the shifting realities.

He straightened and the corner of his lips tugged up. "Full of surprises."

Oops. He'd never seen her transform before. He must've assumed she had only one bird. Guess the secret was out now.

Like waves to a shoreline, Cole lured her ravens in. The shadows lurking around him pulled with invisible ropes. She yearned to go to him, to touch, to taste, to feel.

He held his hand out, palm up, in open invitation. The nearby lamp flickered in his dark, expressive gaze.

With a simple, single thought, her birds launched from their various perches and merged. The chaos slowed down until its manic twisting stopped and solidified. Her human body reformed, bone for bone, flesh for flesh, until she stood in front of Cole on two, normal-sized, human feet.

Naked.

The light in his eyes danced. His shadows swept in to surround them. With feather light touches, the darkness caressed her bare skin.

"We should talk," he said. His deep voice did little to break the spell of his magic. Instead, the rumble vibrated along her senses. The shadows ran down her arms and up her legs in warm, smooth waves—tempting, offering, wanting.

"I don't want to talk." Not right now. Not here. She didn't want to hear anything he had to say that might ruin this moment. He'd rescued her from a dangerous fate. He protected her. He helped her. She wanted to be his, if only for a night. Explanations could wait.

Cole took a step to close the distance between them.

"I want to feel," she whispered.

His mouth clamped on hers before she finished her breath. His arms circled her, and large rough hands pressed into her back. The shadows continued their slow exploration. Cole's tongue delved into her mouth. He tasted sinfully sweet, like a cinnamon bun slathered with icing—something she shouldn't have but inhaled anyway with no regard for consequences. She could, and probably would, feel guilty later. Maybe even regret rushing into things.

The dark energy ran up the insides of her thighs, igniting the sensitive skin with wicked promises. The shadows wrapped around them, a dark cocoon of exquisite energy. Her body lifted. Cole's hands explored her body, stroking, gripping, caressing. The air spiraled up. Her hair whipped around and the shadows released them by the foot of the mattress in her dark bedroom.

"Neat," she said.

Cole smiled against her neck and he trailed kisses down her body. She grabbed the hem of his shirt and tugged up. Cole grunted and pulled back far enough and long enough for her to slip the stretchy cotton over his head. Muscle corded his body—not I-work-out muscle, but the well-honed strength created from a lifetime of drills and fighting. His warm mouth and hands were back on her the second the fabric passed his face. The flow of shadows crashed all around her, rolling her like ocean waves.

When she was younger, a riptide caught her, tumbling her out to open ocean. Her lungs had burned with the need for oxygen and when she finally pulled to the surface and gulped fresh ocean air, relief had swept through her entire body. Cole felt a little like the breathless tumble of the riptide, but instead of fear, anticipation consumed her.

Cole's hands teased and tempted, demanding her nerves to respond. They lit on fire, burning her senses, pooling heat in her core and limbs.

She ran her hands along his broad chest. His skin was smooth and hot to the touch. She traced the hollows of his muscles and trailed her fingers along his back. She sat on the edge of the bed and kissed her way to the waistband of his jeans. Somehow, he managed to kick off his shoes and peel off his socks. She unclasped his belt and looked up.

Cole's gaze seared her own. Dark, swirling pools of black and gray. She pulled his belt free, sliding it past the loops, and tossed it on the floor. The belt buckle hit the thin laminate with a loud clank. Raw need stared back at her as she unzipped his jeans and pulled them down. They fell to the floor with a soft whisper.

Raven sucked in a breath.

Cole didn't wear boxers or briefs. He went commando and he was huge. His large erection jutted out. Before she could reach out and grip the thick shaft, Cole hauled her up and pulled her into his inferno of heat. His hands continued to stroke while his mouth explored, hot and wet. His forest scent curled around them as wave after wave of sensation rushed over her body. He stepped out of his jeans, now pooled at his feet.

In one seamless move, he splayed her over the bed. His mouth covered hers. His tongue delved in. He tasted of sin. His hard, naked body pressed her into the soft mattress. The shadow bands ran along her sides until they cupped her breasts. Warm pressure built. The shadows slid to her nipples and pinched.

Raven moaned. Cole caught the sound with his mouth. One hand smoothed the skin along her face before threading through her hair. The other travelled down her body. He propped up on a forearm. She wrapped her legs around his waist and tried to pull him close again.

He leaned back and grinned wickedly. His hand cupped her and all thoughts of trying anything fled. He explored her while he watched her face, gaze blazing. Her fingers dug into his back as the pressure built, waves continuing to roll, over and over again, until the pressure peaked and broke, crashing over her entire body. The tension released and bone-melting delight spread through her limbs, radiating from her core.

Cole's weight shifted and pushed her into the mattress again. His knees spread her legs as he settled between her thighs. The head of his shaft pressed into her. As she continued to ride the crashing waves of her first orgasm, he drove into her.

Raven gasped.

"Who's TDD?" he asked.

Who? What? Where? When? Why was he asking questions right now? Her brain barely functioned.

He waited.

Her body pulsed with need, his inaction agony to her nerves. More. She wanted more.

"You," she breathed. "It's you."

Cole's mouth found hers again, his lips soft and gentle, his tongue teasing, contrasting with the rough, hard rhythm he set. She ran her hands along his broad back and rippled muscles to his hard ass. With each pump of his hips, the muscles bunched. She dug her fingertips into the smooth skin, gripped and pulled him closer.

"What's it stand for?" he growled in her ear. The deep rumble sent vibrations down to her core.

"What?"

"What does TDD stand for?"

"Tall, dark and dangerous."

His lips curled up and he nipped the skin at her

neck. Not once did he slow his pace. This time the pressure built, hard and fast, intensifying with his increasing pace. Her release exploded along her skin. Raven cried out.

Cole's rhythm faltered. He gripped her hair and his head dropped to her neck. She clutched him as the aftershocks of her orgasm continued to rock her. Her entire body clenched and released, clenched and released.

Cole grunted and pumped into her a few more times, jerky and uninhibited as he came. For a moment, they lay there, panting. A thin sheen of sweat glued her body to his. She gulped in air. Her heart started to slow and her body settle. Her mind on the other hand whirled around at breakneck speed, trying to catch up with what just happened.

No! Don't think about it. Don't process. Don't overanalyze. Not yet. Her brain would ruin the moment. It always did.

Cole rolled to the side and gathered her in his arms. She relaxed into his chest. His heartbeat thudded against her ears. As she listened, it slowed to match her own, beating in tune.

Cole's fingers continued to run down her bare arm. His expression grew serious, his face drawn.

"What's wrong?" she asked. Oh hell. There was a whole lot of wrong with what just happened. No protection. No discussion about birth control or health screens. Sweet baby Odin, she was an idiot.

"Bane took you," he said.

Oh. Totally not where her brain went.

"I didn't like that." His hands stilled and gripped her skin. "I don't like that."

"I didn't like it either. He's pretty fucked up."

Cole tightened his grip. "What did he do?"

"Nothing. It's what he said. He suggested Bear was my soulmate. My own brother. The very thought is disgusting. The last time I checked, we're not in some twisted game for a throne." She ran her fingers along his arm.

"Raven."

"What?"

"Bear is your soulmate."

"Excuse me?"

Cole gave her a strange look—part sympathy, part exasperation. "Why is it so hard to understand soulmates aren't the same thing as mates for werewolves, or what your trashy fantasy novels depict? It means exactly as Huginn and Muninn said—you are two halves to the same coin. You're each other's match. You're twins for a reason. This ensures balance. Most Others are born as twins. The powerful ones at least. I think that's why Odin spared you."

"Are you a twin?"

He pursed his lips. "I do not wish to speak of my twin."

Geez. He probably offed him or her in some sadistic, pagan ritual to gain power. And she'd just slept with him. No. Not slept. That didn't accurately describe what transpired. Mind-blowing, reality altering, bone-melting sex.

She sighed.

"I don't wish to speak at all." Cole's gaze smouldered. His hands slipped down her body, gripped her butt and pulled her close again. "I wish to do other things."

"You're going to distract me with sex?" Oh, please. Yes.

"Is it working?"

"One hundred percent."

Raven rolled to fully face Cole. Something about him still called to her, even now, after what they shared. She should be sated and content, yet, she wanted more. She'd take everything he had to offer.

Cole's dark gaze met hers. Deep pools of melding shadows. She could fall into the depths of his soul. She'd drown there, undoubtedly, but she wouldn't put up much of a struggle. She wouldn't attempt to swim or stay afloat. She'd let the shadows rise all around her and let them consume her.

And that's what scared her.

"Cole?" Her brain finally screeched to a halt, fixated on a thought and poised to ambush this blissful moment.

"Mmm?" He ran his hand along her bare arm, smoothing down the goosebumps.

"Whose feather did I find in my brother's hideaway?"

His hand stilled. He took a breath. "Lloth. The Corvid Queen."

Chapter Twenty-Five

"If Monday had a face, I would slap it...with a tire iron."
~Raven Crawford, every Monday morning

Odin's ominous voice replayed over and over in Raven's memory as she worked. *Are you here for Lloth?*

Lloth, the Corvid Queen, ruled the Realm of Shadows. Did Cole work for her? The titles of queen and lord didn't translate well into Mortal Realm understanding of hierarchy, so though Cole was a lord, it didn't mean he served a queen. It meant he had a shit-ton of power. If the lords occupied a position of power or ruling, they were called queen or king.

Raven wanted to grill the Lord of Shadows on the

mysterious Lloth and why Odin would assume Cole was her messenger boy, preferably with clothes on, but then she glanced at the clock.

"Shit!" She had scrambled out of bed and found the closest, cleanest work clothes she could find. She pulled the polyester black pants over her legs and quickly buttoned her blouse. The clothes weighed no more than any of her other outfits, yet, every time she donned the work uniform, she felt heavier. Sadder. After throwing on her work clothes, she had stumbled to the door like a drunk sailor.

Cole had leapt out of bed and stopped her. "Have a quick shower. I can take you to work."

Now, she found herself at said work and though she'd grabbed the quick shower Cole offered, the deluge of mist-scented water didn't alleviate any of the bitterness from working at Dan's Diner or the uneasiness of Bear's disappearance. Here she stood, clad in polyester, tired, confused, a little scared and a lot angry. Not just at Cole for the unknown, and concern for Bear, but because of the twat-waffle who sat at table five.

"Where's your date?" Raven placed the loaded breakfast plates on the table in front of Robert. Nothing killed an after-sex glow faster than having to serve the ex she despised and his latest fling.

Robert glanced over his shoulder toward the restrooms. "She'll be out in a minute."

His overpowering cologne rose from the booth like a stink bomb and punched her nose. He reached into his man-purse, or murse, and pulled out a vape pen.

"You can't do that in here."

Robert's hand froze with the mouthpiece inches from his mouth. "Excuse me?"

"Put the douche flute away."

"It's just water vap—"

"Put it away."

He held his hands up, one still clutching the vape, in mock surrender. "Okay, okay. Don't get your panties all twisted up."

"Can I get you anything else?" Raven spoke through gritted teeth. If she clenched her jaw any more, she'd crack another filling. Robert had no say or impact anymore on her panties or how twisted they got.

Her ex knew she worked here. This awkward "run-in" was staged, not an accident. The sooner Robert found his balls and got to the point, the sooner she could tell him to fuck off and get on with her day.

"Listen," Robert started.

Finally. She winced as another oldies song serenaded the customers through the scratchy speakers.

"I'm glad I ran into you."

"Yeah, sure." The bright artificial lights paired with the summer sunshine streaming through the windows burned her eyes. She rarely worked days. She preferred the night shift.

"No, I am. I wanted to talk to you."

Her fingers twitched. She swallowed and ignored the urge to flap her hands in exaggerated circles for him to speed up.

Robert glanced at the restroom doors again. The clinking of cutlery and plates along with the general din of conversation almost drowned out Robert's next words. "I feel bad."

Aww, he wanted to clear his conscience. How nice. Unless it came with a cheque for fifty large, she wasn't interested.

Robert waited.

She sighed and rocked back on her heels. "About what, exactly? Leaving me with fifty thousand dollars in debt I had no way of repaying while you declared bankruptcy and somehow went on with your life with no apparent repercussions?"

Robert's gaze shifted back and forth.

"While I had to ditch my dreams to work day and night in order to pay off your loan and prevent the bank from going after my parents?"

"Well, actually..."

She folded her arms. "Oh. Not that?"

His cheeks grew pink and he looked down.

"Or do you feel bad for being a prick the other night when I brought in Mike for a cast? Your selfish little stunt could've cost Mike his ability to shift."

He opened his mouth to start speaking.

She held her hand up. "Don't bother. Although I'm surprised you made it through med school, which I'm essentially still paying for, your behaviour wasn't unexpected."

He shut his mouth and glared.

She placed both hands on the smooth surface of the

table and leaned in. "What you should feel bad about is knowingly showing up at my place of work and parading your latest lay in front of me with some sick pretense of *feeling bad* and wanting to talk about it."

"Sarah isn't my fuckbuddy."

Raven raised an eyebrow.

"She's my fiancée."

As if someone punched her in the gut, her stomach sucked in and the air flew out of her lungs. She straightened from the table. The air buzzed and her head grew light. "Has anyone warned her not to co-sign a loan with you?"

"I honestly do feel bad...for you." Robert's annoying voice broke through her fuzzy vision.

Wait. What? "For me?"

Robert nodded. "You're obviously still upset about how things ended. I should've provided better closure, and I should've told you about Sarah sooner."

The fuzzy film cleared from her vision, replaced with red. Blood red. A knife sat on the table mere inches from her reach. She could pluck it off the table, grip the cool metal in her hand and plunge the blunt knife deep in his chest in a matter of seconds.

She paused and ran over the option again. No. Knowing her luck, the knife would bounce off that awful gold medallion he insisted on wearing under his shirt, and she'd end up getting cut.

Robert waited for her reply, a serene smile plastered on his face. How had she not realized she dated a sociopath until now? Where did she begin to answer him?

Fuck off? Like she originally planned? No, too abrasive for work and not after he made it out like she was the one with the problem. Although, it would feel fantastic and he certainly deserved something offensive.

Don't be sorry for me, be sorry for yourself? Ugh, too childish. Too similar to "I know you are but what am I." She may as well kick his shin, stomp on his foot or stick out her tongue.

She paused. No. No. Not viable options either.

She glanced at the kitchen. Mike watched from the service window in his stained chef's whites with his good arm crossed over the one with the cast, offering silent support with a death glare aimed at the back of Robert's head. Dan wasn't in today. No regulars. Maybe she should go with the option number one anyway and tell him to fuck off.

"Who was that guy?" Robert asked.

"What?"

"The guy with you and Mike. Who is he?"

"He's none of your business." She clenched her hands and straightened her arms. Maybe she should kiss and tell. She certainly could list off Cole's bedrooms skills and the number of—

Robert shrugged.

"What?"

He fiddled with the fork in front of him. "Doesn't seem like your type, that's all."

Her scalp prickled. "I tried a sociopathic asshat, but

that didn't work out so well for me."

Robert's hold on the fork tightened. "That's uncalled for. You better—"

"I better what? You already screwed me over. What more can you do?"

Robert's gaze met hers. For once, she found something other than cold indifference there. Hate. Pure, simple, direct.

Her spine straightened. She might have called him a few names and spewed some swear words at him in the aftermath of their relationship, but last time she checked, she'd done nothing worthy of such uninhibited rage.

Had he always felt this way? Covering it up with his fake veneer?

"Hey, honey." Sarah flounced in. Wavy chestnut hair bouncing around. She leaned in and planted a kiss on Robert's pale cheek before sitting down. A subtle wave of fragrant flowers followed her.

Raven inhaled slowly. Huh. Not just flowers. Dirt and the faint tang of fur. So faint, Raven almost missed it, and probably would've if she hadn't lived with a skulk of foxes. Robert's fiancée was some kind of shifter.

"Oh!" Sarah's eyes widened as they fixated on the food. "This looks great, thank you."

"You're welcome." Raven managed a smile and turned to the obviously clueless woman. Not her fault she was engaged to a narcissistic jerk. Could she warn the poor thing without coming across jaded?

The brunette smiled and Raven walked away from the table. She'd finally off-loaded a lot of what she wished she'd said a long time ago. Instead of feeling elated, or simply relieved, though, confusion and doubt plagued her mind.

Had something happened between her and Robert? Something she was unaware of? Something that drove him away? Something that allowed him to feel justified and unapologetic for screwing her over? She'd labelled him an asshole and tried to move on with her life, while cleaning up the crap he'd dumped on her. What if all this time she'd been wrong?

Calm washed over her like a cool wave on a hot day. No. No she hadn't done anything wrong. Robert was a grade "A" jerk.

And just like that, the anger returned.

She walked through the kitchen, past her brother and the sizzling hamburger patties, and headed for the back storage area. Without a word, Mike followed.

"He...She...He said...So angry..." she sputtered.

Mike held his arms open and she fell into them. Despite his lean frame, his presence warmed her and helped ease the swirling emotions. Sometimes, family love was the best therapy. But as good as Mike's hugs were, she missed her twin.

Chapter Twenty-Six

"I'm getting tired of waking up and not being on the beach with a mojito."

~Raven Crawford, every morning

Still reeling from her run in with Robert, Raven watched from the counter and held her breath. One by one, each customer at table six stood and threw cash down on their separate cheques for each person. Normally, Raven hated large tables that demanded separate payment, but not this time. From the looks of the bills flittering through the air, they were leaving generous tips.

Raven bit her lip. She might actually have enough money to pay for her filling tomorrow instead of having to use credit. She'd called the dentist's office on her break before the lunch rush. The dreaded appointment needed to happen. Since she cracked her filling, mid-shift on the bathroom of Bane's Cabin-of-Horror, her mouth ached, and a constant throb plagued her gums. Food hurt to eat, and coffee hurt to drink. Raven was miserable.

The last member of the group stood up and smiled at his friends. "I have to use my credit card," he said. "I'll meet you outside."

No!

"Yeah, okay," one of the others said as the rest of the group headed out.

The last customer collected all the separate cheques and the money his friends had left and brought it to the counter where Raven stood.

No. She gripped a paper napkin in her fist.

He beamed a hundred-watt smile at her as if the sheer brilliance of his veneers would hide his true intentions. "I may as well put the whole thing on my card." He winked at her. "For the points."

Noooooooooooooo. She squeezed the napkin with both hands so hard it ripped.

The dreaded Seagull. Server Pet Peeve Number Three, not that anyone else cared.

Raven's shoulders slumped as she watched the man pocket his friends' cash and her hard earned tips with it. She balled up the destroyed napkin and chucked it in the nearby waste bin, before plucking the card from the seagull's hand. She ran his card and handed the slip over for him to complete. She didn't need to see what he scribbled on the little piece of paper to know he left her a shitty tip.

He smiled magnanimously again while he signed his name.

She managed a facial twitch and grunt.

He frowned, obviously unused to someone not falling for his charismatic demeanour and left the diner in a hasty retreat. The chime jingled with the door opening and closing and a blast of summer heat rushed into the diner.

Good riddance.

Seagulls were one of Raven's top pet peeves. They swooped in, gathered all their party's money including their generous tips, and then paid for the entire bill under the guise of wanting points, needing cash for something, or some other bullshit reason, when really, what they were doing was stealing from their friends and robbing the server of his or her tips in order to partially pay for their own meal.

Scammers. Fraudsters.

They could smile with all their pretty teeth as much as they liked, but Seagulls were thieves, and she could never be friends with one.

Raven snatched the credit card slip from the counter and scowled.

Sure enough, a ten percent tip. Each of his friends had left her at least twenty.

"Argghhhhh!" Raven clenched her hands into fists and snarled at the ceiling.

The elderly couple at table two jumped and turned their wary gazes in her direction.

Mike's head popped up at the service window. "What's wrong?"

"Another Seagull."

"Vermin."

"My thoughts exactly." She plucked some miscellaneous food from her blouse and turned to start cleaning and stocking behind the counter. The lunch rush had ended, and the diner was slowly clearing out.

"Are you going to tell me what else is wrong?"

She dumped the used coffee filter in the garbage and rinsed the holder out. "What do you mean?"

"Come on, Rayray. You haven't been yourself all day."

She rummaged in the supply cupboard for new filters. When she straightened, she hiked up her pants. In her haste this morning, she'd forgotten a belt and now her pants insisted on trying to slip off her ass every time she bent or squatted. She placed a new filter in the holder and avoided her brother's knowing gaze. She loved Mike but discussing her morning after glow wasn't happening. Ever.

"I mean, besides Bear missing."

With an expert tug, she ripped open a pack of pre-measured coffee. The smell of fresh grounds rose to caress her face. She closed her eyes for a second and inhaled deeply. Ahhhh. Though she knew from experience this particular brand of coffee tasted closer to trough water than delight, it still smelled like heaven.

She emptied the coffee in the filter and shoved the holder back into the coffee machine.

"And besides Doctor Douche."

Raven sighed.

"And finding out your biological father is really two mythological birds created by the God of War."

Raven snorted.

Mike's lips twitched. "Maybe I should ask what's going well, instead."

The tell-tale jingle of coins interrupted her response. Raven turned and watched the elderly couple pull out a large plastic bag of coins. She leaned forward and squinted. Small coins. Were those pennies? The one cent copper coins had been discontinued by the government and taken out of circulation years ago.

The man peeled the bag open and started counting the change. The coins flashed under the bright lights.

Yup. Pennies.

Mike slow whistled behind her. "Bad luck."

Raven's shoulders sagged and she continued to watch as the couple stacked the coins in neat columns. Each coin plucked out slowly made its way to a stack with a clink. *Clink, clank, clink.* Each tinker a nail in Raven's poverty coffin.

Raven swallowed a groan.

"Think they'll leave exact change?" Mike whispered from behind her.

"Of course, they will." Raven turned back to her brother. She generally had more tolerance for elderly shenanigans, especially considered the majority of them were on fixed incomes, but their payment option meant she'd have to sit in a booth rolling coins after her shift ended.

The elderly couple were the last in the restaurant. When they hobbled past the front counter, Raven smiled and waved, wishing them a pleasant evening.

When the door shut, Mike turned back to her. "So, what's up?"

"What do you know about Lloth?"

"The Corvid Queen? Not much. Why?" Mike wiped the sweat from his brow with his unharmed forearm.

"Just something Odin and Huginn Muninn said."

He tugged his stained uniform down and waited.

"Odin asked if Cole was visiting him on Lloth's behalf, and when I showed him the feather I found in Bear's safe house to Huginn Muninn, he confirmed it wasn't his. He suggested I ask Cole about it." Raven took a deep breath.

"And?"

"And Cole said it was Lloth's."

Mike's eyebrows rose. "What did Cole say when you asked him about Lloth?"

Raven wrung her hands in her apron.

"Raven?" Mike growled.

"We got..." She looked away and heat crept up her neck. "Distracted."

Mike groaned. "Are you kidding me? If you were in a horror movie, you'd be the one who'd jump in the serial killer's truck."

"That's not fair. While I admit, I occasionally have brain farts—"

"Raven. Your brain doesn't fart. It completely shits itself."

"That's crass."

"Crasser than getting too distracted by the bad guy's dong to say: 'Hey! Did your boss abduct and possibly kill my brother?'" Mike vibrated. "I told you we couldn't trust him."

"He said he wouldn't harm Bear. He swore a fae oath."

"That doesn't exactly protect brother Bear from others hurting him, now does it?"

Raven rocked back on her heels. Son of a banshee. Why did her baby brother have to constantly make logical points?

"He won't harm our brother, but he can get someone else to do it for him." Mike's face grew red. "He's the goddam Patron Fae of Assassins for fuck's sake."

"He wouldn't do that."

"Because you shared a moment?"

Raven clamped her mouth shut.

Mike sighed and some of the red in his cheeks drained away. "Cole is working with or for the Corvid Queen. She most likely learned the general location of Bear's safe house from your Prince of Penis in advance and used some hocus pocus magic to locate him before you arrived. The only question remaining is whether

Cole was complicit in her abduction of Bear or whether he's played you from the beginning."

As much as she didn't want to think Cole betrayed her trust, the idea of the Lord of Shadows being vulnerable or naïve enough for someone else to use him was unfathomable. Sometimes, the simplest explanation was the best one. Even if it tore her heart out.

Cole was a dark fae lord, and dark fae lords couldn't be trusted.

When the barrier between the realms fell, fae lords had been some of the cruelest Others. They had already squabbled and fought amongst each other, carving out realms within the dark and light domains to manipulate and preside over. The Mortal Realm represented new territory, and they scrapped to seize control. A lot of people died. If Odin hadn't stepped in, Earth would still be a battleground. Or maybe even a graveyard. Now, it was home for the mundane, and the supernatural, like shifters and witches, who'd already existed in the Mortal Realm.

The naming and classification of the realms and domains didn't make any logical sense. A hundred years ago, they were probably convenient, but now they misled the ignorant. The Mortal Realm implied the Other Realms were immortal. Fae lords and Others may have inspired the literary portrayals of fae, angels, demons, and even gods, but they could be killed, and they aged, just slowly. And although they were a mix of these mythical beings, and shared characteristics, they weren't the same thing. They were darker, and in some ways, more formidable.

Two main Other Realms existed, and they mirrored the Mortal Realm's religion and myths of heaven and hell. Beings from the Realm of Light, or Rollers, rarely cavorted with the mundane, but the Underworld was another circus entirely. Many smaller realms, including the Realm of Shadow and the Realm of War resided within the Underworld. It was a place of darkness, deadly deals and scandalous secrets, with promises of naughty sex, lies and everything in between. The dark realms held a certain appeal with the mundane, and many travelled there to seek their inner sinful desires. The fae lords, displeased with Odin's earlier intervention, brutally punished anyone who dared to enter their territory without permission or something to barter with. In other words, people entered at their own risk, and often paid for their stupidity with their life or servitude.

Not only had she slept with a powerful fae lord, she'd entrusted the safety of all her loved ones to him. Mike was right. A bad guy's dong had distracted her.

Only time would tell what the true cost of her actions would be.

Chapter Twenty-Seven

"My knight in shining armour turned out to be a loser in aluminum foil."

~Unknown, but also Raven Crawford,
after one beer too many

With everything else in her life going crazy—Bear missing, Cole's potential betrayal—she needed to keep some normalcy around her. What better way to stay grounded than to meet with her financial planner to discuss how broke she was? After all, she'd questioned her life choices repeatedly, maybe it was time to pull up her adulting pants and do something more proactively about it.

After her day shift ended, she dragged herself home

for a shower and change of clothes. Now clad in a T-shirt, shorts and flip flops, she walked to the local bank branch. The afternoon sun bore down on her and the heat from the pavement bathed her legs.

A heavy weight settled in the pit of Raven's stomach. Her financial advisor, Lucy, kept talking, but Raven's brain and pride had already taken a beating. At her current rate, she'd pay off the remainder of the fifty thousand dollar loan in another five to ten years assuming no more large financial burdens popped up their ugly heads.

Raven didn't need a reminder of her lousy run of luck.

Jean Claude was on his last leg, or tire, and she had a cracked filling to repair. If she wanted to go back to school and pay off this loan, she'd have to move back into her parents' place.

She sank farther into the chair.

She didn't see any way around it.

"Any questions?" Lucy asked. Her expensive lash extensions fluttered as she blinked and waited.

"No. No thank you."

Lucy's kind smile faltered. "You know, it's not my business, but..."

Raven straightened.

"Have you ever considered going after your ex-boyfriend in small claims court?"

Raven frowned. "I thought because he declared bankruptcy, he was essentially expunged of any responsibilities to pay off the loan."

Lucy nodded. "If you hadn't co-signed this loan, he'd still have to make payments depending on his income, but if he is making bankruptcy payments, it isn't being applied to this loan. So, with the bank, yes, he's off the hook, but not necessarily with you. I'm not a lawyer, so I'm not sure how it works, but it doesn't seem fair that he gets a slap on the wrist while you get saddled with one-hundred percent of the loan repayment."

Raven sighed. "No. It doesn't seem fair at all." Story of her life. "He gets to go on as per usual, and my life has been drastically affected."

"You said he's a doctor now? He could afford to pay you back."

Raven pursed her lips. Lucy had been helpful in setting up a manageable repayment plan with the bank and offering helpful financial advice over the last few years.

"But sue him?"

"I know it's not really the Canadian way, and it may not even be an option because he declared bankruptcy, but..." She sat back in her chair and tapped the forms on her desk with her pen. "It's not like he doesn't deserve it."

Raven snorted.

"At least look into it."

Raven dropped the boxes in her living room and let

the grocery bags and purse slide off her arms and shoulders. The weight didn't lessen. Sure, she could've slept on the idea of moving back to Crawford Central with a skulk of foxes. Sure, she could've dwelled and dawdled. But no amount of pouting would change the inevitable. Her need for independence and a place of her own prevented her from changing her circumstances. She didn't want to be a server for life. She needed to be proactive and take advantage of her parents' offer. Not everyone had a loving family to fall back on, so despite having the luck of a funeral director who purchased a mortuary the day before a zombie apocalypse, she was still more fortunate than a lot of other people. Now she had a little more than a month to enjoy the last of her independent living before she returned to her old room in her parents' basement.

The shadows poured from the edges of the room, pooling in front of her. The lighting dimmed.

Raven held her breath. She needed to talk to Cole, but she feared the answers he'd give her. She feared he'd distract her with his large, magnificent...

Focus, Crawford!

The shadows spiraled up into a tower. Beul na h-Oidhche gu Camhanaich stepped from the Shadow Realm to stand a foot away from her. Fully clad in fae garb, his leather and metal armour, and along with a billowing cape, emphasized his imposing stance.

She still wanted to pull him into her bedroom. Her gaze drifted down his body.

The shadow portal faded away and the late

afternoon sunlight streaming into her apartment returned.

His smouldering gaze scanned the room. He frowned. "Boxes?"

"I'm moving back to my parents' place." She kicked off her flip flops. They bounced off the baseboard with a smack and settled by the door.

"Does this have anything to do with not being good at *adulting*?"

"Sort of."

He folded his arms in front of his chest. One hand splayed across his other bicep. Those hands. Those masculine, strong hands had worked her body and made her moan. Heat crept up her neck to her face.

He cleared his throat.

"It has to do with taking back control of my life. I need to move home to pay off my loan faster."

"What did you buy?"

Raven nudged an overturned box with her toe until it stood upright. "A lie and a whole lot of heartache."

"Explain."

She rubbed her bare arms. "I co-signed a loan with my now ex-boyfriend."

Cole blinked. "The doctor?"

She nodded. "He needed money for med school but didn't qualify for a student loan, so I co-signed a bank loan with him because I was naïve and thought of it as an investment for *our* future. He defaulted on the payments and the bank came after both of us. Honestly, looking back, I doubt he had any intention of paying off any of it.

"He declared bankruptcy, but somehow avoided jail and kept his spot in med school after a hiatus. I didn't get off so lucky. They'd recently changed the law in Canada, so you're not considered financially independent from your parents until you've been living on your own for at least four years or you're over the age of thirty. Under the law, Robert was independent, but I wasn't. If I had declared bankruptcy, the bank would've gone after my parents. That wasn't an option. They would've lost the business and possibly the house, and frankly, I'm a grown-ass woman. I needed to fix my own mistakes."

"So, I dropped out of school and started working full time to make the payments. Shortly after all this ugliness unfolded, I discovered Robert was cheating on me with pretty much any woman who'd have him."

Cole's expression hardened. "You should've let me hurt him in the hospital."

"That wouldn't have helped Mike at all."

"Mike doesn't require medical assistance anymore." His body tensed as if ready to spring forward.

Raven straightened. The hairs on her neck stood up. He wasn't suggesting what she thought he was suggesting...was he?

"But I could make sure your ex does."

Oh. He wasn't suggesting, he was flat-out offering. Raven licked her lips. That would feel so good.

"Just say the word." Cole stepped in and plucked a strand of errant hair that had escaped her messy bun.

His earthy scent surrounded her. "Let me do this for you."

The tempting promises of the Underworld. Would she lose her soul if she took Cole's offer? Raven still didn't think of herself as a violent person, but the thought of Robert getting mauled by her fae lord lover sent warm fuzzies all through her body. Ah, the seduction of the Underworld.

She never understood how regs ended up making deals that landed them in servitude to a fae lord. She *felt* it keenly now.

Cole's gaze darkened. The gray bleeding out to leave swirling pools of black. She had no doubt he would disappear on her word and visit her ex-boyfriend. But it wouldn't be a sound beating, like he deserved. It would be annihilation.

Would he kill her ex? Leave him permanently disfigured? Extract money for her loan repayment and leave him destitute?

"So tempting," she breathed.

"He deserves it."

"Not arguing that, but..."

"That's not your way." He let her hair slip from his fingers. His expression softened. "Let me loan you the money."

Her brain stalled. "Absolutely not."

"We could sort out a less aggressive, more flexible repayment plan, and I wouldn't charge you interest."

Oh no. He was serious. "You don't even know how much I owe."

He shrugged.

Her tongue knotted in her mouth.

He stepped forward, now only inches away. He ran his finger down her face.

"I can't," she said.

He nodded. "It's not your way either."

She swallowed. Her body thrummed with need. His understanding and acceptance were more potent than his lethal prowess.

He leaned down to kiss her.

"What's up with you and Lloth?" she blurted.

Cole sighed and straightened. The air between them cooled. He took three steps to move from her entranceway to her living room and sat on her small couch. He almost took up the whole thing. He patted the cushion beside him. "I guess we should talk."

"Yes." Yes, talk. They needed to talk. Her body and heart wanted to do something else entirely, something requiring no words. She worked her wooden legs and moved her lead feet until she reached the living room. Luckily, she only had to take five steps. She plopped down on the couch and turned to face whatever he had to say.

"A long time ago, Lloth helped me rip a portion of the Underworld away to create the Shadow Realm. We were...involved. Romantically."

Her blood heated and spread through her veins like a toxic substance eating away at the tissues it passed. "And now?"

"And now we're not."

"But Odin asked about her."

"Fae have long memories and longer lives. The ancient ones lose track of time. To Odin, my relationship with Lloth was yesterday."

Raven leaned back into the cushions. "We're not related, are we?"

Cole started. "We are definitely *not* related."

Raven rolled her eyes. "Not you and me. Am I related to the Corvid Queen?"

He shook his head. "Not that I'm aware of."

"It's just that—" Her brain scrambled for the words. "You're both connected to ravens?"

Guess that was a bit obvious.

"Lots of Others have some sort of connection with corvids."

Mike's similar comments from a previous conversation flooded back. "Because ravens are connected with death?"

Cole peered down at her. "Not always."

"How'd she find out about Bear?"

Cole grunted. "Spies for the Others are everywhere. We already knew we weren't the only ones looking for the Claíomh Solais and your brother. Now we know who was behind the mercenary attack."

"Oh. I thought..." She looked away.

"You thought I betrayed you."

Well, technically Mike thought that, but she couldn't deny his reasoning. Instead, she fell into a pit of despair and self-doubt. "How'd she find Bear's safe house before us?"

"There's more than technology and PI tricks to find someone, Raven. Lloth is an adept sorceress. She uses death magic and corvid energy to fuel her spells."

His answers seemed so reasonable. The weight on Raven's shoulders didn't slip away, though. It intensified. She was missing something. Something she should ask but couldn't quite grasp. She'd love to accept his answers and melt into his arms, to let his shadows take her to a world of ecstasy and bliss.

"Why are you here?" she asked instead.

"To see you."

"Yes, but why?"

Cole frowned.

"I'm not an idiot, Cole. I know now you didn't really need me for information. You could've just followed me or found another 'adept sorceress' in the Underworld to help you."

Cole leaned back into the couch cushions. His hands splayed on the arm rest and along the cushion beside her. His large, capable hands. The same hands he ran along her body to make her nerves sing. He'd strummed her like a guitar.

Warmth crept along her skin. If only he'd reach forward and stroke her again. She wanted him on her, around her, in her.

But, somehow, she held back. Something kept nagging her. Like Mom when Raven didn't put her dishes away, the voice wouldn't leave her alone. Yes, he'd made sweet, sweet love to her, finding a magical rhythm all their own, but had he played her as well?

"You probably already tried the magical route, and when that failed, you found me. You're using me as bait, just as Bane intended. Although, I appreciate your gentler approach, I don't understand why it was necessary to seduce me. You'll get what you want regardless."

"*Get what I want?*" Cole's eyes narrowed. His lips flattened. "What is it you think I want?"

"I don't know, exactly. Originally, I thought you just wanted the Claíomh Solais. Now, I'm not so sure." She ran her hand along the worn fabric of her couch. "What are you really after?"

"You."

"No, seriously."

"I am serious."

He couldn't be serious. He had to be lying, somehow. Maybe he really was after her, but for some other reason. Maybe some twisted fae worship ceremony where he needed an extremely gullible half-fae woman to sacrifice as a tribute. "You should be with someone as powerful as you are."

"Who I *should* be with and who I *want* to be with, are two separate things, and I don't care about the former. Besides, you haven't tapped into your full potential yet. You could be powerful if you wanted to be."

"So, you're banking on my potential development into someone to fear?" Her skin prickled. She'd spent most of her life hiding her talent and using it sparingly. Now she could alter how she shifted. Did she have

313

other undiscovered talents? Would Huginn Muninn provide tuition to the Underworld's private school for underachieving halflings for her to reach her full magical potential?

"I'm not banking on anything." His deep voice rumbled over her skin.

An ambulance siren wailed down the street, intensifying as it passed her apartment before fading away. The bright flashing lights briefly illuminated the room and the fire sparking in Cole's dark gaze.

"I'm a fae lord, Raven. I don't think about *why* I want something. I *feel* and I take." His gaze smouldered like the hot embers in a bonfire. "And what I want is you."

"But...why?"

"I feel good when I'm with you." He reached over, gripped her arms and pulled her to him.

He moved so fast and smoothly, Raven blinked and found herself sprawled in his lap. His dark gaze danced with laughter. His hands slipped down to caress her back in warm circles.

Her heart fluttered. Her fingers itched to run along his satin skin, to reach out and thread through his hair, to pull his face, with all its hard angles, to hers.

"Who's the Claíomh Solais?" she asked instead.

Cole's smile faltered. His circles hesitated.

"I know he or she belongs to you, somehow, and Bane paid my brother to steal him or her. I want to know two things. No evasion. No distraction. How does one 'own' another person, and who is the Claíomh

Solais?" She bit her lip and tried to breathe through the crushing pain in her chest.

Cole sighed. "Both those questions have the same answer."

She crossed her arms and waited. Her scalp tingled. Maybe she should've asked these questions before she straddled the Lord of Shadows' lap. The urge to squirm against his thighs and groin rose. If she leaned forward and opened her arms, she could rub up against his chest and feel his strong arms around her.

Gah! This was important. Bear's survival depended on her. *Don't let the dong distract.*

Cole's hands slid down her back and settled on her hips. His fingers pressed in, then relaxed, as if he, too, fought the urge to do more.

"I'm waiting," she bit out.

"I don't own the Claíomh Solais. She's my sister."

Chapter Twenty-Eight

"Wouldn't it be great if we lived in a world where insecurity and desperation made us more attractive?"

~Albert Brookes

Raven sat in a plastic chair in the dentist's waiting room, Doctor Kim's office. Those three little words ignited a gamut of emotions. Now firmly in reality, instead of memory, the smell of latex gloves and antiseptics bombarded her. The strong scents brought the taste of bubble gum flavoured fluoride foam to her mouth as if it coated her tongue.

Raven gagged.

Her family hated this office because fox shifters smelled everything. Mike called Dr. Kim's the

"Burning Bone" place. Raven called it the only dental office open on Sunday mornings—a rare find, even in the age of alternate and extended business hours.

Raven waited in the plastic chair and pressed the heels of her feet into the floor to fight the gravity trying to pull her to the clinical white tiles.

She couldn't breathe.

How much longer? She glanced at the clock. Her appointment should've started ten minutes ago. That meant she'd been waiting here for twenty minutes in total. Half the torture of this place was the waiting, yet, she showed up early every time. Every. Single. Time.

The young girl across from her fidgeted relentlessly. Her pigtails swung with each head bob and leg swing. Her father sat stoically beside her with a pinched expression.

The high shrill sound of a drill travelled from behind the front counter.

Raven jumped and looked over at the desk. The receptionist made eye contact and smiled with perfect white teeth. "It shouldn't be much longer."

Raven grimaced and caught her reflection in the large mirror sitting on the front counter. Placed prominently, the dentists probably intended to show patients their great work. Right now, it highlighted Raven's pale and drawn face, with sunken eyes, dark bags, and pinched lips.

Not her best day.

Or week.

Or year.

She still had to process the Claíomh Solais bomb Cole dropped on her last night. His sister! Her name was Chloe and as his twin, she had a power complimentary to his own—absolute light.

Raven had asked if Chloe could shoot laser beams from her eyes. Cole hadn't found it funny.

Apparently, his sister had been staying in a secure compound in the Mortal Realm due to recent abduction attempts.

One day she was there, the next she was gone. It didn't take Cole long to track Bear down as the thief. He'd installed a multitude of safeguards against Others but hadn't considered a mortal theft. The hard blaze in his eyes suggested he'd never make that oversight again.

"Branwen Crawford?" A soft, comforting voice broke her thoughts. "Dr. Kim will see you now."

Raven's breath caught in her throat. A dental assistant wearing bright blue and pink floral print scrubs walked through the frosted glass doors to stand beside the receptionist's desk. With her blonde hair tied back in a tight bun, the young woman smiled brightly. "Right this way."

Raven swallowed and stood up. The skin on her thighs peeled from the plastic seat. She winced and pulled down her sale rack jean shorts before following the assistant through the doors. They passed stall after stall filled with patients sprawled on their backs on recliner chairs with their mouths gaping open. Professionals huddled over them with obscure instruments and mumbled dental jargon to each other from behind their masks. The drilling grew louder, and the potent smell of chemicals, cements, molds and scorched teeth intensified.

"Here we are." The cheery assistant waved her bony arm at an empty seat, resembling more of a contraption for torture than a medical chair.

Raven's throat tightened. Her stiff legs somehow managed to carry her the short distance to the chair where she sat. The bright lights above bore down on her. Her skin slid along the cool tan leather until the seat encased her. Dr. Kim walked into the room, sat on a short stool and rolled the remaining two feet to stop by her side. "Raven. How've you been?"

She placed her hands gently on the flat of her stomach and forced air into her lungs. "Fine, thank you. And you?"

"Can't complain. Can't complain." He tugged two latex gloves out of the nearby box and pulled them onto each hand with a dramatic snap.

Raven wasn't a doctor, but she was pretty sure the snap wasn't required.

"So. What brings you in today?" When the dentist chortled, his belly contracted and danced a little jig. His pinstriped shirt brushed her shoulder. He stepped on a pedal. The chair lowered and the leather groaned.

"I cracked a filling."

"Which one?"

Raven opened her mouth wide. Both Dr. Kim and his assistant leaned in, mere inches from her face.

"Dat un." She tapped one of the teeth at the back of her mouth.

"Thirty-seven," the assistant murmured.

Dr. Kim grunted. And ran his fingers along the tooth and the surrounding gums. The gloves made a squeaky sound. "Sensitive to hot and cold?"

Raven nodded. A pool of saliva built at the back of her mouth.

"Let's run a few tests." He pulled his fingers from her mouth but gripped her bottom row of teeth with his fingertips. She couldn't close her mouth. The saliva pool continued to build.

"No x-rays, please," she said. Or at least that's what she tried to say.

"No coverage?"

Raven nodded.

He winced.

The pool of saliva deepened.

"Let's have a closer look then and do a couple of diagnostic tests to make sure before we start doing any work."

"I see some wear right here." He reached for one of those pointy dental instruments and leaned over her face. He flipped down the two black magnifying glass extensions over his regular thick glasses and his owl eyes peered down at her. With a gleam in his eyes, he brought the tool to her mouth and poked her tooth.

Pain lanced down her jaw and neck.

"Did that hurt?"

Of course, it fucking hurt.

"How about this?" Poke. "Or this?" Poke. Poke.

With each jab and prod, she twitched uncontrollably. Her eyes watered, and the pool of saliva deepened.

"Let's try some cold."

The assistant handed him something ominous and he placed it on her tooth.

Cold encapsulated her tooth. Ice seared her veins. Her body jerked.

"Definitely some sensitivity there."

He repeated the process using hot water. Raven's body arched out of the seat. Sweat broke out along her skin. The pool of saliva threatened to drown her.

Dr. Kim sat back with a satisfied smile. "Yup. I think you have a cracked filling, and maybe some new decay." He pulled off his gloves with exaggerated snaps and tossed them in a nearby bin. "Now. Did you want freezing?"

Of course, she wanted freezing. Who in their right mind got fillings without freezing? She nodded and tried not to whimper.

Dr. Kim looked up at his assistant. "Let's get her started then. I'll check in with some of the other patients."

Raven drooped into the chair and swallowed the pool of saliva. The thick fluid slid down her throat slowly. Raven gagged.

"And give her some suction."

The assistant turned on the mini-hoover and stuck the plastic nozzle in her mouth. "Close."

A little late for suction. Raven closed her lips around the instrument anyway and let it suck up the remaining drool. The air rushed through her nose and left her nasal passage and the back of her throat dry. A headache bloomed behind her watering eyes and her mouth throbbed.

"I'll be back soon," Dr. Kim assured her.

That's what she was afraid of.

Sprawled in a dentist chair for forty-five minutes with no escape from the smell of her teeth being drilled down and packed with porcelain gave Raven some time to reflect on the information Cole unceremoniously dumped at her feet.

She couldn't blame him for wanting to protect his sibling. After all, wasn't that exactly what she was doing? If anything, his revealed secret gave her more of a glimpse at his true self. She understood him better now, and not only his motivation for finding the Claíomh Solais, but his tangible anger for the "theft."

"That will be fourteen-hundred twenty-nine dollars and fifty-five cents."

Raven dropped her wallet.

The receptionist's eyebrows rose to her hairline.

"Uh." Raven squatted to pick up her wallet. Her hands wrapped around the soft black leather. She straightened gradually. Her head still throbbed. The freezing in her mouth slowly wore off and made her swollen cheek prickle and tingle as feeling returned. "Sorry. How much?"

The receptionist repeated the same total. Clearly, Raven heard her correctly the first time, but her brain still stumbled over the total.

"Why is it so much?"

"Let's see," The receptionist clicked some things on her computer. "It was a 37MOD."

"And in English?"

"Three surfaces. If you look here, you'll see the charges broken down for freezing, supplies and the dental work."

"Didn't they just spackle the existing filling?"

The receptionist clicked something on her computer. "No. Says here, there was some infiltration and a new cavity site. They had to redo the entire filling."

Odin's left testicle. Doctor Kim had mumbled something about that from behind his surgical mask. "I, um...I'll put that on my credit card."

"Of course." The receptionist held out her hand and completed the transaction in record time. The slip streamed out of the machine, a visual confirmation Raven had been robbed of any disposable income for shopping or a night out. Ugh.

"Thank you," Raven said, though she didn't mean it. She smiled. Her puffy, half-frozen cheek responded sluggishly.

The receptionist recoiled.

Raven said goodbye, yanked open the door and

stepped into the heat of the summer afternoon. She had a short time left to enjoy the solitude of her own apartment and she planned to enjoy it as much as she could with a missing brother and no concrete plans to retrieve him.

Saliva trickled down her chin. Raven ducked into a narrow, dead-end alley and pulled out a napkin to wipe the drool away.

"Miss Crawford?" A shadow passed over Raven as a man stepped forward to block the exit.

Raven jumped and her head snapped up. Instantly, more throbbing bloomed behind her eyes. Drool ran from her swollen mouth. "Huh?"

The large man, wearing a simple shirt and jeans, neither of which fit him very well, stepped forward. A clear sticker with 3XL in black bold letters ran down the right pant leg. The sun hit his face, illuminating the paleness of his skin and blackness of his Other gaze.

Raven tensed.

He lunged forward. Heart racing, she dodged to the side. He was so broad, though, it made no difference. She couldn't go around him. His hands clamped over her wrists. His Other energy vibrated against her own, rattling it before squashing the power down. He pulled her roughly into his gargantuan chest. His shirt smelled brand new, like he'd pulled it off the hanger, ripped off the tags and threw it on five minutes ago.

Raven thrashed. Her legs flailed and smashed against his shins.

He grunted but held on. Like a manic boa

constrictor, his beefy arms squeezed her tight, the pressure unyielding.

She screeched for help.

He jostled her around so one massive hand slapped against her mouth while somehow pinning her body and arms. He rummaged in his pocket.

Sweat broke out across her skin. She was completely useless and ineffective against Tank man. Her heart hammered. She strained against his vise-like grip. His hand on her mouth shifted a little.

Raven wrenched her head up and sank her teeth into the meaty flesh of his hand near his thumb. She bit down. Hard.

The man yowled. He dropped the portal disc in his hand and grabbed at her hair. He pulled sharply, but she didn't let go. Flesh tore. Blood coated her throbbing mouth.

Pain exploded across her face. Her world tilted and she released her grip.

"Fucking bitch," the man seethed. He shook the blood from his hand and picked up the portal disc.

She teetered by his side, in danger of capsizing. Her head pounded. Her limp body sagged toward the concrete. She spat the blood from her mouth, and whispered, "Beul na h-Oidhche gu Camhanaich."

The man swore and threw the disc to the ground. Wind blew by them and whipped through her hair. A portal snapped in place. The powerful energy from the Underworld spiraled out and entwined with her senses.

A dark thick band of misty gray streaked out from the wall and Cole emerged from the shadows to stand between the man and the portal. His stony expression turned to Raven and searched her face. His gaze blazed.

He turned back to her abductor. "You will pay for that."

The man shoved Raven out of the way. She flailed as she slammed against the wall. Her head exploded with pain. Her stomach rolled. She couldn't shift now if she tried.

"Lloth wants the bird girl," the man growled. His clothing ripped as his body expanded. "It's unwise to cross the queen."

"I like my odds." Cole stood his ground, large and imposing. His lips tugged up in a small smile. Shadow bands darted out and circled them both. And then they were gone.

Raven staggered to her feet, now alone in the alley. Her heart convulsed. Her head hurt, and her legs stung from newly acquired scrapes. She bent to pick up her wallet. Her vision blurred. The man's one punch probably gave her a concussion. Great. Fan-flipping-tastic. This day couldn't possibly get worse.

Most people mistakenly assumed a concussion meant losing consciousness, but that wasn't the case. A person didn't have to get knocked out to sustain a life-altering brain injury. Robert had shared this little tidbit when they were still together. The only helpful thing she'd learned from the douche canoe...other than not blindly trusting your partner with your finances.

She stumbled forward and caught herself on the wall. Her stomach rolled again. Blood still coated her mouth. Leaning in she rested her forehead against the cool brick. A gentle breeze trickled down the narrow alleyway. The sea scent washed over her. Raven focused on breathing. In and out. In and out.

With a shaky hand, she pulled her napkin from her pocket and wiped the drool from her chin. The white paper-like material came back bloody. Hopefully, it all belonged to the other guy. If she cracked another filling because of this, she was going to be pissed. Maybe she could sue? Raven groaned. If she couldn't take her loser of an ex to court—she'd looked into the possibility after speaking with her financial advisor—she doubted she'd successfully sue Lloth's minion for damages.

Her whole body ached, and her lead-like appendages refused to move.

Maybe she'd stay here for a minute longer. Or two. Or sixty. Mike would be done with his classes soon. She could call him and ask him to pick her up in Jean Claude. That was worth the extra gas.

She pulled her phone from her other back pocket. Her hands shook. Her phone clattered to the ground. Raven sucked in a deep breath and turned to find it.

Cole stood three feet away. A swirl of shadows lifted the phone from the dirty ground and brought it to her. She plucked it from the air.

Cole remained still. His jaw clenched, his gaze fierce, his expression murderous. A thin red line marked the otherwise perfect skin on his neck.

He wore combat fae leathers and armour, a more simplified version of his court attire, yet, somehow more captivating. His cape billowed behind him. His disheveled ink-back hair curled around his ears.

Her body grew warm.

"Einin." His deep voice wound around her with a low-vibrating caress.

She sniffed and wiped drool away from her chin and lips again. She forced her mouth to move, but the words came out with a lisp. "What happened to the man?"

His open hands curled into fists. The shadows pulsed and rushed out from the crevice of the alleyway. They engulfed her.

"You'll never have to worry about him again." Cole's voice rumbled from every direction.

Her body sagged. Her head grew light and she fell. Cole's shadows caught her, pillow soft. He stepped forward and gently collected her in his arms. His hand stroked her swollen cheek.

"I hurt," she said.

"I know." He continued to caress her skin. "Do you want me to take you to the hospital?"

She shook her head and regretted it.

"Home? Your parents' place?"

"No," she whispered. The idea of sitting alone in her apartment no longer appealed to her and neither did an interrogation session from her family.

"If you want, I can take you away and make you feel

something else."

"Yes." She leaned in and rested her face in the crook of his neck. His forest at dusk scent surrounded them. "Yes," she repeated.

The shadows rose up to surround them, and their feather-light touch carried them away to the Realm of Shadow.

Gentle hands set Raven down in a shower. Cool air with a fresh meadow scent surrounded her. Cole reached behind her and turned the nozzles. A stream of cold water hit her back. She flinched. The water quickly turned warm, then hot. Scalding hot. Just the way she liked it. A cloud of heated steam rose around her. She kicked off her flip fops and clung to Cole, the smooth tiles still cool against her feet.

The dark energy of the Shadow Realm spiraled around her, drawing out her own power so, it pushed against the inside of her skin, and muted the pain.

Cole's gaze blazed under the soft lighting in the shower. He peeled her wet, sweat-soaked, blood-stained shirt from her body and flung it away. His mouth clamped on the smooth surface of her stomach and along with the hot water, trailed down her body, inch by slow, delightful inch. He pulled off her shorts. Cool air rushed over her. Cole's mouth instantly returned, chasing away the cold. Her panting and the sliding of Cole's hands along her wet body merged with the sound of water.

Her heart thudded in her chest, heavy and powerful, and the pain in her head eased. The phantom hands of Cole's shadows caressed and soothed, gently kneading at the knots in her shoulders. Cole removed the rest of his clothes, all the while, kissing and licking every peak and valley of her body. Fabric slapped against the tiles. Her breasts grew heavy. Her stomach clenched. His mouth travelled lower and lower. The promise of his skilled mouth sent shivers racing along her skin.

With each surge of dark Other power brushing her skin, the nausea and pain from her concussion and recent dental work faded away, driven to the background until it disappeared altogether. Replacing the pain, the beguiling pressure continued to ebb and flow, until it filled every cell of her being and demanded release.

Cole's breath fanned her core before his mouth explored. He watched her writhe in tune with his tongue. His dark Other eyes bled out to cover the white. They caught and held her gaze, hypnotizing and seducing. Water ran down his face and slicked his hair, dripping from the ends.

She leaned back into the tiled wall of the shower. A moan escaped her lips. Yes. There. He needed to be there.

His tongue plunged in. She cried out as an unexpected orgasm ripped through her. She arched against the wall and he gripped her hips. He continued to tease, taste and thrust with his tongue as the aftershocks of her orgasm travelled to the tips of her fingers and toes.

Her limbs grew languid. Her body, content, slid down the tiles. Cole slowly rose along her trembling body, his naked skin slid along hers.

He paused to caress the bruised and swollen side of her face.

"What happened to the man?" she asked.

His lips twitched. "That's what you're thinking about right now?"

"I need to know."

His face grew hard, cheekbones rigid, mouth compressed. "I killed him."

Not waiting for a response, he lifted her against the wall with her legs wrapped around him, flexed his hips and thrust into her, hard.

She gasped.

He caught her cries with his mouth and continued to pump into her. All she could do was grip his broad back, dig in her fingers and hold on. He'd killed a man for her, and she didn't even care. She couldn't find any emotion to feel other than the pleasure he stoked inside her and the safety he provided in his strong arms.

Chapter Twenty-Nine

"We are all broken...that's how the light gets in."
~Ernest Hemingway

Raven's face regained feeling two hours later, but this time the throb had dulled, and the headache and drooling stayed away.

"I thought you didn't claim healing capabilities," she mumbled. Her damp hair stuck to her face as she rested on a plush pillow in a cloud of bedding with a fresh linen scent.

"I said I didn't think I could claim that ability." He ran a finger down her arm. He rested behind her, spooning his body against hers. "Now I know I can...for you."

"You're better than ibuprofen."

"Don't tell your dentist. They'll try to bottle me." His mouth moved along the back of her neck. His warm breath fanned her skin and sent a shiver of goodness running down her spine. He'd carried her from the shower after toweling her dry. His muscles flexed and his hold tightened. He pulled her against his chest.

Spooning with the Lord of Shadows.

A lone, black feather rested on the nightstand closest to her. "Is that mine?"

"Of course." He dropped kisses on her bare shoulder.

He'd killed a man for her, and she didn't cower in fear or become plagued with guilt What did that say about her? Did that make her as heartless as the Others? Was she becoming the very thing her mom feared from the Underworld? Was her friend right to want the Other Realms separated from the mortal one?

Raven pushed the troubling thoughts from her mind. "Cole?"

"Yes."

"Can you get me an audience with the Corvid Queen?"

He sucked in a breath. "No."

"Why not?"

"She's crazy. Crazy and dangerous. Let me take care of this, Einin."

She tensed in his arms. "She has my brother."

"She might've killed your brother. Or your brother

might've escaped."

Raven shook her head. She refused to believe her indomitable brother was dead. Her brain couldn't compute that possibility. No body. Not enough blood. She needed to keep moving forward with the assumption he lived. She'd crumble otherwise. "She wouldn't have sent a thug to get me if he was dead."

"All the more reason to avoid her."

"I don't think she wants me harmed. The man you killed only hit me because I was hanging off his hand like a rabid squirrel."

Cole's arm relaxed. "I wish I could've seen that."

A question flickered in and out of Raven's mind. No. Not today. She needed to work through this and understand.

She turned around in Cole's arms. "We know Lloth found out somehow about Bear stealing Chloe. How did she use death magic to track him? Doesn't she need something of his?"

"She would've used my blood to track Chloe."

Ravens mouth snapped shut. She counted to ten. "How'd she get your blood?"

Cole's mouth pressed into a straight line.

She waved the question away. "You're right. I don't want to know."

Another question clicked in place. The question eluding her from before. She'd been asking all these "how" questions that she forgot to ask why. "Why did she steal your sister?"

"To control me," he said.

"She already has your blood. Isn't that enough? Can't she control you with that?"

"Not as well."

Raven took a deep breath. "Does she control you now?"

"Not in the way you're asking. She governs the realm I exist in."

Instead of the tension easing from her muscles, the tightening of muscles intensified. "Why does she want to control you?"

"I'm powerful, and she's crazy, which is why you should stay away from her. She feeds off corvid energy."

"At the very least, sneak me into her court."

"No."

She pulled away from the warm cocoon of his body, slid from the bed and searched for her clothes. They lay draped over a chest. Cole must've wrung them out and hung them to dry. He sprung from the bed to stand in front of her. One of his feet landed on her bra. It must've slipped off the nearby chest. "Just because she didn't want you harmed en-route doesn't mean she has good intentions."

Raven ducked down and grabbed her bra. She tugged. "I get that, but what she does have is my brother."

"Maybe." Cole folded his arms across his chest. His abdomen rippled with muscle which corded in a distinct V down to his groin. His groin, which hung very close to her face in this position.

She bit her lip. If she shifted her weight to the left, she could change the tone of this conversation with one flick of her tongue. She tugged at her bra instead.

He lifted his foot and released the strap. She sprawled backward and landed on her butt. Raven shook her head. Mike was right. She got too easily distracted by Cole's large, beautiful, silky-smooth, powerful...What was she saying?

Focus. She needed to focus.

"Can't you arrange some sort of parlay?" She clambered to her feet.

"Parlay?" His tone was incredulous. "We're dark fae, not pirates."

She scooped up the remaining pieces of her outfit.

"Raven."

"Cole." She pulled on her underwear and clasped her bra.

"You can't do this."

She pulled her shirt over her head. Still damp, the thin cotton clung to her body. "I can and I will." She shoved her legs through her shorts and yanked them up. Goosebumps pebbled along her skin against the clammy material.

"How?" Cole glowered at her.

"I'll find a way. I'm going with or without you."

"Right now?"

Raven checked the time on her phone. "No."

His dark brows bunched inward.

"Right now, I'm going to Sunday night dinner with the Famjam. Tomorrow, I'll figure out a way to reach

Lloth's court."

"I can't let you do that."

"You can and you will. Our deal was to work together to find my brother and your sister. We know where they are and who has them. I'm going to get my brother."

"I distinctly recall adding the caveat disallowing too-stupid-to-live moments. Going after Lloth falls under the TSTL clause."

"I'm asking you to come with me so, your point is moot."

"I'm not taking you."

"Then, aside from not hording your sister all to myself, which I have no intention of doing, I owe you nothing."

Cole growled and stepped forward. "Is that how you want to leave things?"

"Of course not, but I won't leave you to *handle* this."

"You don't trust me."

"Yes. No." She ran a hand through her hair. It snagged on a wicked knot. She winced and pulled her hand free. "I don't know. You haven't been fully honest with me and I think you're still hiding something."

He placed his hands on his bare hips. "Do I have any redeeming qualities?"

Her gaze drifted down. Nope. Not commenting on that. "I trust that you won't hurt my brother."

"But?"

"But as Mike pointed out, you can work around that

promise."

His eyes narrowed. "If either or both of us walk into Lloth's lair, we'll walk into a trap."

"Maybe. But I can't leave my brother's fate in someone else's hands. Instead of trying to stop me, you could help me so, I'm more prepared."

He shook his head. "I will not deliver you to the Corvid Queen."

"Fine." Raven folded her arms and looked away from the still naked Patron Fae of Assassins. For the first time since her arrival, she examined his bedroom. Old, heavy furniture with tufted backs, rich in textures and colour. He didn't have anything tacky like red satin sheets or a mirror on the ceiling. Instead, muted blacks, grays and whites tastefully decorated the room and covered the bed. Soft, natural light filtered into the room through the blinds.

The energy of the Shadow Realm continued to curl around her and call to her power. It hadn't stopped since she stepped out of the shadows with Cole.

Raven had no way home.

Cole continued to do his best fuming naked statue impersonation, as if the sheer force of his glare would change her mind.

No. She needed to get home. She couldn't allow his glorious penis to distract her any more than it already had. Her brother was injured and most likely held captive by a crazy Corvid Queen, and here she was going to O-town with a fae lord.

She cleared her throat.

Cole's expression shuttered.

"Will you put some clothes on and take me home, please?"

For a second, she thought he'd refuse her request. His calculating look suggested he considered the idea. After the longest twenty seconds of her life, he threw on some dry clothes. His shadows spiraled up and did their shadow portal thing and he dropped her off unceremoniously in her parents' front yard. His shadows withdrew, whispering threads against her skin, before carrying him away without a word.

No goodbye. Nothing. He was pissed.

Her stomach sank. What did she expect? She essentially told him, his dick, and his integrity to fuck off.

Her shoulders dropped. She was such an idiot. How could she let him go? Why did she have to push the whole Lloth thing?

Pepe bleated at her as she walked by. She patted his head. Though early evening, the sun still shone and heated the path. She dragged her concrete feet up the final steps to the front door.

Because Bear needed her. That's why.

"Rayray!" The door flung open and Dad stepped out on the landing. He scooped her up and squeezed her. "You're just in time."

"Like I'd miss roast night."

He pulled back and held her by the shoulders an arm's length away. His smile faded. "What the hell happened to your face?"

"Dentist, then failed abduction. I'll tell you about it over dinner." She left out the sweet, sweet loving à la Cole. There were some things dads didn't need, or want, to know.

His fingers dug into her shoulders. "Are you okay?"

She beamed up to his open and honest face. "I am now," she said, and meant it.

"Good." He hugged her again and pulled her into the warm comfort of her childhood home. The savory smells of butter, garlic and seafood floated through the air from the kitchen.

"What's going on? No roast?" Not that she was complaining. She loved seafood.

Dad grinned and led her to the dining room. Her entire family, minus Bear, had taken their seats.

"About time!" Juni shouted and reached forward to spoon some vegetables onto her plate.

Raven clamped her mouth shut and watched her sister dish food onto her plate. Juni, the notorious salad-dodger, voluntarily selected something green to eat. What in the Underworld was going on?

Mike rolled his eyes. "She's eating 'healthy' because Robby Feathermore likes 'healthy' girls." He used air quotes when he spoke.

"Who's Robby Featherhead?" Raven asked.

"Feathermore!" Juni burst out, then turned red.

"Whatever." Mike flapped his hand for the potatoes.

"He's just the most handsome, smart and—"

Mike groaned loud enough to drown out the rest of

Juni's adjectives.

"Hey." Raven poked Juni's neck. "Your hickey is healing nicely."

Her sister batted her hand away. "It was a rash."

"Sure. Sure."

"It was! The doctor figured it was the new detergent. Mom switched back and it's going away."

"Told you so," Mike bellowed from two feet away.

"Take a seat, dear." Mom smiled. "We have a special treat for tonight."

"Not that I'm complaining, but why?" she asked, taking the vacant seat beside Mike. Normally, Juni sat here.

A mild odour wafted from her brother. She leaned over and sniffed him. Body sweat, sugar and pizza permeated around his favourite metal band T-shirt in an unpleasant combination. Raven recoiled.

"When did you last shower?"

"Midterms are coming up. Back off." He glared at her and snatched the dish holding the fish from Juni. It looked like halibut, Raven's favourite. His gaze flicked to her damp shirt. The shower hadn't removed all traces of sweat or blood. He wrinkled his nose. "Like you're a bed of roses."

Raven slumped in her seat. She probably didn't smell too great after the dentist, failed kidnapping, and sexual healing session. The shower helped, but they probably picked up Cole's scent on her skin. Her face grew warm. *Please, please, don't bring up Cole.*

Cole's dark Other gaze flashed through her

memory, intense and focused as he held her in his arms and made her body sing.

Her heart convulsed. Sharp stabbing pains attacked her stomach. She pushed the painful memory away. She didn't want to revisit thoughts of Cole any time soon.

"To answer your question, dear," Mom said. "We're celebrating your decision to move back home. We're all very excited."

Mike coughed.

"That's not true," Juni blurted.

Everyone's heads snapped to her direction. Raven froze. What did Juni mean by that?

"Not the excited part, the first bit," Juni explained.

"You need to start making sense," Raven said.

A wicked smile spread across her sister's face. "Dad's exact words were, 'We're celebrating Raven's decision to stop being a stubborn mule.'" She deepened her voice to impersonate their dad perfectly.

"Sounds about right," Raven said.

Their mom sighed. "She didn't need to know the precise wording, Juni, dear."

Juni and Mom glared at each other.

"Oh, come on." Her dad beamed. "Dig in. We're going to have a *halibut* time."

Raven and Mike groaned, loudly, while Dad crumpled in a fit of giggles. Juni and Mom cancelled their staring contest and turned to Dad with wide eyes.

The banter continued as they ate. The sun set outside, casting the dining table in the soft glow of the chandelier above. Mom had begged Dad to buy one for years and he finally relented last winter. He hated the fixture and referred to the light as a monstrosity when Mom wasn't around.

If anyone else noticed the bruises and swelling on Raven's face, the blood staining her shirt, or Bear's continued absence, they didn't comment. Evidently, they were content to focus on the good in their lives instead of the lurking, but ever present, unknown.

Mom had cooked the halibut perfectly. The tender white fish melted in her mouth with buttery goodness. Raven sat back in her chair and soaked up the feeling of having her family surround her. Utensils scraped almost empty plates and the conversation lulled periodically while everyone focused on eating.

Juni gave up "healthy" eating five minutes into the meal. The remains of the "repulsive green things" pushed to the side, she now focused on shoving garlic and cheese mashed potatoes into her mouth with wild abandon to feed her fit and lean figure. If Robby Featherbottom, or whatever his name was, didn't like Juni for the awesomeness that she was, he could go kick some boulders with bare feet.

When did she become a young adult? Only moments ago, she was a rampaging child expressing every single one of the five thousand thoughts flying through her brain and asking Raven what her third favourite dinosaur was.

Mike grunted and tossed in burns whenever the conversation needed it. Although he'd always be her baby brother, Mike was well on his way to becoming something greater than she could ever hope to be. He just needed a shower.

Though the dining table lacked the ominous empty chair, one voice, one presence was notably absent. No one asked Raven for an update on the investigation. Bear had stopped attending Sunday night dinners almost a year ago, but now his absence was involuntary, and as much as his withdrawal stung before, his current absence bore a hole in her chest. It hurt.

Her gut twisted. Stomach acid bubbled up her throat. If she didn't find a way to extract Bear from the evil clutches of the Corvid Queen, she'd lose her brother forever.

She gripped her dinner knife. No. Losing Bear was unacceptable.

"Raven, dear. What's wrong?" Mom asked.

Everyone stopped talking and turned to her.

"I, um." She forced her fingers to uncurl and placed the knife gently on her empty plate. "I miss—"

A knock on the front door interrupted her.

"I'll get it." Juni leapt from the table and bolted to the front door with a grace and speed defying the amount of food she inhaled.

The front door opened and cool air from the summer night flowed into the dining room. The sound of voices murmuring traveled down the hall.

"Raven!" Juni called out. "It's for you."

Raven frowned and pushed away from the table. Who the heck would come to her parents' place for her? One, she didn't have much of a social life to begin with, and two, the few friends she did have would text her, not show up unannounced during Sunday night dinner. This time with her family was sacred.

Her chest tightened. Cole? Had he changed his mind? Or did he decide to patch things up after their argument?

She turned the corner and walked down the hall. Juni moved to the side, her smile wide, her gaze gleaming with a side of crazy.

What was wrong with her?

Two warriors stood at the threshold. They wore similar fae garb as Cole, but not as fancy, and certainly not as dangerous looking. Their dark Other gazes assessed her coldly as she completed the final steps to meet them. The air thickened near the door and she moved through a soft bubble of space. Magic billowed around the entrance.

Wait. Why had she kept walking? Why hadn't she cried out a warning?

The answer hit her in the face. Because a skulk of foxes wouldn't hold up long against two experienced fae warriors, and she knew her family well. They wouldn't run. Not when Raven or Juni faced danger.

Her scalp prickled more and more with each step she took toward the dark fae warriors and the Underworld energy radiating off them.

"The Corvid Queen commands your presence," Warrior One said in a deep gravelly voice. Unlike Cole's sensual voice, which held dark promises, this guy's voice sounded like it had been beaten up one too many times during sword practice. He didn't whisper. Nor did he peer over her shoulder to check for the cavalry. The entrance must be spelled.

"Come with us now, without a fight, and we'll leave your family unharmed," the second warrior said in a matching tone.

Raven glanced at her spelled sister and gulped. Dark Other magic curled around Juni's throat in a silent threat.

Raven stretched up on her toes to peer over the warriors' shoulders to the dark yard outside. No spite goat. No Cole. No guards.

"Camhanaich's assassins will be of no help to you," Warrior Two said.

Well, fuck. What did that even mean? Had Cole pulled the guard detail in a silent tantrum, or had Lloth's warriors neutralized them?

"Decide now."

There was no decision to make. Raven stepped to the side and kissed her sister on the cheek. "I love you."

Juni blinked and her smile widened.

With her heart wedged like a giant, halibut bone in her throat, Raven straightened her spine, pulled her shoulders back and stepped forward.

Chapter Thirty

"It's Thursday...or as I like to call it: 'Day four of the hostage situation.'"

~Unknown, but probably a fellow hostage

Raven's neck ached as she looked up and took in the tall, dark towers. The black brick gleamed in the moonlight. The nearby ocean crashed against the rocky shore. The castle perched ominously atop a cliff, which dropped down to the tumultuous water below on all sides save the entrance. The offshore breeze teased her hair like a lover's fingers and carried hints of the sea and soft summer florals. Ravens, magpies, jays, crows and other birds she didn't recognize circled the spires and entrance to the stronghold of Lloth, the Corvid Queen.

A loud groan echoed across the ravine. Wood creaked and chains clanked as the drawbridge shuddered and lowered.

The birds croaked and continued to soar overhead.

Raven smoothed her sweaty palms down her shorts. With this setting, she would've preferred something more fae-ish, like a glorified bustier, some kickass knee-high leather boots and a cape. Definitely a cape, and definitely not sporting bedhead while wearing some ugly shorts and a shirt soaked with dried sweat and old blood. She needed a wardrobe overhaul. Sure, it was summer, but she wore the same look almost every day.

Her scalp prickled. Odin's dried nuggets...she was turning into her dad.

"Come," One said. "The Corvid Queen awaits."

Raven shook her head. She should be worried about survival right now, not clothes. Why couldn't she focus like normal people? She ran through her mind and made a list of why the Corvid Queen shouldn't chop her head off.

They pivoted without another word. Raven's legs refused to move. She froze where she stood, lock-kneed and tongue-tied. The warriors on each side of her gripped her arms tighter and hauled her down the bridge. Her lead feet dragged against the iron and stone. Her heart hammered in her chest. Cole's constant warnings played through her mind. She shook them away. After Cole's refusal to seek an audience with Lloth or help infiltrate her lair, she'd decided to find a way to sneak in and steal her brother. Now, she didn't have much choice in how she met the big, bad, and psychologically unstable Queen.

Time for Plan C, whatever that was.

Stay positive. Her brother might be here, and she wanted, needed, to see him safe. There still might be a way out of this. She needed to keep her head clear and not dwell on the circumstances.

They walked in silence through the courtyard and grand hall entrance. The ceiling opened to the night sky and natural red moonlight shone down. Though open to the outside, the delicate smell of flowers faded, overpowered and replaced with iron and something menacing. Pillars and walls of black brick and flooring of midnight granite composed the ominous décor. Their footsteps echoed ahead of them. Beady eyes of the corvids perched on the ramparts tracked their progress.

She'd never seen so many ravens in one place. Their essence pinged against hers.

Her heart convulsed. Bear? Had he called them here as a sign, or had the Corvid Queen? Although she intended to visit this court, she'd planned on fully researching Lloth before making an entrance.

Did Lloth know what skills Bear possessed? Dread slithered up her spine. The Corvid Queen fed off raven energy. The implication of Cole's words smacked her in the face. If Lloth learned of Bear's ability to call the birds to him, she'd never let him go. He'd provide her with a bird buffet of power.

At the end of a black runner, a woman sat on a throne constructed of large metallic feathers. They fanned out behind her. When she stood, her black gown flowed around her, seeming to melt into the floor like a cascade of falling ink. Her black hair, pulled up behind her in intricate braids, accentuated her severely angled brows and stern expression. Her black Other gaze remained trained on Raven.

Familiarity smacked Raven in the face. The snooty mystery woman from the restaurant. The Corvid Queen had lowered herself to enter Dan's Diner to scope out the competition, and Raven had been so clueless she tried to serve her.

"Branwen Crawford." The queen's silky-smooth voice rolled down the steps to meet them. A voice of seduction and dark promises. She could lure young men to their demise with her sultry voice.

Raven gulped. Bear? No. No. She refused to believe her serial-dater of a brother would fall for a sweet voice. Grandma Lu raised them better than...Cole's voice strummed her memory. She gulped again. Or maybe not.

"We haven't officially met. I am Lloth, the Corvid Queen of the Shadow Realm. Welcome to my court." She reached down and plucked a large scythe with a skull etched into the metal from where it rested against her throne. The blade was as long as Lloth's body and probably just as dangerous.

Raven nodded. This chick didn't seem so bad, so far. Her fashion choices were on point.

Silvery gray mist streaked through the room from the walls and crashed together a few feet from her. A familiar forest scent flooded the air, along with blood. Cole stepped out of the shadows, wearing a scowl and similar attire as he had to Odin's court. This time, instead of the male embodiment of fatal shadows, he appeared more regal, the matte black metal replaced with shining silver.

He studied Raven and his jaw clenched. His mysterious scent flooded the room.

What was he doing here? He said it himself—if they walked into Lloth's lair, they'd walk into a trap.

His hand clutched the light brown, blood-caked hair of a severed head. The man's glazed-over eyes were wide, and his mouth gaped open in a perfect "O." Blood dripped from the cross-sectioned neck and hit the dark stones with tiny splats. He looked vaguely familiar.

"And who's this?" Lloth tittered and pointing the scythe at the decapitated head. Light reflected off the sharp point of the weapon.

"A former employee tasked with guarding something of importance to me." Cole chucked the head down the black runner. The surprised expression on the dead man's face turning over and over as the head tumbled along the ground with sickening wet thumps until it settled at the base of the stairs to Lloth's throne. "And a traitor."

Raven winced with each thud. At least she no longer had to wonder how Lloth's men got past Cole's assassins.

The queen studied the severed head before turning to Cole. "Camhanaich."

"Laidain." He hissed.

The queen smirked and sat back in her throne, resting her arms on each side. "Beul na h-Oidhche gu Camhanaich, Lord of Shadows, master of darkness..." She paused, letting her voice trail off in the middle of his accolades.

Cole grunted.

She continued. "Minion of the Corvid Queen."

Chapter Thirty-One

"I have licked the fire and danced in the ashes of every bridge I ever burned, I fear no hell from you."

∼Nicole Lyons

Raven's heart plummeted. Her stomach twisted into a knot. Cole was Lloth's minion? A foul taste coated her mouth. Betrayal. So, this is what it tasted like. No wonder he refused to help her.

She swallowed and avoided Cole's gaze when he turned to her. Heat flooded her cheeks. Her hands balled into fists. Her muscles tensed. Memories of their time together flashed through her mind. Had it all been a lie?

Lloth's gaze moved from Cole to Raven. "Oh, don't

worry, little raven. Or should I call you Einin, like he does?" She leaned forward and squinted. "You're not the one betrayed here."

Wait, what?

Surprise shocked the overwhelming pit of sadness pulling down her heart only moments before. Cole hadn't betrayed her? What did that mean? She whipped her head toward Cole.

His jaw clenched.

He'd knowingly walked into a trap. For her.

"You appear confused." Lloth smirked.

"Uh." Huge understatement. Raven balled her hands in the thin cloth of her shorts.

"When I learned of your abilities, I asked Cole to bring you to me." She paused. "He didn't."

Raven gulped.

"When asking didn't work, I ordered him to bring you to me."

The fire in her veins cooled.

"He still didn't obey and chose instead to ignore me. Then I compelled him..."

A hollow pit grew in her stomach. Cole had warned her about the Corvid Queen and her questionable sanity. He may as well have double-dog-dared her to go ahead as planned, though. Fear of the unknown paled in comparison to fear of her brother's death.

Lloth rose gracefully from her chair again. "Even then, my minion defied me. Turns out, he was my minion in name, only, and *somehow* evaded my control. His formidable acting skills granted him access to my court, and...sensitive information. I don't know why he needed this ruse, but I intend to find out. I should thank you, little raven. I never would've discovered his betrayal and duplicity, otherwise."

The Corvid Queen shook her head and slammed the end of the scythe against the stone floor of the dais. The sound echoed down the grand hall.

Cole drifted toward her while Lloth turned away. His gaze raked Raven's body, as if searching for damage. His eyes narrowed, his jaw clenched again.

A door to the left opened and guards ushered two figures into the room. The red-tinted moonlight illuminated the black cloth bags over their heads. The large brawny man she recognized on sight. Raven didn't need to see her brother's face to know him. The dark energy inside her vibrated with more intensity the closer her twin got. It always did that. She'd recognize him in a dark room, blindfolded.

He stood stiff with his shoulders slightly hunched. He wore a pair of jeans, but no shirt. Bear rarely flaunted his muscles. They must've shredded the clothes from him. Black ink marked his body with symbols. Raven leaned forward. She had minimal knowledge of runes, but they looked like amplifier and connection symbols from her textbooks. Not good.

The other figure, long and lean, with ebony skin and snow-white hair cascading down her back from beneath the hood, walked with a lithe grace. The Claíomh Solais. Cole's twin.

She wore jeans and a tank top. Unfamiliar runes in

white marked her arms and collar bones.

Cole swore under his breath. "Chloe."

The woman straightened and her covered head snapped in their direction.

"You would use absolute light to control him?" Raven risked another glance at Cole. The Lord of Shadows' eyes blazed.

"The brightest light casts the darkest shadow. She cannot control Cole, she empowers him." Lloth considered Cole, gaze raking his body up and down. "The only reason Camhanaich doesn't rule this realm is because he chose not to, and it was my price for helping him. Now, I will harness his power and bolster my own claim."

This woman was really crazy if she thought she could control Cole. Raven paused. If Chloe's power couldn't be used against Cole, then why had the trinket Luke threw on the floor like a kid in mid-tantrum worked? Maybe momentary surprise? Raven replayed Lloth's words. Cole's explanation of soulmates pinged along her neurons. That's what he was getting at. Did Bear empower her as well? He certainly couldn't be used to control...Oh. "You'll control him by threatening to harm his sister?"

Lloth tilted her head back and giggled delightfully. The twinkling, bell-like sound grated Raven's nerves. "You understand. That is good."

Raven frowned. Good for what? Lloth wasn't a friend of Raven's. If the Corvid Queen thought something was good, it probably meant something very,

very bad for Raven.

Cole's scowl deepened. He stepped toward the queen. His shadows coiled around him.

"Uh, uh, uh." Lloth waved her forefinger back and forth as if scolding a child. The runes on Chloe flashed.

Cole froze, his gaze calculating.

"I'm so glad you understand the importance of twins," Lloth turned to Raven and prattled on.

"Imagine my delight when I arrived to retrieve Chloe and found a gem all on his own. So ignorant to his own power, he hasn't learned how to wield it. I could sense his twin nature immediately and Cole's reasons for hiding you became crystal clear. Your power is so unique I changed my plans." She licked her lips.

"You plan to threaten my brother to control me, too?" Raven's voice cracked. Damn. That would work.

Bear stiffened.

"Silly child." Lloth giggled. "I plan to destroy you and control him with your power."

Cole's warnings of Lloth's sanity continued to beat Raven's brain cells to a pulp. She wanted to punch Cole in the gut. Why couldn't he just say Lloth was the big bad villain?

Okay, so maybe he did, and she already figured that out. But why hadn't he mentioned how Lloth still thought he was her minion? He could've explained how he had a connection to her court.

Then again, would the information have changed anything?

"You swore to serve me," Lloth growled at Cole, completely ignoring Raven and the impact of her last words. Lloth's dark gaze flashed. "But that's not quite true, is it?"

Cole's expression said he didn't like where this was going at all. Join the club. Raven hadn't liked this situation the moment Cole used a pet name for Lloth. And she really stopped liking this little visit when Lloth explained her plans to kill her.

"You swore to serve the 'Compeller of Corvids.' I thought it sweet that you used one of my titles, now I know the reason. You somehow changed your allegiance to this little hatchling, didn't you? No matter. I will rip the corvid energy from her inferior body and leave your latest infatuation a dry husk. You will serve me again. You will bow to my commands."

Whoa, hang on. Not only did Lloth plan to kill her, but she body shamed and insulted her, too? Raven balled her hands into fists. She needed a way out of this. How could she overcome this tyrant? How could she twist things to her advantage? There's no way she could physically flee unless she shifted into her conspiracy.

That would do it. Assuming Lloth couldn't control her or consume her corvid energy when she was in that state, she could fly away.

Movement near the dais caught her attention.

Raven sucked in a breath as a guard removed the hood over Bear's head. Her body tensed. Her brother's dark Other gaze met hers.

Nope. No fleeing in bird form. She couldn't leave her brother with this madwoman. There had to be another way out of this for both of them.

They'd removed Bear's contacts, probably forcibly. He'd never take them out voluntarily. He hated having the eyes of an Other. He said he didn't have the power to back up the look.

Her brother stood twenty feet from her, with the doodles from a psychotic bird queen slathered over him in black ink, like some raver at a foam party. A dark bruise marked his left cheekbone, and the left side of his face looked swollen.

Bastards!

Anger rippled through her body. She clenched her fists. They'd pay for this. The dark energy inside her surged up. She choked the power down. Shifting into birds and flying away might save her, but it wouldn't help anyone else she cared about.

"Cole," a woman's delicate voice drew Raven's attention away from her brother. She hadn't noticed the other guard removing the hood from Bear's female companion.

Light where Cole was dark, and dark where he was light, Chloe appeared the polar opposite of her brother. Even her voice—light and twinkling, like a fairy on ecstasy—contrasted with his deep rumble. Instead of standing large and imposing, her slender frame appeared willowy, as if a gust of wind would knock her over. Only her dark Other gaze resembled her brother's—deep and powerful.

"If only you stayed with me," Lloth tittered. Her lean figure swayed on the dais at the top of the stairs, as if she fed off the conflicting emotions in the room and found them overwhelming.

"Now you shall be mine for good." She flicked her finger at Chloe, and the runes flickered again. Chloe cried out.

Cole tensed. His mouth clamped shut and his shadows drew in around him.

Raven had no knowledge of runes, but Lloth's actions needed no explanation. She'd threatened Chloe's life. Cole couldn't interfere. He couldn't help Raven. She was on her own.

Lloth held her hand out toward Bear. The runes on his skin glowed.

Bear grunted.

Lloth swayed more, like a lethargic top hat. The more Bear's runes glowed, the more she rocked. The metal blade of the scythe glowed.

The dark energy inside Raven, the source of her power and Other nature, pulsed. This close to Bear always seemed to heighten her awareness, but now, with him glowing, her power burned.

Ravens croaked as more corvids swooped into the room from the dark summer night above. Bear's expression grew pinched. Yes, he tapped his power to bring them here, but not by choice. Cole said she fed off corvid energy, and her brother's power provided the queen with her favorite food.

No wonder the Corvid Queen wanted him. No

wonder Lloth wanted Raven. Her life probably looked like a fat cupcake slathered with icing to Lloth.

"Yes!" Lloth screeched. She threw her hands up in the air, still gripping the weapon. "More."

Raven gulped. Like standing in front of a tsunami, overwhelming helplessness consumed her.

Cole stepped forward.

Lloth's head snapped back. 'One more move, shadow scum, and your sister's life ends." To emphasize her point, she held her hand out toward Chloe.

The Claíomh Solais gasped.

"No." Cole clenched his jaw and rocked back on his heels. He glanced over at Raven, a war of emotions battling in his deep gaze.

Of course, he'd choose his sister. Raven would pick her sibling, too. She couldn't hate him for the same decision she'd make if their roles were reversed. Twins before wins. Always.

Sweat poured down her brother's face as hordes of corvids flooded into the grand hall. The Otherworld energy within her twisted and spiraled, aching to emerge, to be set free. The Corvid Queen continued to sway, gaining energy and sucking up power.

Raven clenched her hands. Like she'd stand here and wait for Lloth to smite her.

"More!" Lloth repeated. Her skin grew dark and her gaze lit as she turned to Raven. All the while, Bear's runes glowed as he continued to call the corvids to Lloth's castle.

Raven's shoulders slumped. With her brother acting involuntarily against her, how could she possibly defeat Lloth?

Bear shook his head. She wouldn't have noticed if she hadn't been glaring at him. Maybe he used Lloth's power to call more birds to him, but not because he *had* to, but rather he *wanted* to. Why would he—

She was an idiot.

Luke and Cole's comments about soulmates rebounded against her skull. Proximity to Bear always made her stronger. Lloth wasn't the only one capable of feeding off Bear's power. She'd never tried to use Bear's skills to amplify her own, but there had to be a way. Her energy pulsed to confirm her suspicions.

If Bear was her soulmate and being close to him made her stronger that meant distance made her weaker. Raven groaned.

She really was an idiot.

All this time, she was losing her birds, not because she was growing older, or sick, but because the distance and divide between her and her brother continued to grow.

"I shall absorb your power." Lloth grinned at her. "Eat it like the tasty morsel it is. Consume it. Master it. And with your brother by my side, I shall be invincible."

Absorb it.

More corvids poured into the room. Bear visibly trembled. His lips compressed and grew white.

Lloth cackled. She waved her arms around and

recited arcane words. The energy in the room grew and called to Raven's power.

Cole tensed beside her. When she glanced over, his gaze contained no fear, only calculation. Did he have a plan? Should she wait for him to save her? Grandma Lu's groan vibrated in her skull.

No.

Crawford women saved themselves.

She refused to stand by helpless and meek while some power-thirsty psychopath consumed her powers and used her brother as a magical battery pack. No. Just...no.

Raven reached down to where the corvid essence lurked deep within her and pulled. Instead of combusting into a large flock of ravens, she pushed the chaotic power to her extremities, and directed the dark energy. Controlled it. Like she had at Luke's cabin, she guided the power to her limbs. The flood of power continued. Pain sliced through her body. She gasped as the corvid essence took hold.

Cole yelled something.

Lloth cackled.

The pain intensified and Raven's body convulsed uncontrollably.

A portal snapped in place somewhere behind her, the shock of power and suck of air unmistakable.

Raven bent over as the pain hammered her senses. Her energy continued to pulse and flood her limbs.

A dark figure walked through the portal. From her crumpled position, she made out his feet, outfitted in warrior boots. The familiar soft scent of cologne washed over her.

"An interesting development," Bane mused. A raven's feather fluttered to her feet. Not one of hers. Lloth's. "You left this helpful clue at your place."

"Too late!" Lloth squealed. "You're too late!"

"Am I?" Bane mused. "I think the show has just started."

Lloth's energy looped around Raven like a demented lasso and pulled. Raven lurched forward, her power still within, but pushing against her skin as if it would burst from her instead of transforming her.

Too much.

Sweat ran down her face. Her heart punched against her breastbone.

Too much power.

Lloth's magic pulled again. This time, it reached inside and sank its hooks in. With each pull from the Corvid Queen, everything within Raven tried to go with it, as if her spine and organs would physically rip out of her body. With each tug, the sensation grew stronger. Lloth would literally wrench out Raven's power to consume it. No wonder Lloth needed to amass power, instead of just gutting Raven with a sword like a normal tyrannical overlord.

The tugging didn't relent. Raven bent over again and threw up. The remains of her celebration dinner splattered the hard flooring and splashed her legs. *Not having a halibut time now, Dad.*

Dad's warm face flashed through her mind,

followed by her mom and siblings.

"Fight, Einin!" Cole hissed from somewhere to her right. "Fight or you lose it all."

Anger welled up along with what remained of her power. How dare he tell her to fight when he stood by her side as useless as her shadow.

"Yes," crooned Bane. "Fight."

Banshee's bastard! The Lord of War's not-so-original advice didn't make the situation any better. He probably got off on it. Sick fuck.

Lloth's power pulled again. Her skin stretched and ached. One more pull and she'd rip apart.

"Use it, little raven." With Bane's words, another energy coated her skin. Scalding, hot, angry power seeped into her skin. She yanked the power in and wound it around her own twisted energy. She reached out and grasped Bear's as well, wrenching it to her core.

Her brother grunted.

Her body vibrated with power. Her vision blurred.

When Lloth pulled again, Raven used the tug and pushed her energy out. Her skin tore. Her power burst from her human body. She screamed. Her mind cracked, threatening to fracture.

No!

With the last ounce of effort still remaining, Raven molded all the power she held. Her body contorted. Bones snapped. Flesh compressed and expanded. Pain stabbed at her skin. Her stained shirt and shorts tore as her body ripped through them like paper. Feathers and scales sprouted. In an instance, her raven essence

365

wiped away what remained of her human form, leaving a large bird in its place.

Larger than Luke and Cole, she towered over the men and women in the room.

"Holy fuck," her brother whispered.

Dark energy radiated from her bird chest. Her blood thrummed with potent power. The Others in the room glowed with their dark essences, the pulsing light a beacon to her heightened raven senses.

Lloth stood, arms out, eyes wide. Her rambling citations cut short. Her followers screamed. Their footsteps slapped the black marble as they fled from the room.

Without hesitation, Raven launched in the air and pumped her wings to move toward the Corvid Queen.

"No," Lloth sneered. She turned toward Raven and raised her scythe, and evil smile spread across her face. She opened her mouth and mumbled a dark spell. The metal of her weapon glowed and pulsed with the swirling Underworld magic.

Lloth's dark gaze cut to the side. She broke off her chant. Abruptly, she whirled around as Cole materialized from the mounting shadows.

Time slowed. Raven's vision narrowed to surgical precision. She hovered above the queen. Cole stepped forward from the shadows. What was he doing? If he attacked Lloth, he risked his sister's life.

Bands of gray snaked around Lloth's wrists. Cole's hand darted out. Silver flashed under the moonlight. Lloth twisted to the side.

Time resumed its fast adrenaline racing pace. Cole's dagger sank deep into her chest, inches away from her heart. He missed.

"Traitor!" Lloth bellowed. She staggered, her back toward Raven and dropped the scythe. The weapon clattered to the ground.

Raven pulled her wings in and dove. She had to help. Failure wasn't an option. They'd pay for the slightest mistake with their lives.

Lloth threw her arms wide, shrieking ancient words.

Raven swooped down. Wind rushed against her face as her strong beak cut through the air.

Lloth turned and gasped. She flung her hands up and screamed.

Raven opened her enormous beak and clamped onto Lloth's head. The queen's skull jammed between her bills like a fragile sunflower seed.

Lloth thrashed and pummeled her fists against Raven's feathers.

Dark energy curled around Raven like a cocoon. This dark fae had planned to kill her and use her brother. Her beak snapped shut.

Bones crunched. Fluids and tissues exploded on her tongue. Lloth's body shuddered. The queen dangled, body limp, from Raven's beak.

Raven opened her mouth and what remained of Lloth fell to the floor with a sloppy wet slap. The dark energy drained from Raven's body. Her limbs grew heavy. Her body withered in on itself, shedding feathers and excess skin. Her fatigued human form slumped to the slick tile.

Raven took in the bloody mess in front of her and fainted.

Chapter Thirty-Two

"I look like the girl next door—if you happen to live next to an amusement park."

~Dolly Parton

A shadow fell over her. Through tears, she looked up. Her stomach rolled. Blood coated her tongue, metallic and tangy. Lloth's blood.

What in the Underworld had she done?

Luke Bane, Lord of War, stood before her, on the other side of Lloth's limp and bloody body. His stance relaxed, face smug. He held two swords, both dripping blood. The prone bodies of what remained of Lloth's loyal guards lay on the floor behind him. Lloth's court reeked of death.

Raven glanced down. Blood. Gore. She swallowed the rising stomach acid and quickly looked away. Her brain scrambled to make sense of the deformed remains of Lloth. Raven's head grew light, and her vision swam.

She *killed* someone.

Bane cleaned his swords with the cape of a fallen guard before sheathing them. He squatted beside her, completely unfazed by her naked, blood-spattered body, and ran a finger through the pool of blood by his feet.

Cole straightened from another guard's prone body a few feet away, bloody dagger still clutched in his hand. Cole and Bane had dispatched at least ten guards together while she lay vulnerable on the blood-soaked floor.

Cole grumbled something in fae before cleaning and sheathing his dagger. He walked over to Raven wearing his shadows as a shroud and side-stepping bodies. His cloak dragged against the stones and hung heavy with blood.

She gulped.

Cole crouched beside Raven, unclipped his cloak and draped it over her shoulders. His intoxicating scent embedded in the thick cloth surrounded her, providing comfort as the cloak provided warmth. She drew the surprisingly soft fabric around her, held it close and ignored the damp hem.

Bane brought his hand up to examine Lloth's blood as it ran down his finger. He tsked and shook his head.

"Little Raven." Bane shook his head again. "What

have you done?"

Cole straightened and Bane's gaze travelled up as he mirrored Cole's actions, his relaxed stance gone.

"Do we have a problem here?" Cole asked.

Raven wanted to laugh. No, she wanted to puke, roll up in a ball, cry...and then maybe laugh hysterically, while rocking back and forth and clutching her childhood doll. A problem? She had ninety-nine problems and no idea how to deal with one. Cole's question, phrased like a line from a cowboy standoff in a bad Western movie, seemed so inadequate for the situation.

Bane chuckled and shook his head for the third time. "A problem? No. You've just handed me the solution."

Bane continued to laugh as he turned on his heel and walked toward a waiting portal.

"Wait!" she called out.

Bane paused.

"My brother? Spare him." Her voice quivered more than she would've liked.

"You will owe me a favour."

Bear shook his head. "I'm not worth it, Rayray."

Oh, shut up, you big idiot.

"Done," Bane said.

Bear groaned in unison with Cole. Whatever. This was her brother. Her twin. She didn't need to think about it or hear all the reasons against agreeing to Bane's offer. Just as she didn't need time to make a decision when Lloth's guards showed up at her house and threatened her sister.

Bane's gaze briefly cut to Bear, who stood frozen with Chloe. "Consider him safe from retribution."

A deep sigh escaped her lips.

"My mercy is payment for a favor owed."

She nodded, not trusting her voice.

Without a goodbye, Bane walked into the portal and disappeared. It snapped shut behind him.

"That was a mistake," Cole grumbled.

"Could you have kept Bear safe indefinitely from the Lord of War if he wanted him dead?"

Cole's jaw clenched.

Relief flooded her. She'd made the right choice. Now, alone in the dead queen's moon-illuminated hall with only her brother, Cole and Chloe, Raven's shoulders dropped. Tension eased from her muscles.

When were these Others going to make sense? Bane had wanted the Claíomh Solais to defeat Cole. He didn't leave with her, and Cole stood nearby perfectly healthy, so why... Her gaze drifted down again to the pile of gore on the black floor. Her stomach rolled again. Understanding clicked in place. Bane's ultimate target hadn't been Chloe or Cole at all. It was Lloth. He'd wanted to use Chloe to force Cole to kill the Corvid Queen, and Raven had unknowingly completed his dirty work for him. Maybe he should've spared Bear's life as payment for her taking care of his business.

But why would the Lord of War want to kill Lloth? And why wouldn't he just kill her himself? He was more than capable, wasn't he? He cleared the guards with Cole in the time it took her to regain consciousness. The more she figured out about the Underworld, the more unanswered questions she had.

Cole's hand fell on her shoulder—large, warm and oddly reassuring.

"Come," he said. "I need to get you and Chloe to safety."

A half-naked man streaked through the air and slammed into Cole. The two large men tumbled over one another. Their bodies hit the hard floor with a loud thump. Bear snarled and threw punches at Cole's body. The impact thudded in the empty hall. Cole growled and shifted his weight to one side, throwing Bear over his shoulder. Her brother's body slapped the blood slathered tiles. Cole rolled with him to land on top of Bear.

"You can't have her!" Bear roared.

"She's my sister, you idiot." Cole's jabs hit Bear's sides with loud thumps. "I was protecting her, not caging her."

"Oomph." The air from her twin's lungs rushed out. Bear curled up and groaned.

Cole continued to pound his fists into Bear's body.

Bear covered up and grunted, attempting to dodge and shift away from the hard impact of Cole's strikes.

"Cole!" Raven shrieked. The sound came out two-toned. Raven spun around.

Chloe stood with her arms crossed and glared at the men. "That's enough."

Cole stalled his fist and paused. In one swift movement, he stood and loomed over Raven's twin.

Bear scowled and slowly stood. Although his name gave nothing away of his supernatural abilities, it fit his physical prowess perfectly. Tall, broad, and heavy with bulky muscles, his shoulders were twice the width of hers, and his trunk three times as thick. Her brother was a massive hulk of a man. Now that she'd met Huginn Muninn, Mom's Scandinavian god-like blast from the past, his physical features made more sense. The likeness between Bear and Odin's spawn was striking, and a little unsettling.

Bear brushed off the dirt from his skin. Blood streaked his chest and the paste used to draw the runes had smeared, making war-like stripes along his torso.

Raven's headache returned. Her mouth throbbed and her limbs grew heavy as if she carried fifty-pound dumbbells in each hand. When would this be over?

"I love Chloe," Bear announced.

Raven blinked. Say what?

"You can't take her from me," her brother said.

Chloe and Raven sighed in unison.

Cole's eyes narrowed. "Like I said, I'm her brother. I have no intention of fighting you, nor any plans to harm my sister."

Deflated, Bear stepped back. "Why'd you keep hitting me then?"

Cole's lips spread into a nasty smile. "Those shots were for your sister."

Bear turned to Raven. The creases around his eyes

relaxed. He took three giant steps and held her in his strong arms. His wooded glen scent wrapped around them and the dark energy inside her hummed. He spoke into her hair, his voice muffled. "Rayray."

With that one word spoken in the soft tone he reserved for her, Bear apologized.

"Brother Bear." She accepted and squeezed her brother before releasing him.

"You're a shitty brother," Cole said.

Bear nodded, his expression drawn. He stepped away from Raven, leaving her cold, to face Cole again. "I am. I hadn't realized how much I hurt her or myself with my absence. I will make it up to her."

Raven started to tremble, then shake. Her vision started to dance. She grit her teeth and fought through the light headedness.

"You better." The shadows drew around Cole, surrounding him like a liquid threat.

Bear straightened and pulled his shoulders back to face Cole.

"How about instead of posturing with one another, you take us home?" Chloe stood with her hands on her hips. "I want to scrub off your psycho ex's doodles, and Bear's sister looks like she's about to fall over."

They all turned to Raven. The light in the room intensified and flared, receding to black. Raven's mind drifted and her body went limp. Instead of hitting the hard, blood-coated stones, the familiar touch of Cole's shadows surrounded her.

Epilogue

"According to a recent survey, men say the first thing they notice about women is their eyes. And women say the first thing they notice about men is they're a bunch of liars."

~Jay Leno

After dropping off Bear, Cole took her home without a word and after assuring him she was "just fine," he promptly disappeared. She might've told him to fuck off. Her memory of the drop-off was still a little hazy.

Now, showered, fed and too amped on adrenaline to sleep, Raven made tea and settled in her dark living room. Alone.

Raven still didn't know what to think about Cole. The mere thought of the Lord of Shadows sent heat racing through her veins. On the one hand, he'd kept the full extent of his relationship with the queen secret. On the other hand, he'd tried to warn her, and he'd risked his sister's life and his own to plunge a dagger into Lloth. The queen's last-minute distraction proved to be the opening Raven needed.

Her heart warmed at Cole's act to protect her. If their roles had been reversed, she wasn't sure she'd risk Bear to save the Lord of Shadows.

Memories of their time together streamed through her mind. Her body clenched.

Ugh. Why did her mind have to contradict what her body and heart wanted? Why couldn't she just feel and live in the moment like Cole apparently did?

Maybe because she only had one human life span to get things right?

She grabbed her mug and stood abruptly. Her baggy pajamas whispered against the worn fabric of the sofa. Rain pinged on the metal roof and splattered hard against the road and her small deck outside. Her top floor apartment was far from a penthouse, but it allowed her easy access to the sky with relative privacy. Sure, she normally drove to remote locations to shift, but emergencies happened.

The steam lifted from the fragrant water in her mug. She inhaled deeply and let the tension ease from her shoulders.

The shadows in her apartment shifted. Her skin

warmed as the dark curled around her. The feeling of seclusion dissipated.

Once, she'd beckoned Cole to step out of the shadows and drive her loneliness away.

Now?

Now, she wanted to reach into the shadows and haul Cole to her. But she hesitated. Her ignorance of the Underworld had almost taken her life and her brother's freedom. As much as she wanted to melt into Cole's strong embrace and the world of dark pleasure the Lord of Shadows offered, she couldn't. A little voice kept nagging her of the potential costs. She knew too little about Cole and his world.

The Underworld was her world, too, the world she'd been born into.

The niggling voice continued to poke her brain. If she had a truly honest moment, she also didn't fully trust Cole's reasons for being with her. He could have his pick of fae women, powerful or otherwise, and mortal women alike. Why would he settle for an out-of-shape, over-worked, broke waitress with a history of making poor decisions? His choice made no sense.

Lloth had said he swore to serve the Compeller of Corvids and somehow changed his allegiance to Raven, or as Lloth referred to her—the little hatchling. Is that why Cole showed interest? To form some sort of bond that allowed him to escape Lloth's shackles? Was she a means to an end or something more?

And why was her attraction to the Lord of Shadows so strong? Did it have to do with Cole switching allegiance to her or did twin nature create some sort of weird twin attraction? Bear's adoration of Cole's sister couldn't be a coincidence. Had Cole used some sort of Underworld love potion on her? Or had her heart jumped in with two feet...brain and past lessons be damned?

The shadows caressed her skin, a voiceless request.

"No," she whispered. "You're not invited. Please leave."

The shadows withdrew, pulling away from the room and from where she stood. Leaving her. A light caress, much like the pressure of a lover's fingers, ran gently along her face.

She whirled at Cole's touch. Only her apartment's regular shadows remained. The feeling of company faded. Cole had left as requested.

She placed her half-finished tea on the kitchen counter and sighed. Time for bed. Her dad had texted regarding a new job in the morning. Life went on. Bills kept coming.

With heavy feet, she padded to her bedroom. She froze in the doorway. There, placed on her pillow, lay the Scythe of Lloth. The soft bedroom light glinted off the skull pattern etched into the metal surface.

The scythe not only held painful memories, it carried a silent promise.

Cole would be back.

~The End~

Did you enjoy reading Conspiracy of Ravens? Please help this author out and tell someone or leave a review. Your support is much appreciated.

Raven and Cole's story continues in
Nevermore
A Raven Crawford Novel. Book Two.

RAVEN'S LIST OF SERVER PET PEEVES

1) Campers

2) Split cheques for large groups

3) Seagulls

4) Finger snappers and wavers

5) Unwanted comments about appearance

6) Old people with bags of coins

7) Vegans

GLOSSARY OF TERMS

Reg: A "regular" human being from the Mortal Realm without any supernatural powers or skills.

Regulators: An organized group of regs who despise Others and hold meetings to bitch about the unfairness of life.

ROL: Realm of Light. An Other realm full of rollers who look down on everyone else.

Rollers: supernatural beings from the Realm of Light

The Underworld: An Other realm, often in direct conflict with the Realm of Light. Contains multiple, smaller realms, such as the realms of War and Lust.

ACKNOWLEDGEMENTS

I'd like to thank Katie and Nathan Guskjolen for all the fantastic trapping information, Alicia P.W. and Meredith M. for their help with Gaelic pronunciation, and the ever-fabulous Cindy RN for the nursing and hospital information. Though this book contains scenes involving a few nurses, one of whom demonstrates less-than-professional etiquette, I personally have only love and respect for nurses.

I'd also like to thank Karilyn Bentley, Katie O'Sullivan, Charlotte Copper, Nicole Flockton, and Hannah Myles for beta reading, Lara Parker, as always, for editing and putting up with my Canadian ways, and Tammy Payne for proofreading.

Any errors contained in this book are my own, despite my best efforts to research and consult experts, and everyone's best efforts to steer me in the correct direction.

Thank you to Eerilyfair Design for the incredible cover, and most of all, thank you to you, the reader, for trusting me with your precious reading time. I hope you enjoyed this story as much as I enjoyed writing it.

ABOUT THE AUTHOR

J. C. McKenzie is a book-loving, gumboot-wearing, unapologetic science geek. She's the author of the Carus Series, an urban fantasy five-book saga published by the Wild Rose Press. Born and raised on the West Coast, J. C. sets the majority of her books in the Lower Mainland of British Columbia, Canada. She writes urban fantasy and paranormal romance with sassy heroines and brutish, alpha-type men.

Visit her at www.jcmckenzie.ca

Amazon: www.amazon.com/author/jcmckenzie
Blog: jcmckenzie.blogspot.ca
Goodreads: www.goodreads.com/JCMcKenzie
Twitter: twitter.com/JC_McKenzie
Facebook: www.facebook.com/j.c.mckenzie.author
Instagram: www.instagram.com/j.c.mckenzie